410 500 701
410 500-601
9601

THE END JUSTIFIES THE MEANS

Family Dentistry
410 922 5500

a novel by
T.H. MOORE

443 858 8122

Grand - 410 496 4758

Published by:
In Third Person Publishing
P.O. Box 2964
Camden, New Jersey 08101
www.inthirdperson.com
www.thmoorenovels.com

Cover Design: Barron B. Steward
                      www.villagezion.com

Book Layout: Shawna A. Grundy
                      sag@shawnagrundy.com

First Edition November 2006

Library of Congress Cataloging-in-Publication Data is available upon request.

ISBN: 0-9779519-0-1

Acknowledgements

First and foremost I would like to thank my mother for doing the best job possible to afford me all the opportunities I needed to become successful. Without you, there's no telling how I may have ended up. I would like to thank my family (i.e. the Jackson's and the Moore's), friends (i.e. St. Barts, T.E.A.M, the Que Psi Phi), and loved ones because part of who I am today is a direct result of the experiences I've shared with all of you.

A few of you deserve special thanks. My little man, Jason. You're too young to read and understand this but when you are old enough, just know that you're my motivation. T. Jackson, for reading my original manuscript so many years ago, and not letting me cheat the story. My editor, Martha Tucker, www.marthatucker.com for your selfless assistance in refining my writing style. You've helped me find my voice. My graphical and web designer, Barron B. Steward, www.villagezion.com for my book cover and other promotional designs. My proofreaders, Yasmin Paula Carlos and Pio Carlo Carlos, http://popecarlos.blogspot.com.

Finally, I want to thank the city of Camden, New Jersey for inspiring me to write this story. It's time the world knew our city has more to offer then embarrassing crime statistics. This story is for all the forgotten High School and College graduates from Camden. For all the overlooked talent that I've had the pleasure of meeting and those of you I have yet to meet. Find your voice and let's make our city better ourselves, for ourselves.

For my son, Jason . . .

Chapter 1

"Where the hell have you been?"

The angry voice startled ten-year-old Jalen out of a sound sleep. His heart slammed against his chest, his eyes shot open, and his mouth went dry. His mother was raging at his father, Terrence. Jalen pulled the pillow over his head, trying to block out the sound. Still, something in the tone of her voice signaled a bad ending to this outburst.

"It's almost three in the morning!" she screamed. "And you can't call to let me know if you're okay, or dead somewhere?"

Jalen could tell that his thirty-three year old, ex-convict father was pushing her last nerve again. He shook inside, not able to understand how they had stayed together for ten years. In all those years, he rarely heard them speak a civil word to each other, let alone stay in the same bedroom long enough to give him a sister or brother. If not for his looks, Jalen could have sworn he was adopted. He had his mother's caramel complexion, bright smile, and naturally straight hair. His father's long slender build, brown eyes, stubby hands, and long feet were the biggest part of his appearance, causing the neighborhood kids to call him "Slim."

"Bitch, how the hell I'ma call you if I'm dead?" his father shot back. "I swear, you don't make a damn bit of sense!"

Furniture screeched against the hardwood floor. Jalen knew his father must have stumbled and bumped into a chair. The argument was their usual for a Friday, but not this early—it was only about three in the morning. His father was the kind that stayed out all night and faced his woman after the sun came up.

"Bitch?" Michelle shrieked.

Jalen grimaced, because usually at the sound of that word, windows shattered, hot grease was thrown, and baseball bats swung. That word, to his mom, was a call to arms.

"That's right! I said *bitch*. I told you before not to be asking where I'm at and what I'm doing. That shit's *my* business. We ain't married, so I don't answer to you. I go wherever I damn well please, and see whoever I want."

Jalen's throat tightened until it hurt. It wasn't the first time he had heard his father yell those words, and he never seemed to care that she would go crazy on him. Even knowing how she sulked for days after he threw Cynthia, Leslie, Cheryl, or Mia up in her face, he would do it anyhow. Jalen and his mother couldn't go to the supermarket or laundromat without running into one of his father's "beck and calls." And he defended his right to do it. Those women always acted like they had the upper hand. Jalen would stand to the side and watch his mother pass them up with only a smirk, like they were low-life jokes.

"That's right, you *didn't* marry me. So maybe it's about time I start going out and testing the waters. Since you don't see anything wrong with running after those chicken head, river rats you like so much."

Jalen balled his body in his arms and tightened the blanket, hoping she would just stop talking. *What is she doing?*

"I don't have to put up with your shit!" she yelled. "I'm doing *your* ass a favor, 'cause staying here is the only thing keeping you out of the pen—"

"What? Doing *me* a favor? You got it twisted, sweetheart. If it wasn't for me, you and that li'l bastard upstairs woulda been on the street a long time ago. I wasn't trying to be no daddy. You the one that started this family thing."

"Bastard upstairs? Don't you talk about my son like that! And since you ain't trying to be no daddy, maybe I'll call your parole officer and have you tested for drugs, and your sorry ass'll never have to worry 'bout being a daddy again!"

Jalen sprang up and glared at the closed door. Then the sound of glass shattering and a blood-curdling scream jerked him out of bed like he'd been stung by a bee. His feet barely touched the carpet as he tore down the stairs. He froze at the sight.

His father had her pinned into the corner, his six-foot-two, 220 lb body towered above her significantly shorter and slender frame. Only a chair separated them. Terrence grabbed the chair and hurled it across the room without taking his eyes off her.

Hoping that neither of them saw him, Jalen inched from the base of the stairs toward them, closer, not sure what he should or could do. Then he remembered his mother's words.

Call 9-1-1. Call 9-1-1 if daddy hurts me.

Jalen ran into the living room, grabbed the phone, and punched the keypad with shaking fingers. Terrence stomped across the floor toward him.

"9-1-1, what is your emergency?"

"Help! My mom . . . " formed inside his throat and the rest tried to come out of his mouth. It just balled up and turned around and around. Finally, the words shot out, but Terrence had already ripped the phone out of the wall. Then Jalen saw his father's hand come down like in slow motion. It landed on the side of his head and hurled his thin body across the room. Jalen bounced against the wall and slid to the floor. Pain exploded in his skull, then shot to his temples and straight down his spine. His entire little body hurt.

A warrior-like scream spewed out of his mother as she jumped onto his father's back and beat him with clenched fists. Jalen scurried to the kitchen. Just as he glanced back, his father slammed her to the floor. He clamped his hands around her throat. She clawed at his arms and face, squirming like a lion's captured prey.

Daddy's killing mommy.

"I'ma end you tonight," Terrence growled, his eyes blazing. "Don't you ever put your hands on me, woman!" Keeping one hand pressed into her neck, he reached into his pocket and pulled out a knife.

Daddy's killing mommy.

"So you and that li'l bastard was gonna call the police to take me away, huh?" He pressed his full weight on Michelle as she kicked and kneed his back. "Gonna have them haul me back off to prison for another stretch, huh? Leave me there while you find another man?"

Daddy's killing Mommy.

Terrence jabbed the knife toward Michelle's cheek. "I'ma cut a hole in ya face. Then nobody'll want you. Even the kid'll hate to look at you after I'm through wit' you."

Michelle's eyes grew wide as Terrence placed the blade on her cheek. Jalen darted toward his father, yelling, "Stop it! Stop hurting her!"

Terrence eased his stranglehold on Michelle, and she gasped for air. His brown eyes were vacant. Shock gripped his face. He slumped forward and collapsed at Michelle's side. A trail of blood inched across the floor.

Jalen stood over his parents, tears in his eyes and a blank expression on his face. Then the red, white, and blue lights flashed through the windows. Michelle composed herself long enough to ask, "Baby, are you okay?"

Before Jalen could answer, something hit the door. Both of them jumped. A coppery smell filled the air and the trail of blood grew longer. Michelle reached over and shook Terrence hard. His limp body moved willingly to her hand, but he said nothing. His eyes stared at her. Then, she saw it. At the small of his back a black knife handle stuck out. She glanced at Jalen, scrambled on her hands and knees, took the edge of her nightgown and wiped the handle, up and down, down and up.

Bang! Bang! Bang!

Michelle turned to Jalen. "That's the police. If they ask what happened, tell them I did this to daddy, okay?"

This wasn't the first time Michelle had played hostess to the police. In the past when she had fights with Terrence, she told her son, "Calls to 9-1-1 are instantly traced and police are sent if the call is suddenly interrupted."

Jalen stared up at her, shaking. *What did I do? What did I do!*

Bang! Bang! Bang!

Michelle shook him. "Say it, Jalen! It's okay. Say mommy stabbed daddy."

Jalen swallowed, staring blankly at his mother's tear-stained face, then he allowed his eyes to find the form stretched out on the brown hardwood floors like he had seen on so many drunken nights before. But this time, he knew his dad wouldn't wake up.

4

Bang! Bang! Bang! "Open up! It's the police!"

"Jalen! Baby, you have to say what I told you, or the police'll take you away from me. You hear me? Say, *Mommy stabbed daddy.*"

"Mommy stabbed daddy," Jalen said to her, expressionless. He closed his eyes and hoped the world would fade away. *Mommy stabbed daddy? No, I stabbed daddy.*

The police broke down the front door and Jalen could feel them coming toward him. Michelle held onto him.

"Ma'am, are you all right? Is there anyone else in the house?"

Michelle didn't answer. She just held Jalen in her arms and rocked him like a newborn as he sobbed. All the while, she whispered directly in his ear, "Mommy stabbed daddy."

The officer inched closer to Jalen, keeping one hand on his holster as he surveyed the room and the motionless body on the floor. "Hey, son, are you all right?"

Jalen looked up at the officer, blinked, and opened his mouth. He muttered three simple words.

Chapter 2

The murder of Terrence Carthane sent shockwaves through the small Southwest Philly neighborhood. The response across the Benjamin Franklin Bridge in Camden, New Jersey was another story. Camden, although a much smaller city, had its own share of makeshift memorials that marked murder sites similar to Terrence's. In some of the more notorious parts, crime was just a part of everyday life. Only a mother's love could wrap the murdered men in a proper farewell. It was also the final resting place for the raped and abused women who had been sucked into drugs and prostitution before ever getting a glimpse of the promise and opportunity that lay beyond the city.

Kevin English knew life in Camden all too well, but managed to avoid its dangers. He was a young man with a natural sense for business that others spent thousands of dollars at universities to attain. His street swagger was unrivaled by his peers. His mother, Rhondella English, and her life-long companion, James Rowen, had raised Kevin. Now, Kevin took responsibility for the family, promising to make life better for himself and his loved ones. That's what kept him out of courtrooms and prison cells. He studied the streets and knew how to maneuver them. But—

Two small words:--"I'm pregnant"—gave his life a new form. He searched his girlfriend's face, looking for signs that the state of her womb was a joke in poor taste. He didn't find any. Fear jabbed his heart as he recognized the responsibility Tamika Randall had just dropped on his shoulders.

He turned to Tamika, who sat in her parent's modestly decorated living room, on a brown suede sofa, his own fear reflected in her dark brown eyes. "We won't tell anyone about the baby right now," he said.

She sighed softly. "So we *are* going to keep it?"

"Yes, Mika. We're keeping the baby."

She cried right then with deep sobs that tore into his soul and made him more determined than ever to make a home for their baby. Tamika was the best thing that had happened in his life and he wasn't going to screw that up by ending their child's life in a cheap downtown clinic.

"What we gonna do after we let everyone know? My parents won't let me stay here," Tamika asked.

"By then, I'll have enough money for a place of our own. We not gonna put this responsibility on our parents."

Tamika smiled for the first time that day. "Our own place? Where?"

"Shhh, don't worry about that now," he said, placing a tender kiss on her forehead. "I'll let you know when the time comes. You just take care of you and the baby. I'll take care of the rest."

Tamika put her head in his chest and closed her eyes. She was one year younger than Kevin, five-feet three-inches tall with full lips, slender waist, fleshy hips, full breasts, an unblemished golden brown face. Her almond eyes framed by long lashes finished off her sultry beauty. He stroked her shoulder.

Kevin knew that finding a decent-paying job at sixteen would be damn near impossible with his limited experience. Fast food restaurants and supermarkets could pick and choose from an ever-growing stack of applications. Not much chance there for a young man to support a family.

He remembered his grandmother telling him stories of how slaves had stolen food from the master's table to feed their young, how beautiful female slaves had laid themselves bare at their master's feet to save their men's lives and to keep their children safe. That story taught Kevin one lesson—the end justifies the means.

Drug addiction was today's slavery. The white powder rushed urban communities like a Mississippi River flood. He wasn't sure if he could stomach becoming a small player in this multi-billion dollar national industry, even if it was just temporary. It wasn't exactly what his ancestors had in mind. But to Kevin, a temporary solution to a pressing problem was just that—survival.

Chapter 3

After hearing Tamika's news about the baby, Kevin spent less time under her and more earning the money he had promised her. Just around the block was a Spanish corner store or Bodegas. There, to earn an honest wage, Kevin swept, stocked shelves, and assisted customers. On the other hand, Mike Randall, Tamika's older brother, had no problem being a neighborhood hustler. The notorious king of 6th Street, sporting clean locked hair and manicured nails, walked into the store to purchase rolling papers for his weed. Kevin had met Mike through Tamika. He noticed Mike checking him out while he was restocking cans on the shelves.

Tamika had told Kevin how her hardworking Jamaican parents were suspiciously naïve about the late-night traffic at home and their son's endless supply of cash, and how they assumed he would leave home after his high school graduation. Instead, Mike pulled up stakes from his upstairs bedroom and drove them down hard into the basement. He kept the peace by forking over three hundred dollars a month to secure his privacy. Bills were paid, family emergencies were handled, and life was good.

Kevin saw Mike's trademark bright smile behind lips blackened from smoking personally-rolled reefers stuffed with quality marijuana. While Kevin made sure the labels of all the Goya cans faced forward, Mike approached him from behind. He sidled up close and talked right into his ear. "Hey, I noticed you ain't been hugged up wit' me sista like you used to. Da girl been spending a whole lot of time in her room. You gwon and broke me little sista's heart?"

Kevin looked over his shoulder and the trademark smile had vanished. Holding his ground, Kevin answered, "Naw, it ain't nothing like that. We still together. Just making a little extra cash. Her birthday's coming up soon."

Mike smiled again. "Ya know brudda, me sister likes nice tings. You doin' good for yaself? Keeping 'er happy?"

Kevin played dumb, not wanting to get into a deep conversation. He had enough on his mind. "What you mean?"

"You know what I mean bwoy."

Kevin turned to face him with an empty box propped under his arm. "Naw, man. I don't do that." He brushed by Mike, making sure not to nudge him out of respect.

Mike scoffed, "Well if ya change ya mind youngin give me a shout."

Kevin disappeared in the back of the store. He had more work to do. More money to earn—*formula, daycare, diapers, baby clothes, hospital bills . . . and I still have to graduate.* The list swirled in his head. It echoed in the front, sides, and back of his mind, all at the same time.

It was Friday, payday. He mentally added every hour, so that Mr. Perez couldn't shortchange him. Mr. Perez played everything by the book, no paying him under the table. Kevin had to fill out an application and was receiving a check, which meant Uncle Sam was getting his piece before one cent touched his pockets. *Thirty hours at $4.95 an hour is 'bout one fifty. After FICA and the check-cashing place, I'm left with 'bout a hundred to go home with.* Kevin shook his head and his lips tightened. He had held his ground about getting his hands dirty making easier money. But after Mike's visit and offer, that ground started to shake.

The word *survival* was weighing heavy on Kevin. Days soon turned into weeks and everything now revolved around how many weeks Tamika was into her pregnancy. Those weeks would soon translate into months. Only seven months before their child would be born. Visits to the free clinic for check-ups and vitamins took part of that hundred bucks and the nausea medicine for her morning sickness looked like it was going to take the rest. And he still had to find the money for a place of their own.

The following Saturday afternoon, Kevin sat in the living room watching TV while the spicy smell of Tamika's mother's cooking filled the house. It was the countdown before he would have to go to work. Suddenly, he heard the music and rushed upstairs. There was Tamika in the bathroom, on her hands and knees, praying for mercy. The small radio she now kept on the back of the toilet was playing to drown out the sound of their secret.

Kevin wet her face and kissed her forehead, then sneaked back downstairs. Somehow, he didn't care if her parents found out now. He felt like a man. Soon, Tamika eased back downstairs in a pair of baggy jeans and a sweatshirt making it only halfway down before she did a one-eighty, darted back to the bathroom, and slammed the door shut. The volume shot back up again.

Mike walked into the living room with a glass of bright red Kool-Aid and a large bag of potato chips. His eyes were marbled red and his movements slow and lazy. He collapsed onto the couch next to Kevin and took a handful of potato chips, shoving them into his mouth. Light from the lamp reflected off his eighteen-karat gold watch and matching oversized dookey rope chain.

I could take Mika to a real pediatrician with the money he spent on them sparkles. Instead of waiting for four hours for a fifteen minute check up at the free clinic.

Mike finally noticed Kevin looking at his jewelry. "Yeeeah mon, I see ya over der eyeing me jewelry. You like?"

"Yeah, it's nice. But not for me, for Mika."

"Yeah mon, me sista like all women. Nice tings keep em happy. You gone have to save bowt two monts worth of checks to buy sometin like dis for her." He reached for the glass of Kool-Aid, taking two big gulps that dripped from his chin to his shirt.

"Yeah, I know." He looked up at the stairs to see if Tamika was on her way back down. "Your offer still good?" Kevin asked.

Mike was struggling with a memory as cloudy as the Kool-Aid he was drinking. "A couple of weeks ago, you saw me at the store and said—"

"Riiiiight, right, mon. I remember now." The smile returned.

Kevin didn't return the gesture. He felt like he had just stepped out of his body, and where he stood was dangerous.

Chapter 4

The last week of school normally caused a joyful rally cry that could be heard all over the city.

No more pencils, no more books
No more teachers' dirty looks
Are you ready for the summer . . .

This year, however, Kevin didn't feel overjoyed. He would be entering his senior year at Camden High School next fall, but he had barely squeaked by. Now summer meant he wouldn't have school as a façade for the hours of street work he was doing. He had quit his job at the Bodegas, but remained in school. Instead of reporting to the store after school, he and his cousins Chub, Leroy, and Eric headed to Mike's to pick up their freight. Mike's smoke-filled haven was furnished with a couch, love seat, fifty-four inch color TV, and a twenty-gallon fish tank.

"Heey, mon. How ya doin?" Mike asked.

"We're good. How things with you?" Kevin shot back.

"Mon, I'm living the good life. Come and soak it tup for a while."

"Umm . . . " Kevin shrugged with resistance.

"Kevin, you're graduating from high school next year. What you gwon do ater you get ya diploma?"

Kevin thought about Tamika. "I'm not sure." He looked around the room, and like every other visit, he saw something new. This time, it was the new surround sound stereo system to match the 5-disc CD player. *Man! That's dope.* "I'll probably find a job like everybody else."

That wasn't completely honest. In Camden, getting a job 'like everyone else' meant that girls aspired to became hairdressers or nurses, guys became manual laborers—that is if the position wasn't already filled by an applicant with a city address other than Camden. Those with a high school diploma and no rap sheet could pass the civil service exam and become one of Camden's finest. Kevin knew the baby wasn't going to wait for him to finish high school or pass an exam that came once every one to two years. He sighed quietly.

Mike took a long drag of weed. "Well, whatever it tis, I know you'll be alright. Jus tink of all dat time and money ya lost holdin off working fir me. Your crew been workin' out real good too. Making more money dan I taught ya could."

Kevin sighed again.

"I would hate ta loose ya to da Yankee mon." Mike slumped into the sofa. "You don't bring no drama wit ya, you ain't no punk, eder."

"Dat da only reason me don't make a big fus bout you being wit me sista? Respect, mon."

"Thanks, man," Kevin said, eyeing the eighteen-carat gold bracelet Mike wore on his right wrist. He wondered what Mike would say if he knew the whole story about Tamika and the baby. "We just come to pick up the package for tonight. You need anything else before we roll out?"

"Naw, for now ya good. Just swing through tonight. I'll see ya when ya get done."

All the cousins turned and followed Kevin upstairs.

"I'll catch ya'll outside," Kevin told his cousins, as he peered at Tamika who was stretched out on the couch. Her long, jet-black hair in a ponytail, curled around her neck. Open textbooks, homework, and notepads lay on the coffee table in front of her. At the top corner of one of the pages was a testament of her love for Kevin. KEVIN -N-TAMIKA 4EVA!

He sat next to her and lightly nudged her shoulder.

She stirred and smiled up at him.

"How you feelin, babe?"

"I'm fine, baby." She squinted at the grandfather clock that Mike gave their parents for their 20th anniversary. "You just got here?"

"Naw, been here a li'l while. Had to see ya brother."

Concern flickered in her eyes. He fingered through the end of her ponytail that ended at the cleavage of her breasts.

"Quit it, nasty," she said, giving him a sly look and arching her body to him. She swept her hand between his thighs and found his erection.

"Hold on, babe," he said, putting space between them. "We gotta take this up a li'l later."

"Fine," she said, sulking. "I'll just go back to sleep and finish the li'l fantasy in my dream."

He laughed, leaned over, and kissed her forehead. "I just wanted to say 'hi' before I left. You need anything?"

"Just wish you didn't have to be out there so late at night," Tamika said, a hint of sadness in her eyes.

"I know." His gaze found hers. "But, with the baby coming, I need to stack as much cash as I can. Don't worry 'bout me, I'll be okay." He took her hand in his. "When I'm done with school, we'll have enough money to carry us for a while. Then, I'll get a regular nine-to-five and we'll be a nice boring family."

Leroy poked his head in the door. "Come on, man. Time's money and my money ain't got time for you to be playing around wit' ya girl."

Kevin leaned over to kiss Tamika, but pulled back. "Damn, girl, you got morning breath like a mutha."

She turned up her nose. "Then don't kiss me no more if it's so bad."

"We both know that ain't gonna happen. I gotta go, but I'll see ya soon." He headed for the door.

"Kevin?"

"Yeah?"

"It's just 'til you graduate, right?"

He understood. "Just hold tight, alright? I'll be back later."

"Be safe. I love you," she said. Kevin smiled at her before heading out the door.

"A'ight y'all, let's go."

The team fell in line with Kevin, heading toward 6th Street. "Yo Eric, you still gonna help Aunt Michelle move, right?" Kevin asked.

"Yeah, my mom said they gonna be ready this weekend."

"How's li'l Jalen? Ain't seen li'l man in years."

"Man, I don't know. My mom said they needed help so she volunteered me," Eric grumbled.

"Ay, y'all listen up!" Kevin said. "Jalen's not the little kid we had to baby-sit back in the day, so keep him away from this shit. I don't wanna hear nothin' 'bout him being around or knowing anything about this."

They walked on until they reached the concrete stretch in front of a three-story brick house with boarded windows. Then, Kevin's mood changed. His eyes peered around and he felt suspicious. His jaws tightened and his senses sharpened.

"A'ight y'all let's work," he said, snapping his collar up high on his neck against the chilly night air. "The block's calling."

Remember, be safe. Make this money and get home. Get back to Mika and the baby. This is short term 'til you get your diploma. Stay alert. You won't go to jail, you won't get killed . . .

Chapter 5

Jalen pressed his back firmly against the seat and gazed out the moving van's half-open window as they passed through Center City, Philadelphia. A car navigated behind the white and orange moving van, where he sat sandwiched between his mother and cousin, Charles. Cousin Charles was Michelle's age and looked more like Jalen's uncle than a cousin. The Benjamin Franklin Bridge, with its freshly painted blue suspension cables and steel beams, came into view.

Although Jalen had lived in Philly for as long as he could remember, this was the first time he'd really seen the Philadelphia skyline—the tall centerpieces of Liberty Place and Mellon Bank Center. From I-76 East he could see Boat House Row. They passed the expressway exit leading to 30th Street Station. *Only a few more miles to go.* When he raised his head and looked outside, the streets were littered with debris and newspapers that people had tossed to the ground.

As they sat at a traffic light on the Philly side of the bridge, a few homeless people flitted from car to car, begging for loose change. Most drivers ignored them, but not Michelle Williams. Reaching into her brown purse, she handed two dollars out the window to buy food. Even Jalen knew better than that. He wondered why his mother was a passenger instead of the driver.

"Mom, don't you have a license?"

"Yes, I do."

"Then why is Cousin Charles driving?"

"I don't like driving on highways or over bridges, Jalen. They scare me."

"Why?" Jalen asked, studying the base of the oncoming bridge for danger signs. "It's the same as driving on a regular street, except you get to go faster and higher. It kinda makes you feel like you're flying." He leaned across his mother to address Charles. "Right, cousin?"

Charles flashed a sly smile.

"Like I said, Jalen," Michelle repeated, "I don't like driving over bridges." Then she lightly tapped his mouth. "And if I have to repeat myself again, you'll be walking to the new house."

Jalen slumped down in the seat and kept his mouth shut.

Charles chuckled. Now Jalen understood why they always traveled to Camden by train. Charles glanced out the side mirror, trying to spot his younger cousin Eric driving Michelle's car behind them. Eric, the ladies' man…tall and stout, not so tough though, but enough charisma for two lifetimes. That's what he remembered about him.

Jalen turned, to the Schuylkill River and took in the light reflecting off the murky water. He wondered if he had seen his friends from Philly for the last time. His mind raced back to that awful night. *Jalen stabbed daddy . . .* Jalen, searching his mother's eyes for comfort, managed somehow to heed her words—*Mommy stabbed daddy*—he had told the police.

Their world became an instant soap opera—a whirlwind of court appearances and newspaper articles followed, and they lasted for weeks.

* * *

"All rise," the stocky bailiff bellowed across the courtroom. "The Honorable Judge Evelyn Hopkins presiding."

The stale smell of cologne and perfume floated off spectators who had come to see what would become of Michelle Williams. Jalen, in full Catholic school uniform, the only presentable clothes he had to wear, scanned the room. He turned from the stares of Black and White faces. Their stark scrutiny pushed him farther down into his seat and his stare rested onto his mother's back.

Jalen had been in this very courtroom before. It felt like something heavy choking him, making a kind of separation from the world. The spot his father smashed years prior had been fixed.

The judge looked at Mr. Baker, the prosecutor, who was noticeably younger than Michelle's attorney. "Will the prosecution please proceed with closing arguments?"

Baker fumbled through the documents strewn on the wooden table. "Your honor and members of the jury, the law does not allow citizens to take the law into their own hands. Ms. Williams did that exact thing when she killed Terrence Carthane. Ms. Williams had plenty of opportunities to remove Mr. Carthane from the home from previous domestic disturbance calls she's had in the past but when given the opportunity to prosecute, she declined every time. If she felt so threatened for her life and that of her child, she could have pressed criminal charges. It is only now, after she killed the boy's father, that she is choosing to play on our sympathy. The only acceptable verdict will be guilty."

Michelle's right foot wiggled nervously as she searched the jury's faces for any indication that she wasn't going to jail. The judge turned to the defense attorney. "Mr. Poindexter, you may give your closing argument."

"Your honor, for the past few days, we have presented the court with documentation and testimony that Michelle Williams acted in self-defense to protect her ten-year-old son, Jalen Carthane, and herself.

"We have provided copies of restraining orders and hospital reports of the beatings received at the hands of the deceased. The deceased's parole officer testified that Mr. Carthane was imprisoned for drug possession, and distribution several times. He was also a habitual drug and alcohol abuser. And it was under these influences that he was most violent with Ms. Williams and their son."

Michelle's attorney, Mr. Poindexter, walked towards the jury, addressing them directly. "What happened was not ideal, but at that time it was the only choice Ms. Williams had. Therefore, under those unusual circumstances, the defense requests that the jury consider the testimony and overwhelming evidence, and return a verdict of not guilty." He strolled back to his seat and gave Michelle a reassuring pat on the shoulder.

Michelle looked at her attorney for some sign of hope.

The judge looked at both attorneys and then at the jury. Then she gave instructions on how they were to reach a verdict. Judge Hopkins dismissed the jurors for deliberation. Hopkins rose and retired to her chambers. Michelle trembled.

Jalen followed the escort, his mother and her attorney to a small, white office, where they sat and waited. Jalen's mind drifted, losing all track of time.

* * *

Jalen stared up at the flag post near the judge's bench, above her head where the City of Philadelphia's seal hung. It was the first time he ever saw Judge Hopkins.

"Mr. Carthane, you have been found guilty of drug possession. You are hereby sentenced to a maximum of five years."

"You dike ass lesbian! Five years for holding a little coke? This is my first offense!" Terrence Carthane had glared at the judge.

"Mr. Carthane, you will shut your mouth before I find you in contempt of court," the judge warned.

"I don't have to shut my mouth, but I'ma shut you up!" He shoved his lawyer out of his way, grabbed the chair behind him and hurled it at the judge. She ducked beneath the bench as the chair hit the wall and splintered into pieces, leaving a hole just beneath the city seal.

The judge rose from under the desk, "Mr. Carthane." She pounded the gavel into the wooden desk. "I find you in contempt! Bailiff, remove him!"

Jalen would never forget the slow burn in her eyes.

* * *

Now, an hour and a half had passed and Mr. Poindexter's assistant rushed into the room notifying them the jury had come to a decision. Jalen wasn't sure how long he had been day dreaming. The bailiff instructed everyone to return and take a seat. The gavel sounded again. Mr. Poindexter reached under the table and grasped Michelle's hand. Michelle swallowed hard; her heart pounded like a jackhammer.

The jury foreman stood at the judge's request and read. "In the case of Michelle Williams vs. the City of Philadelphia, we the jury find the defendant not guilty of murder in the second degree."

The minute the Carthane family heard the verdict, Terrence's mother locked eyes with Michelle. Rage flooded her face. "I'll never forgive you for taking my son away from me, and if I ever see you again, so help me God, I'll send you to meet your maker."

Murmurs erupted, causing the judge to bang her gavel again. "Order! Order! On a more personal note, Ms. Williams, it is my sincere hope that you have learned the kind of men to avoid. If by some strange coincidence you happen to appear before this, or any court in this jurisdiction, again, we will have no sympathy for you. Is that understood, Ms. Williams?"

"Yes ma'am—I mean, Your Honor. You won't be seeing me here ever again."

* * *

In the months that followed, Terrence's relatives and mistresses refused to leave Michelle and Jalen alone. Michelle filed restraining order against them all, but ultimately decided to move to Camden in a hurry.

Things also got tough for Jalen at school. Kids started calling his mother "psycho." Such incidents were so frequent that he was sent to the library instead of going outside for recess.

After three months of lying low, Jalen was eleven and they were moving to a new life. Driving to Camden, New Jersey. He looked out of the corner of his eye at his mother. She never lied to him, not even when it pained her. But she had lied for him. *Mommy killed daddy.* He would never forget what he would come to know as her sacrifice. A single tear pooled in the corner of his eye. Maybe she saw it. She smiled at him. "It's okay, baby. It's okay now."

Jalen nodded without a word. It had been years since Jalen's last visit to Camden. Michelle put a stop to them after he landed in Cooper Hospital. Although he was five years younger than his cousins, he always found ways to tag along with them during his visits. They introduced him to street games such as Truth-or-Dare and Questions. His favorite was Hide and Go Get It. In that game, girls were given about twenty seconds to run and hide. If a boy caught one of them, he had a minute to grind or dry hump her. Unknown to his mother, that game and the events that followed nearly made him pay with his life two years ago.

Now Jalen was heading back to Camden for good. And that spring day in 1986 brought back memories of Hide and Go Get It. *Oh, yes*! The truck pulled onto the bridge, Michelle closed her eyes, and dug her nails into her thighs.

"Mom, you gonna be okay? If his driving is making you nervous, I can drive us the rest of the way."

Michelle didn't open her eyes, but still managed to pop Jalen in the mouth with a precision that would make a sniper jealous. "I warned you about your mouth."

Jalen rubbed his mouth to dull the pain and embarrassment of the blow. He redirected his attention to passing traffic, and then to the Schuylkill River directly below them. They were at the peak of the bridge, where downtown Camden spread out before them. As they rolled off the bridge, Jalen spied Camden's littered downtown. *Just like Philly.*

Charles pointed to the only tall building in the entire area. "That's where I work, Jalen. City Hall. I know the mayor and most of the city officials."

Jalen wasn't impressed. The only noticeable difference between Philadelphia and Camden was that his new city was much smaller and had fewer white people walking or driving around.

"Hey, isn't that the transportation center where we used to catch the train, Mom?"

"Yes, it is. All I'll have to do to get to Philadelphia is catch the speed line to Eighth and Market and I'll be at work." She leaned her head back against the seat.

When they arrived at their new home right off Haddon Avenue, girls were clustered on the stairs. They waved. Jalen smiled and waved back.

21

Chapter 6

As Jalen walked toward the house, he hated the sight of it and slowed his pace. Their new home was the only porch house on the block, but the railing had been torn down. He could tell red brick had once paved the front walkway but now most of the brick was missing. The vacant lot across the street was a graveyard for abandoned cars, and behind it, a highway stretched for miles. An eighteen-wheeler honked as it rumbled and its great power vibrated through Jalen's body. His Philly neighborhood didn't have those kinds of noises. *If I couldn't sleep through the fights in Philly, for sure I won't be able to sleep through the sound of these trucks!*

Charles cut into his thoughts. "Okay, let's get this stuff unloaded."

Jalen scanned the area as he unloaded, nearly buckling under the weight of the first load of furniture. He hadn't expected the house to be worse than the one in Philly, and tried to mask his disappointment for his mother's sake. He smiled.

"I know it's not what you expected, but once we put a little work into it, it'll feel just like home," Michelle said.

Jalen looked straight ahead, soundless. He'd already been smacked in the mouth twice today, no need to make it three times. Jalen followed in his cousin's footsteps. Eric lugged in a large box, dragging it across the worn carpet while Jalen flipped on the light switch. The darkness deepened. Jalen straggled into the kitchen. "Ma! Nothing works around here."

"What you mean?"

"None of the lights work."

"What? I called the gas and electric company before we left Philly."

Charles and Eric went to the basement searching for the circuit box while Jalen ventured upstairs. He peeped in two bedrooms, then found the bathroom and stared at the filthy, rust-streaked, claw-foot tub. No showerhead. *I have to take a bath in that nasty thing?* As he peed in the rusty toilet, his gaze scrolled from the ceiling downward. It stopped on a shiny piece of metal glistening from behind the tub. "What the—?" He zipped up his pants and leaned in for a closer look.

"Michelle, we found the circuit box. I'm gonna start flipping switches and you let me know if any lights come on." Charles yelled from the basement. "Anything?"

"No. Nothing," Michelle answered.

"Now?"

"Nope. Still dark."

"Charles, can I call PSE&G from your house tomorrow?" Michelle asked. "Our telephones won't be on for another week."

"Just come by whenever you're ready."

"Jalen! Where are you?" Michelle yelled.

Jalen sprinted downstairs to meet Michelle, who pointed a flashlight directly in his eyes.

"What's that?" She asked.

"Found it in the bathroom," Jalen said, handing her the gun.

Michelle's brown eyes widened as she snatched the weapon from his hands. "You found this here?"

"Yeah, behind the tub."

Michelle clenched her fists and exhaled slowly. "I don't *ever* want to see you with a gun in your hand! Next time you see a gun you go in the opposite direction. You hear me?"

"Okay, ma," he said. "Are we staying at Cousin Charles's house tonight?"

"No. We'll go to the supermarket to get some candles, and something to eat and stay right here."

Jalen didn't argue; he wasn't going to provoke her again. He headed for the front door and sat on the porch. Eric joined him, but Jalen looked straight out into the darkness. "What else can go wrong?" he mumbled.

23

"Hey, little cousin, it's gonna be a'ight. It'll just take a little getting used to. In no time, you'll be all settled in like you never left Philly," he said. "But hey, your mom is right about the gun thing, man. I don't wanna see you fooling around with those things either, a'ight?"

"A'ight."

A few minutes later, Michelle, Charles, Eric, and Jalen squeezed into Michelle's car, made a quick trip to the Pathmark on Mt. Ephraim Avenue and finally to the Golden Arches across the street. He ordered a double cheeseburger, fries, hot apple pie, and soda. That made up for his day.

The next morning, footsteps and knocking played games in his sleep. They got louder and louder until they woke him. The sunlight hurt his eyes.

"Jalen! Time to get up!"

Time to get up? Already? Michelle was already in his room with her blue bathrobe and matching slippers. He looked up and saw the knocking came from her knuckles hitting the wall. Then he remembered, his bedroom had no door, just an open threshold that once held a door. Pink plastic curlers held her hair high on her head, giving her intimidating height.

"I have good news and bad news," she said.

Jalen turned to his mother. "Give me the good news first."

"It's Sunday and it's time to go to church."

Jalen buried his face in his pillow, but sprang up when a cloud of dust choked him. "Then what's the bad news?"

"We have to clean this place as soon as we get back."

Jalen stared at her. *This evil woman isn't my real mother. My mom wouldn't move the child she carried in her womb for nine months to a bad house, without any electricity, hot water, and no way to cook a good meal, then wake me up at 8 o'clock and force me to go to church.* Jalen pursed his lips. *And, we get to clean after church.*

Michelle's small hand whipped out to her right hip. "Something you wanna say to me, Jalen?"

Jalen took a breath, and thought about voicing his concerns but the no-nonsense look in Michelle's eyes changed his mind. "Oh, naw, ma."

"Well get up, then."

Jalen had stopped arguing about going to church after the last time his father took him to play baseball instead. It turned out to be a cover for something else . . .

* * *

Jalen sat in the front seat, anxious to get to Fairmount Park. "Dad, how long 'til we get there?"

Thump. Thump. Thump. Jalen's feet hit the dashboard.

"In a sec, Jalen. And stop kicking my dashboard."

"Sorry, dad." He was happy he didn't have to go to church, and hoped the park trip would be fun. He'd gotten used to his dad dropping him off at an aunt's house, driving off and not getting back until 8 o'clock that night. Every once in a while, they ended up doing something fun, but that was usually on the way back, *if* his father was in a good mood.

"When we get to the park, you can run around and go crazy with the other kids. We just need to make one stop and pick up my friend first." Terrence pulled the car over to the curb. A man about his father's age stood there waiting.

Terrence turned to Jalen. "Get in the back and let Junior sit up front."

While Jalen slid over the seat into the back, a man dressed in powder blue sneakers and a dusty pair of jeans slipped into the front seat. His clothes smelled of cigarettes.

"What's up, Junior?" Terrence asked as he drove off.

"Nothing much. Just happy to get away for a few hours, you know? Hey, you got any weed on you?"

"Man, watch your mouth! My son's in the back."

"Oh, my fault." Junior looked over his shoulder. "Hey, little man. You gonna hang out with your old man and uncle Junior today, huh?"

Terrence glanced at Jalen in the rear view mirror. "Yeah man, we're headed to the park. I rescued him from his mother and church. He's gonna play in a kids' baseball game. So we'll just hang out until it's over."

"Cool with me."

The second his father parked the car, Jalen darted to the baseball diamond where a group of kids were being assigned to teams. Terrence and Junior found a place to sit on the metal bleachers. After Jalen was assigned to a team, the coach looked at him.

"Yeah, umm . . . Jalen Carthane, you're playing centerfield, but you can't play without a glove and I don't want your parents ringing your neck if you get those clothes dirty."

"They're in the car. I'll go get 'em."

Jalen's legs ran as fast as he could push them. At last, he reached the car and checked the backseat. He rummaged around and found his clothes in the backpack, but no glove. He yanked off his penny loafers and put on his sneakers. He kept looking for the glove. On the front passenger side, he checked the seat and floor. No glove. He opened the car door and scanned the bleachers, looking for his dad. He didn't see him. He just couldn't be left out of the game. He yelled out of the open door. "Dad, I can't find my glove."

Junior shouted back, "I put it in the glove compartment, little man."

Jalen ducked back inside the car and opened the glove compartment. The worn leather glove! He snatched it and a miniature yellow folder came with it. A flurry of white powder floated onto the floor.

From school, Jalen knew what drugs looked like. The white powder was cocaine. He had often heard his parents argue about his father's coke, but had never seen it.

Terrence ran up, out of breath. He glanced at Jalen, then the floor. "What the hell you doing? Did I tell you to go snooping in the glove compartment?"

"Mr. Junior said he put my glove in there. I just wanted to find it."

"I don't care what Junior says. It's my car and you listen to what I say."

"I'm sorry, dad. I'll clean it up." Jalen scrambled to scoop the powder up with a piece of paper and shove it back into the envelope, but his hands shook, and he made an even bigger mess.

Terrence yanked him by the collar and flung him to the ground. Before Jalen could stop rolling from the force of his father's toss, Terrence was already holding him by the seat of his pants. That big right hand came down across his face. Every time Jalen moved his hand to protect himself, his father hit wherever he could. Each wallop sent a thousand lines of pain through Jalen's body. He cried, coughed and gurgled. Blood smeared the creases of Terrence's right hand. It trickled down Jalen's nose and slowly dropped onto his shirt. Junior ran over and looked down at Jalen with helpless sympathy. The kids on the baseball field stopped the game and stared at his misfortune.

Terrence yelled, "Get in the car. I'm taking your ass home."

Jalen leaped into the back seat and sat quietly, blood dripping in steady little drops down his nose. It winded off his chin and fell between his fingers. He feared reaching for the handkerchief his mother had given him because he didn't want to do anything to upset his dad again. Every once in a while he would sniff to stop the blood.

"You'd better not tell your mother what happened today, you hear me?"

Neither of the men mentioned the white dust on the floor. They rode in silence until Junior spoke.

"Hey man. You can drop me off back at my pad and we can catch up later."

"Naw man, I'm gonna drop him off to his mother and we'll do our thing. He ain't goin' to go tellin' nothing. Huh, Jalen?"

"No—"

"And stop crying like a little sissy!"

Jalen sat quietly. He'd never kept anything from his mother, but one thing was for sure—from now on, he was going to church.

* * *

Chapter 7

Jalen never understood how his mother got up *before* him and still never beat him out the door. He stood on the porch waiting. Michelle finally came out of the house and gave him the once over. He always had to be presentable for his grandmother Edith and the family. And none of Edith's kids or grandkids ever missed church or came out of the house looking sloppy, with shirttails hanging out and spots on their Sunday clothes.

Michelle ushered Jalen inside New Miracle Baptist Church, quietly. The inner doors were already shut and they were officially late. Jalen peered through the glass doors and spotted Kevin, Eric, Chub, and Leroy in the last pew, whispering, laughing, and punching each other. The choir sang and the congregation united in that ethereal sway of Ray Charles while the rhythm of the song took charge.

"*Jesus, Jesus, Jesus,*
Sweetest name I know,
Fills my every longing,
Keeps me singing as I go . . . "

Finally, the song ended and the doors opened. The usher pointed Jalen and Michelle toward the only empty seats—up front. Jalen grinned, made a quick right, and headed toward the last pew. Michelle jerked his arm and frowned. Sitting with his cousins wouldn't be happening this Sunday.

Leroy pointed toward Jalen and laughed. Kevin smacked his cousin, smiled, and nodded at Jalen. He returned the gesture and trudged behind his mom to the front pew. His aunts, Rhondella and Janet, scooted over a bit, making room for them while the women whispered compliments and smiled. Aunt Janet waved to Aunt Rachel, who sat in the soprano section of the choir.

Jalen's mind wandered. *Who wants to hear about turning the other cheek, Moses, and the burning bush, when a bright sunny Sunday was going to waste?*

His mother nudged him and handed him the silver collection plate. He dropped in the dollar she had given him before they left the house. Jalen watched as the plate passed from pew to pew until it reached the back row. Then he heard a noise.

"Pling! Ting! Ting!"

"Aw shit—I mean shoot. My fault." Chub said as change from the plate hit the hardwood floor and bills scattered everywhere. The usher scrambled to pick up the offering. The pastor began the sermon as Leroy whispered and pointed. Then everything became absolutely quiet.

After the service, Jalen's mother and aunts, along with other members congregated on the front steps. Jalen painfully stood nearby, enduring aching feet that were stuffed inside his too-small penny loafers that pinched his toes. His cousins headed toward the corner store and Jalen peeked at his mother. She was deep in conversation. He inched away, a little bit at a time, until he was out of sight, then he broke into a sprint and caught up with his cousins.

"Sup, man? How things going at the crib?" Kevin asked.

"Man, that house is like a hundred years old and jacked up. No gas, no electric, no phone. I took a cold bath this morning," Jalen said.

Eric and Chub laughed. Kevin snickered.

"Aww, man, you lucky," Chub said, giving Eric an elbow. "Eric didn't wash his ass at all today and was smellin' up the whole church."

Eric didn't think it was funny. "At least I brushed my teeth and my breath don't smell like hot garbage, Chub."

A small Asian man and a young girl with yellow ribbons in her straight black hair peered suspiciously over the counter at the boys when they walked into the store. Jalen followed Kevin down one aisle; Leroy and Chub took off down another. A Snickers bar disappeared into Leroy's pant pocket.

"Why y'all stealing when y'all got money?" Kevin asked.

"Shut up before you get us caught," Leroy growled, looking over Chub's shoulder to see if anyone else heard him.

Eric strolled over to the boys. "Look, I got five dollars from the offering plate. *I'll* pay for it."

"What's the difference between you stealin' from the offering plate, and him stealin' now?" Jalen asked.

"The difference is the church didn't catch us and they won't be calling the cops," Eric answered.

"Yeah, but God's watching. He's worse than the cops," Jalen said.

"Yeah? Well you keep an eye out for God and tell me when you see Him, so I can run as fast as I run from the cops."

"A'ight big spender, if you're buying, then I'm getting in on this," Kevin said, demanding the others to hand him the candy bars. He strolled to the front counter.

Jalen followed while Leroy thumped the back of his head. He grabbed a handful of jawbreakers and big box of Lemon Heads at the front counter and piled them on top of their other bounty.

The young girl in yellow ribbons rang up their purchases. The man stood behind her and watched the register. "That will be $3.60," she said with only the slightest accent.

Eric pulled out five dollars and waited for the change. All the cousins grabbed their pick and scrambled outside. Soon, Jalen could see their mothers talking to the pastor and the usher.

Eric froze. "Damn, one of y'all need to say you bought this stuff. My mom didn't give me no money, so she's gonna think I stole it."

Leroy answered, "Our mom didn't give us no money either. You gonna have to take da ass whippin' for this one."

They didn't even have time to swallow the evidence. Eric's jaws were clenched. The rainbow flavored Now & Laters stained Kevin's tongue. Jalen spotted Michelle's warning face. The women walked forward like a posse and pulled the boys in different directions. Jalen was sure he had nothing to worry about, since he had done nothing wrong, but Michelle's slightly made-up face had turned a brilliant red. Her fists were clenched by her side—not a good sign. She grabbed his collar and power-walked him toward her car.

Aww man, she's mad. "Mom, is everything OK?"

"Just wait 'til I get you home." She pushed him ahead of her.

Jalen's heart pounded. His mouth felt like a cotton ball. *She's gonna wait 'til I get home so she can kill me. When she hits you, fake an asthma attack. Wait, I don't have asthma.*

Michelle slammed the car door and threw him an angry glance.

As they were about to drive off, Kevin ran up to the car waving a ten-dollar bill. "Jalen, if you wanna get some more Lemon Heads, I work at the corner store near your house and you can get whatever you want for free." He shoved Jalen the bill. "Here! Just in case I'm not around the next time you want to go to the store." His gaze locked with Michelle. "Bye, Aunt Michelle." Kevin waved politely and ran to catch up with his mom.

Michelle's eyebrow shot up as she peered at Jalen, who was trying his best to look innocent—hands folded on his lap, eyes bucking wide. Kevin had just saved his tail. He wanted to release the laughter caught in his throat, but he knew he'd better not.

Then it hit him! They were on their way back to the house to give it *a thorough cleaning*. That was punishment enough.

Chapter 8

Jalen dragged himself out of bed and into the bathroom. Hot water flowed from the old faucet, the tub was clean, and dust that had covered everything like beach sand was gone. He still preferred their home in Philadelphia.

After three months, Jalen still hadn't made many new friends. He dashed out of the house carrying a sack lunch and wearing the Catholic School approved uniform—navy blue slacks, white shirt, and a navy blue, red, and green striped tie. The walk up Haddon Avenue to St. Bartholomew Catholic School would take twenty minutes. On the way, he joined other kids who wore uniforms as identifiable to the public school kids as a bull's eye to an archer. Hatch Middle School kids took special pleasure in tormenting them with evil looks, stares, and verbal abuse. As he walked toward the back streets, four boys, wearing T-shirts and jeans, trailed him.

Jalen picked up his pace, but the Hatch kids were gaining on him. He clutched his lunch, and broke into a sprint, hoping the next few seconds would give him a chance to escape. They picked up the pace while the wind seemed to be under Jalen's arms, lifting him and pushing him forward. His book bag twisted and the strap slid down his shoulder as his thin legs pumped the earth beneath his feet—harder, faster, faster.

Jalen could hear the boys' footsteps beating the pavement right behind him. He could feel their breath against his back, hear them panting. Then, all at once, something charged him. His book bag dropped and a football tackle knocked him to the ground. The kicking felt like pellets from a hailstorm. They became more violent. Punching, kicking, and slamming. His head hit the ground and the pain tore his insides. Jalen thrust his hands and feet out to fend off the attack, but the beating continued in full force. His knuckles and elbows connected with nothing but the cement as he fought to get back on his feet. A kick to the groin sent him crashing flat on the ground again, killing whatever fight he had left in him.

Fetal position . . . fetal position . . . ball up and ride it out. Pain shot through his stomach, back, and ribs as he tried to cover his head and face with one hand while protecting his throbbing scrotum with the other.

"A'ight, that's enough." someone said.

But they continued kicking him.

"Stop before we kill his ass!" the voice yelled.

Jalen peeked up and matched the face to the voice. *Puerto Rican. Not Black.*

"Y'all know I'm on probation. I'm not going back to juvie." The Good Samaritan said.

Jalen lay before them dazed and confused. *Should I run? No, keep playing possum. They'll go away soon.* Then one of the boys walked over while the Puerto Rican kid was calming the rest of the crew down.

"Hey, you okay?" The dark skinned thug asked.

Are you fucking serious? You just kicked the shit out of me. Jalen said nothing. He was wobbly, shaking, and bleeding as the dark skinned boy with nostrils spreading from cheek to cheek, yanked him to his feet. "Got any dough? Jewelry?"

Jalen just stood there.

"If you do, give it up." He fiddled his fingers.

The kid patted his pockets and checked Jalen's wrist and neck. Finding nothing, he swung once more and knocked Jalen back to the pavement. He laughed and joined the rest of the crew who had already started walking off in the direction of Haddon Avenue.

Jalen just lay there sprawled out. *Ain't no way in hell I'm going to school after this.*

The next day was worse than the day before. His entire body was bruised. It ached and throbbed like a burn. "Ma, I can't go to school today."

"What you mean you can't? If you still breathing, then you can go to school. Especially since you can't seem to remember who did this to you."

Jalen knew better than to tell her anything. There was no way he was gonna make things worse by having his "mommy" go around the neighborhood threatening the guys who beat him down.

"Okay, fine. I'll let you stay home one day, but tomorrow you go back to school, understand?" Michelle said. "I'll call during my lunch to check up on you."

Jalen propped himself up on the sofa to watch "What's Happening." Even his favorite television show didn't help because his ribs hurt when he laughed. His back hurt when he walked. It even hurt to think. Soon, he was drifting in and out of sleep.

Later that afternoon, a knock on the door woke him up—the best sleep he'd had all day.

Jalen didn't answer.

The knock got louder. Then a yell. Jalen pulled himself off the couch and peeked out the window. He pulled back when he saw Kevin's face.

"Boy, I see you peeking through the shades. Open the damn door."

Jalen dragged to the door and opened it. Kevin took one look at Jalen. "Who did it?"

Jalen inched his way to the sofa, slumped onto the cushions, and didn't answer. He lowered his gaze to the floor.

"Never put your head down! You have to look a man in the eyes to gain his respect."

Jalen lifted his head, but not eyes, because he was still embarrassed.

"Now tell me who did it!"

"I don't know their names. I just know what they look like and where they hang out at."

"Well that's all you need to know. You don't miss another day of school. And you take the same way to school you did when they jumped you."

Jalen looked at him like he was insane.

Kevin sighed and rubbed his hand across the top of his head. "Look, li'l cousin, you can't be hiding in the house your whole life. You got to face your fears like a man. The pain you're feeling now will go away if you man up, but if you keep running, the pain's gonna last forever."

Jalen nodded. "A'ight. I'll go to school tomorrow. But they just gonna beat me down again. I can't fight all those guys by myself."

"Then bring a weapon with you. Before they get the drop on you, you make sure you take down at least one of them. Make 'em feel your ass whuppin' first."

Kevin reached in his pocket and pulled out a pair of homemade brass knuckles—fashioned out of duct tape, loose change, and two strategically placed pieces of metal sticking out. This would definitely harm a person's face. He handed it to Jalen.

Suddenly, Jalen didn't feel so small.

The next morning, he was still in pain and struggling with fear but he knew he'd never convince his mother to let him stay home again. Also, he had promised Kevin.

"You want me to walk with you to school, Jalen?" Michelle said as he left the stairs.

"No!" *You can't be serious.* He rolled his eyes.

The moment she walked out the door to work, he placed the brass knuckles in his pocket and left the house. When approaching Haddon Avenue, Jalen could see the gang in its usual spot. He noticed that the Puerto Rican kid that saved him was missing. *One less person I need to worry about.* Jalen slowed as he came closer to Haddon Avenue. The boys huddled like a football team, then headed straight for him. Jalen kept walking and slid his right hand in his pocket. They met right at the corner of Haddon Avenue.

"How you doin', my man?" one boy asked. "You went missing in action yesterday."

Their laughter grated Jalen's nerves. His right leg shook uncontrollably. He tried to calm himself, but he was too scared.

"So, you got any money for us, Catholic school boy?"

Jalen started to put his head down and not answer, but he remembered what Kevin had told him. With his fist still clenched in his pocket, he raised his chin and looked the boy right in the eyes. "I ain't got shit for you."

They were caught off guard. One boy's eyes widened. Another's jaw dropped.

"You gonna let this geek diss you, Kareem?"

Kareem's face flushed with anger and those wide nostrils flared even wider. His two buddies joined him and formed a half circle around Jalen. Suddenly Leroy, Chub, Eric, and Kevin tore from the corner store across the street carrying chains, bats, and pipes. Kevin led the pack with clenched fists the size of softballs. The boys didn't see them coming. Jalen did.

Jalen couldn't help but smirk before he punched Kareem with all his strength just before his cousins reached them. Then the brawl kicked into full swing. Kevin grabbed one of the boys by the waist, lifting him off the ground. He slammed him onto the pavement. Leroy kicked another boy in the side of his face with his tan work boots. Jalen's head was on a swivel, watching the fighting all around him, landing punches to Kareem's ribs and the back of his head. Kevin climbed on top of the boy he slammed using his knees to pin him down to the ground while he battered him over and over. The boy would occasionally throw his legs up trying to wrap them around Kevin, but his legs eventually stopped moving.

"Oh God, please stop. I'm sorry. I can't breathe! I can't... Oh, God!"

Jalen *almost* felt sorry for him. Then, Eric grabbed Kevin off of him. The boy just lay there, shirt torn, one sneaker missing, face mangled in a bloody mess. Jalen tried to imitate Kevin and wrestled Kareem to the ground, hoping to pin him down. Leroy came and held the big boy in a standing "full nelson" as Chub and Eric took turns pounding his mid-section. The boy twisted, turned, and kicked. Leroy kneed him in the back and side hoping to take some of the fight out of him but the boy kept fighting back.

Jalen finally pinned Kareem down, ignoring the pain of yesterday's injuries. Revenge rose up and strengthened him to throw a barrage of pathetic punches that barely connected. Pointing and snickering, Kevin and Eric watched him, but Jalen didn't care. He threw a punch with the makeshift knuckles and blood shot out of Kareem's cheek. Kareem yelled and grabbed his face. Kevin pulled Jalen off. Jalen saw the damage and felt victorious, throwing his hands in the air. He shouted, "You want some more? You want some more of the champ?"

The whole fight was over in no more than sixty seconds, and Kareem was the only one that remained on the ground, one hand over his cheek. Kevin towered over him.

"Listen up, man! This is my li'l cousin, and I don't wanna hear nothing else bout y'all giving him problems. 'Cause if I do, the next time, I won't be empty handed. Feel me?"

"I feel you," Kareem whimpered, looking the way Jalen had a day ago. He nodded.

"Now get the hell outta here," Leroy yelled.

Jalen felt like a new person. He brushed off his school uniform, inspected his pants, then he and his cousins headed towards his school.

Still savoring their victory, Kevin and Jalen tread quietly. Then Kevin spoke. "A'ight Jalen, you see that corner right there? If you have to walk this way to school, walk on the opposite side of the street like we are now. If anything crazy happens, I don't want you getting caught in the middle of some bullshit. Always be aware of your surroundings and you'll be a'ight."

Jalen noticed that every one of the hustlers that passed by greeted Kevin with a nod, or a "Sup?"

"Stay away from those corners, too," Kevin warned.

When Jalen reached the school grounds, his classmates were already lined up for class. "Aw man, I gotta go, but thanks for today," Jalen said.

"It ain't nothing, li'l cousin. We won't be there tomorrow though, but I doubt you'll have any problems from now on," Kevin said.

Jalen reached into his pocket and offered the weapon back to his cousin.

"Naw, you hold onto that, just in case."

Jalen smiled.

Kevin reached into the pockets of his blue and grey two-toned jeans, pulled out a roll of cash, pealed off a ten-dollar bill, and gave it to Jalen.

"Man! Can you get me a job at the store with you?"

Leroy laughed. "Dis guy ain't worked at that store since—"

Kevin's face tightened and stared Leroy down. Jalen ran off and fell in line with his classmates. He watched his cousins walk back toward Haddon Avenue.

At recess, Jalen rushed outside to play touch football and one of the older boys stopped him. "How you know Kevin?"

Jalen was surprised that the boy knew his cousin. "He's my cousin."

"Oh, a'ight," the boy said, and walked toward the fence separating the schoolyard from the street. Jalen noticed the older boys had gathered outside the fence and were eyeing and pointing at him.

A few seconds later, Jalen's classmate J.C. walked up behind him. "I know your cousin, Kevin. Him and the rest of your cousins be out on the corner of my block doing their thing."

"What you mean?"

J.C. glanced over his shoulder. "They be selling drugs and making plenty of dough."

"You don't know what you're talking about!"

"Whatever you say."

Jalen walked away, down the long narrow hallway and into his classroom. He thought about the money Kevin gave him after church. The roll of money he pulled out before he went to school today. How the guys on the corner knew him. *Kevin sells drugs? The same shit that messed up my father? No, that couldn't be right!* He pulled the ten-dollar bill from his pocket and stared at it. Nothing inside him could explain where that money came from, *except . . .*

His gut told him all he needed to know. He balled up the bill and tossed it in the trash.

Chapter 9

The next five years all seemed to have swept by like a Midwest tornado. Instead of landing like Dorothy and Toto in the Land of Oz, Jalen found himself stepping off a yellow school bus two blocks from his home. Two of Pennsauken High's prettiest girls walked on each side of him—Tysheina Mack, his new girlfriend on his right, and Asia Carter, her best friend on his left. When Asia stopped to say goodbye to a friend, Tysheina leaned against his shoulder.

"Sorry you guys didn't win today. If you don't want to be alone you can come by my house. My mom's working the night shift at the hospital. We can be alone for a change."

Jalen looked straight ahead. "Wish I could, but I've got to get home before my mom leaves for her second job. I can probably come by later, after I eat. A'ight?"

"Sure, baby. Just give me a call when you're ready."

Asia caught up and sighed. "I guess I'll be the only one alone tonight. Omar doesn't like to see anyone after he loses a game."

"Why?" Tysheina asked, grinning.

"He gets all depressed. We don't even talk about it the next day. I just give him his space and wait until he comes out of his funk."

"Are you two still going to apply to the same college next year so you can stay together?" Tysheina asked.

Jalen turned to Asia. It was the first time he noticed the small round beauty mark on her right chin that danced up and down every time she spoke.

Asia hesitated. "Um . . . yeah, but it's more like we're hoping to get accepted in the same area. We don't want to smother each other, being at the same school and all, so we're just applying to colleges in Philly, Jersey, maybe New York, so we're close enough to see each other."

Whenever Jalen passed that corner off of Haddon Avenue, the sour taste of dried blood flooded his memory. He touched the scar he still carried near his right eye. Who would have thought that something as simple as walking to school could be so dangerous?

Jalen dropped both girls at Asia's house, kissed Tysheina, and then walked across the street. All the way home, he thought about losing the game. He walked inside and flopped in the straight back chair at the table.

"Hey, Jalen. How did the game go? Did you win?" Michelle said, reading the mail.

Jalen reached for a plate. "Naw. Lost 98 to 111." *They were really good.*

"Well you can't win them all, besides that's the first game you lost all season. You can still make the playoffs."

"Yeah, I guess. Can we talk about this later?"

"Sure, I need to talk to you about something else anyhow."

We'd better not be moving again. Jalen got up, fixed his plate and came back to the table.

After five years, the worry lines had disappeared from his mother's face, and she had settled into a comfortable routine of work and family. She wiped her hand on her apron. "Your Aunt Marlene is getting a divorce," she said, "and she's having problems with Sean."

Jalen braced himself for the rest of her revelation.

"How would you feel if Sean came to live with us?"

Jalen relaxed and scooped up a mouth full of rice. "Sean's the closest thing I have to a brother. It's cool with me."

Michelle let out a long, slow breath. "Good. We need to make it as easy as possible."

Like the transition from Philly to Camden? As much as his mother wanted him to stay away from violence, Camden wasn't the type of place where a guy walked away from fights and intimidation with positive results. There are times in every man's life when he has to endure hardships like a good soldier.

That meant manning up to kick ass or get your ass kicked—didn't matter if he was outnumbered and scared to death.

Jalen assumed Aunt Marlene had exhausted all efforts to provide discipline for her only son. He also assumed that all the reform schools and counseling had failed. Now she was ready to pass the job on to someone else who would at least love him.

Jalen was on the phone with Tysheina when he saw his aunt's car drive in front of the house. "Hey Tysheina, my cousin just got here. I'll call you later."

Jalen rushed downstairs grinning from ear-to-ear, sticking out his hand. Sean grabbed it and the boys wrestled the way they had when they were younger.

"You better not rip my shirt, punk." Sean yelled.

"Boy, you better watch your mouth," his mother said.

"Ha-ha, yeah, you better watch your mouth," Jalen mocked, giving Sean a playful shove. "Come on, grab a suitcase and I'll show you your room. It's right next to mine."

As they took the stairs, Jalen noticed how much Sean had grown. He was built more like his father, short and stocky, with a big head that wasn't proportionate to his frame. He was much shorter and darker than Jalen. His dark brown eyes were deep, cold, and intimidating.

While the boys unpacked, Michelle and Marlene's laughter turned into a heated argument downstairs. Before the boys finished unpacking, the sound of a car engine starting up sent the boys back downstairs. Disappointment flashed all over Sean's face. He gazed at the ground where his mother's car had sat.

Jalen didn't move, didn't say a word, although he thought it was odd that Sean's mom didn't say goodbye. He tried to imagine how Sean felt, but couldn't.

"Hey Sean, what do you want for dinner?" Michelle asked.

"Huh? Oh, um, macaroni and cheese and baked chicken."

"I almost forgot how much you like Mac and Cheese," Michelle said.

Jalen bounced the basketball as he and Sean walked outside. Sean sat on the porch.

"My mom will probably put you in my school." Jalen kept bouncing the ball.

Sean reared back. "Man, I ain't goin to no booshy ass school. I'ma make some money. You go on gettin' them A's my mom keeps braggin' about with yo White ass."

"Who the hell you calling White?" Jalen shot back, tucking the ball under his arm, charging toward him.

"You! White boy," Sean said, standing to show off his developed chest.

"Nothing's wrong with passing classes besides gym," Jalen said.

"See, that's how yo White brain think. Who you know black, got money, and don't play sports?"

Strangely, Jalen couldn't name one person. All the millionaires he saw on television wore sports uniforms, or entertainment costumes.

"You don't know shit. I'm blacker than you!" Jalen said.

"See, that's how dumb you are." Sean slapped the ball from under Jalen's arm.

"You don't even know who Malcolm X or Hughey Newton are," Jalen yelled.

"I got enough sense to know I ain't White."

Sean dribbled the ball between his legs but Jalen stole it back.

"Like I said, White boy, don't sweat what I know, cause I'm dat same Nigga that beat ya ass when we was younger and I'm still dat nigga now."

Jalen reared in his face. "Who da fuck you calling White?"

Sean sized Jalen up. "Aw shit, look who got a li'l heart now. That must be ya pops coming out in you. Now ya pops . . . that Nigga was straight hood. Did time and everything. If he was still around, you might a turned out a'ight."

Jalen squinted at Sean like seeing him for the first time. He thought about his father. The power it took to stab a man. The power it took to kill someone who tries to kill your mother. The flesh resisted the point of the knife, and yet he did what he couldn't help but do to save his mother. And Sean was in his face. *If he only knew.* Sean backed down.

"You do ya school thing. I'ma find Kevin and get down with the *family* business." He turned his back on Jalen. "You know where I can get some weed?"

Weed? It's jus a matter of time for you. Jalen brushed past Sean and walked inside. He rushed past Michelle's wide questioning eyes and up the stairs to his room.

Chapter 10

Since their argument, the two cousins rarely spoke outside of necessity. Jalen kept "being white", going to school, counting down the days until he would leave for college. Three weeks later, though, Jalen and Sean walked out of Ali's barbershop on Haddon Avenue to music blaring and vibrating from every other car that rolled by. Guys hung out, talking to ripened girls walking home from Camden High. They were a billboard for ghetto-fabulous hair do's and bright nails painted in elaborate designs. Camden High School's basketball team had just won a playoff game, so the gymnasium crowd spilled out onto the Avenue.

A navy blue Toyota, street named a "Point Eight", rolled by with the back trunk rattling from the WU-TANG Clan's debut album.

Boom! Boom! Boom! Boom!

Boom! Boom! Boom! Boom!

The young ladies waved their bodies to the beat of the bass while singing along with the Clan's leading member demanding people to *get off his cloud*. One of the young men jumped out to spit some game at her. Jalen led Sean across the street to avoid the corner Kevin had warned him about years ago. The crew's faces had grown older, but they were the same. Jalen quickened the pace.

"Ay! Why you in such a hurry?" Sean asked.

"Got things to do at home. Come on, man." Jalen kept moving.

"Damn, we just got out da barbershop. Chill. I might see a chick I like."

Jalen turned back to the Point Eight. Both the guys and the girls were now chanting lyrics about Method Man's *bags of skunk* and *White Owl blunts*.

Jalen knew the longer they stayed, Sean was going to run into Kevin and the rest of his crew, and he wasn't going to contribute to Sean's delinquent nature. "Come on man, it's chicks around the way I can hook your desperate ass up with."

"Jalen! Ay, Jalen!" a raspy voice hollered from across the street. Both boys turned to Leroy standing just outside Kim Sue's Chinese Take-Out. Sean took off, dodging oncoming traffic. Jalen reluctantly tailed behind him.

"Sean, what you hangin' in Camden for?" Leroy asked, swaggering down the block to where one of his colleagues, Bucky, was posted.

"I'm squatin with Aunt Michelle and Jalen." He smirked at Jalen.

Jalen nodded.

"Ay, cousin, where's Kevin?" Sean asked.

Jalen's whole body tensed. This was the one thing he didn't want to happen. If Sean gets involved, drugs will end up in his house—*just a matter of time.*

"I'm tryin' to get put on to the game, 'ya mean?" Sean said.

Leroy crooked his neck in Jalen's direction and stared hard.

"Don't look at me. I didn't say anything," Jalen said as a group of girls walked by.

"Damn mami, let me talk to you real quick," Leroy asked but his advances were ignored. "Fuck you den!"

Bucky, a light-skinned pretty boy about as tall as Sean, but much wider, snickered at Leroy's lack of game.

Leroy noticed and interrupted. "Oh yeah, dis is Sean, my li'l cousin from Philly."

Sean grinned. "Yeah, dat's right, nigga, you heard. Philly up in here. You'll be seeing a lotta me around."

Leroy let out a loud laugh.

Jalen shook. "Sean, you coming back to the house, or what?"

"Naw," he said, draping an arm around Leroy's shoulder. "I'ma hang wid Leroy, I'll get up witcha lata." He turned his attention to Leroy. "Ay, cousin, where da smoke at?" A predatory glint flashed in his eyes. "Hey, Jalen, tell Aunt Michelle I'ma be home before midnight. And make sure you do ya homework."

Sean and Leroy's laughing exploded as they took off.

At least he didn't call me White boy 'cause cousin or no cousin, I'd have to jack him up.

Chapter 11

In the three months since Sean moved in, Jalen had grown weary of him confronting his mother. After Sean convinced her to enroll him into Camden High, Michelle received daily phone calls about his truancy and fights. That evening, Jalen sat at the kitchen table doing homework as his mother searched the refrigerator for something to fix for dinner. The phone rang.

"I'll get it," Michelle said.

Jalen's eyes followed his mother's house slippers sliding across the tile. He could tell by the way she cocked her head the phone call was about Sean again.

"Yes. I understand. I'll talk to him. Sure will." His mother walked back dispirited toward him, deep worry lines puckered her brow. "Lord, if I had a dollar for every time that phone has rung about that boy and his mess, I could afford to send you to Harvard. I'm 'bout two seconds from sending his behind back to his mother."

"How come I couldn't go to the 'High' like Sean?" Jalen asked.

"Boy, I don't wanna hear that mess today! You're at Penn-sauken High and that's where you're going to stay. Don't work my nerves."

Jalen sneaked Michelle a look.

"Don't think just because you're bigger than me I won't beat your ass." she said. Jalen looked up from his textbook in disbelief.

O shit, she cussed!

"That's right, you heard me. A belt might not work but that broomstick over there will." Jalen refocused his attention back to his Physics textbook.

Yeah, okay, and I'll have the Department of Youth and Family Services up here watching me fake a seizure. I'll even chew on a couple Alka Seltzers and start foaming at the mouth, and see how long it'll take em to lock you up.

"Thank God I never had these worries with you. How many days has it been since he's been home?" Michelle asked.

"Um, about two," Jalen answered. But the truth was that Sean hadn't been home in three days. He downplayed it, hoping to keep his mother's anger under control. He knew how she could be.

"Two days? Oh no! Not here, not at my house. Do you know where he is?" she asked.

"I'm not sure. Maybe he went back to Philly to visit a friend. I'm sure he misses being over there. He'll probably be back tonight."

"Well, he better be back here tonight because if he's not, I'm changing the locks and he can find himself another place to stay."

Man, now I gotta go find that fool.

After dinner, Jalen was out the door, headed up to Haddon Avenue. Fifteen minutes later, he spotted Sean on the corner with Leroy, Chub, and Bucky. They were laughing and joking. Sean was impressing. He had been officially *working the block* for about a month. His clothes reflected it. His new white Reebok Classic sneakers and matching athletic jogging suit made him stand out like an ink spot on white linen. A modest gold chain around his neck completed his ensemble. Sean noticed Jalen first.

"Hey, what's up, Cuz? What you doing out in these parts so close to your bedtime?" Sean mocked.

Jalen ignored him. He had more important things to deal with than trading shots with him. He grabbed Sean by the shoulder. "Look, my mom's pissed about you not coming home at night, and all the trouble you're getting into at school." His gaze locked with Sean's cold, arrogant stare. "If you keep this up, she's gonna kick you out!"

Sean shrugged off Jalen's hand. "So? Let her kick me out like my mom did." He grinned and took another pull from his blunt, and held the smoke in his lungs while he talked. "Da... only reason . . . I came . . . was so . . . I could get . . . put on by Kevin . . . phooooo." He exhaled the smoke and his body moved in a little shiver. "O, shit. Dis dat killa." He glanced at the crew on the corner. "I told you. I ain't feeling that school shit."

"Well—," Jalen started.

"I mean, don't get me wrong, I got love for you and Aunt Michelle, but I'll just stay with dis chick I been fucking til I get my own spot."

Jalen knew the number of men in his family who wouldn't find their way to jail had just decreased by one. *How do two people who grew up side-by-side decide to go in two completely different directions?*

"Five-O, Five-O!" Bucky yelled.

Jalen's heart pounded his chest. Sean smiled and raised the roach to his lips, inhaling the last drag. The noise screamed in his ears like a battle alert. The shrill deafened him. Three squad cars screeched in from different directions. Two runners sprinted into two separate alleys, jumping over trashcans while dogs howled in the backyards.

Bucky, Leroy, and Chub stood on the corner and stared at the officers. "Just chill y'all, we ain't dirty. All we doing is loitering," Bucky said calmly.

When the police car door slammed, Sean ducked in an alley that local stores used for dumping garbage. Jalen froze and slowly walked toward Sean, just in time to see him stash a chrome .38 revolver and two small bags of weed near a trash bin. Sean glared at Jalen and walked out of the alley. His dark eyes twinkled with excitement; his chest rose and fell. The flashing lights didn't seem to scare him.

A young man with features far too familiar stomped toward them. His image became clearer. "Is that Fatar?" he asked Sean. Sean didn't answer.

The cop that looked more like a professional football player than a police officer patted Fatar down for weapons. "Oh yeah, I got one and the dummy was still holding." He kept patting.

"I bet I can guess what you got in your pockets, Carl Lewis." The cop said, inspecting the bag. He tossed it to another cop.

The officer placed the few bags onto the hood of the cruiser and dug into Fatar's pockets. More small bags. "Eleven, twelve, thirteen, and the cash . . . One-sixty, one-seventy, one-eighty, one-hundred and eighty-five dollars." He clicked on handcuffs and led him to the squad car.

"His slow ass shoulda tossed dat shit." Sean boasted.

Jalen looked at Sean. *Just a matter of time.* As for Fatar, he'll be getting "three hots and a cot" for the next few years. *Sean could have all of the same things on the outside, but that would be too White.*

"Whew! Look at what I found, fellas," another police officer said, walking out of an alley. "I found me a big ole stash." He held up four plastic sandwich bags, with smaller bags inside. "Let's see what we got here."

Sean groaned. "Fuck . . . Kevin ain't gonna be happy 'bout dat."

The cops had Bucky, Leroy, and Chub up against a wall, searching their pockets, shoes and even had them open the front of their pants.

Leroy laughed when they found him clean.

"OK, you guys can go for now. Move it down the street. When I come back later, this corner better be clean or I'll arrest you just for the hell of it," the cop said.

Jalen didn't know where to place his anger: his cousins for putting Fatar on their payroll or Fatar for getting involved. *Idiot! Now they gonna try and pin everything on you. You didn't even need the money. Your grandmother spoiled you with the latest of everything. Clothes, sneakers, video games.*

"Sean, I gotta go. When you coming to get your stuff?"

"Man, fuck that shit, y'all can keep it or throw it out. I got all new stuff now."

Jalen turned to walk away. Sean's hand snaked out of his pockets and gripped Jalen's shoulder. "Make sure you thank her for letting me stay. A'ight?"

Jalen nodded. Even though Sean was messing up, Jalen still felt for him. He headed home to give his mother the news. *Just a couple more years and I'm done with this city. Off to college. I can't wait to leave . . .*

Chapter 12

Kevin sat on the sofa with his son sleeping soundly on the other end. Chasing after three-year-old Ronald had worn them both out. Now Kevin was hoping he could steal a quiet moment while Tamika was in the kitchen washing dishes. He was dozing off when his cell phone rang.

"What, man?"

"We just got hit by Five-O," Chub told him.

"Hold on!" Kevin said, rising from the couch, heading to his front steps. "Round up the crew and meet me at the basketball court near the 'High' in five. And Chub, everybody better be there."

Kevin rolled up to the area high school in his black SUV. He got out and as the truck's interior lights shut off, he started striding toward them. Everyone went silent as he stood there taking mental attendance.

"Everyone inside," Kevin ordered and headed for an abandoned brick shack twenty yards behind the courts. "So what happened, Eric?"

Eric, his captain, faced him, not altogether squarely. "Cops came from everywhere, man. They found a stash and arrested one of our runners. 'Na mean?" he spoke nervously.

"No! I don't know what you mean. Tell me what you mean. We've never been raided before. Why now all of a sudden? Can you answer me that simple question?"

Leroy stepped up. "Hell naw, he can't answer 'cause his ass wasn't there. He was messin' around wit' some chick. Only reason he know what he know is 'cause Chub called him."

"Shut da hell up, Leroy!" Kevin said.

Leroy bit his lip and shuffled in position a little.

"What about it, Chub?" Kevin asked.

Chub nodded.

"How much did they get?" Kevin asked.

Eric glanced at Chub and Chub stared up at the ceiling while counting on his fingers. Bucky stood to Kevin's left and intentionally cleared his throat.

Kevin nodded in his direction.

"They got one of the two stashes and a few bags off one of the runners. About a grand and sixty five in product, and one eighty-five in cash," Bucky said.

"So, the runner got caught holding, gave up a stash, and probably snitching right now? That about sums it up?" Kevin asked.

No one answered. Kevin surveyed the room, waiting.

Footsteps interrupted the silence and everyone jumped. Sean reached for his gun.

Jalen spoke from the doorway. "It's not Fatar's fault. The other runner did it."

"What da f—? How'd you find us?" Kevin demanded.

"Everyone knows you all meet here. Eric used to bring girls here before he made enough money for motels," Jalen answered.

Everyone snickered.

"So, how you know Fatar ain't a snitch?" Kevin asked.

Jalen took a deep breath, feeling the weight of everyone's stares. "It's simple. They only caught Fatar with thirteen bags and the money from what he sold. The big cop who brought him out the alley didn't find the stash," he said. "Another cop found the stash in a *different* alley closer to the corner. The other runner got caught, too, and gave up the stash so they would let him go."

Jalen watched how intensely the crew accepted his report. It was working. "They arrested Fatar because he *didn't* give up his stash. The cops know they have a better chance at a big fish by rolling him onto their side. If Fatar plays ball, he gets no charge and little or no time. Smacking him with jail time for the bags would be their last resort if he keeps his mouth shut." Jalen clasped his hands behind him. "Y'all need to get Fatar a lawyer.

Spring him out before they start messing with his head. Then find the runner that got away."

"You figured all this out in the last twenty minutes?" Kevin asked.

"Yeah, I'm smart, remember?"

Kevin addressed the crew. "Eric, you owe me twelve-hundred-fifty dollars. We never meet here again and you work with Leroy now. See if you can get that right. Chub, you're my captain now. Report only to me. From now on, two youngins to a stash, one runs for the package and the other handles the money."

"Bucky, you collect every half hour, depending how heavy traffic is. Then you turn the money over to Chub."

Tension was mounting.

"Chub, tomorrow, you get a safe. Find an apartment, but one that isn't close to the kitchen.

The scar on Jalen's leg was a constant reminder of what was really cooking in the kitchen. He had learned the drug game without ever touching it. He reached down and rubbed his calf, recalling an event that changed his life—

* * *

"Jalen! Come here and give me a hug before I go."

Jalen ran to his mother and gave her and his aunt Rhondella a goodbye hug. It was girls' night out. Jalen was going to spend the next few hours with his cousins, Kevin, Chub, and Eric. He trailed behind them as they made their way around the corner. Some neighborhood girls, including Mike's sister, Tamika, were standing there. Kevin and Chub disappeared down the alley with Tamika and her girlfriend. Jalen stayed with Eric who was flirting with a girl he didn't recognize. Mike came around the corner.

"Yo, what up, Mike?" Eric asked.

Mike kept coming. "Nuting much, mon. Jus' gotta run in da house and git sumting."

When Mike passed by, the kids parted like the Red Sea. A few minutes later, Mike was back. He summoned Eric. "Eric, come here for a second, mon."

"Who's ya shadow?" Mike asked, pointing to Jalen.

"Aw man, that's my li'l cousin from Philly. He gotta go with us wherever we go."

"No problem, well look, li'l cousin from Philly, don't tell nobody what tum bout ta show ya, hear?"

Jalen nodded, wanting to sound like his cousins. "A'ight."

They single-filed into the basement, where there was a table with a portable hotplate, a couple of coffee pots, and a sandwich bag full of white powder.

"Oh shit, you cooking?" Eric asked.

"Kevin told me how you showed him, but he don't wanna teach me. Hook me up, Mike. School me on how it's done!" Eric said.

"Hold on and I'll show you a ting or two. I showed Kevin 'cause he jus here when he come ta see me sista. Him ain't puttin in no work for me."

What's the big deal? My mom makes coffee every morning, but I never saw it done with flour. "How you gonna make coffee with flour?" Jalen asked.

The others laughed.

Eric walked over to the powder, stuck his finger in it, and put a sample on his tongue. "Hey, Jalen, come here."

"Hey, Mon what cha doin?" Mike asked.

"Nothin', it's cool. I'm jus' gonna put a li'l on his tongue to make it go numb." Eric put the tip of his finger back in the white powder and turned toward Jalen.

Kevin tore down the steps of the basement, accidentally knocking Jalen to the floor, and tackled Eric to the floor. "Are you fucking stupid? You don't give that shit to no kid."

"I was jus playing around, man. I wasn't gonna give it to him for real."

"Man, you ever do some dumb shit like that to Jalen again, I'ma beat the shit outta you." Kevin growled as he punched Eric in the nose. He turned to Jalen. "Get ya li'l ass outta here!"

Jalen ran, turning to look at Kevin. "It was just flour!" he said, trying to understand why Kevin was so mad.

Jalen darted out the door and into the street. Kevin was charging him, calling him. Suddenly, he heard honking horns and screeching tires. The sounds vibrated in his head. Kevin pulled the back of his shirt and jerked him off the ground but the momentum threw his leg in the air into an oncoming car. He felt the power of the car knock his sneaker off his foot and the shoe landed 20 feet down the street. Pain shot through his leg. Kevin picked him up in his arms and ran two blocks to the hospital emergency room.

Soon, Jalen's mother and her sister came flying through the door like a tornado. "Where's my son? Where's Jalen?"

She found Kevin and Eric waiting at the nurse's station talking to the doctor and the driver that hit Jalen. "Kevin! How did this happen? Doctor—"

A middle-aged white man with a comb over turned to Michelle. "Hello ma'am, I'm Dr. Banks, your son was very lucky that he was pulled from the path of the car. He's suffered a laceration on his leg and he'll be sore for a while, but he'll be fine." Dr. Banks led her to Jalen's curtained room.

Michelle threw the curtain back. "Baby, are you OK?"

"Yeah, mom. My leg just hurts, but I can still walk on it, see?" Jalen hopped off the bed to prove he was OK.

Michelle stormed out of the examining room with Jalen hobbling behind her.

"Aunt Michelle, I'm sorry. I tried to grab him but—" Kevin said.

"I don't wanna hear it, Kevin! Y'all don't have to worry about watching him again for a long time. Let's go, Jalen."

Jalen stopped in front of Kevin on the way out. "I'm sorry I made you mad, Kevin. I won't say anything to get you in trouble. I promise."

* * *

"Chub, put the safe in the new apartment and collect from Bucky every hour. Only me and you will know the combination. Understand? *Only me and you*! That apartment is our bank." Kevin made it clear.

Chub nodded.

Jalen knew he had no reason to listen to any of this, but didn't dare move until Kevin gave him the okay to leave.

"Sean, you and that new soldier, Norris, y'all go back and forth to the apartment with Chub and watch his back." Kevin scanned the crew. "Any questions?"

The only sounds came from night insects, leaves blowing in the wind, and horns of the cars in the distance.

"Good. Now get the hell out." Kevin said. Then he turned around once more. "The corner's hot! Leave it alone 'til we get a handle on what's going on and we square this thing with Fatar. And Bucky, find that damn runner!"

As everyone started to leave, Kevin called, "Hold up a minute, Jalen. I'll take you home." They walked silently until they reached the car. "Damn, I knew you were smart, but you're damn near psychic."

"Nothing psychic about it," Jalen answered.

"Ain't spent one day hustlin', but you got it all figured out before anyone else." He tapped Jalen on the shoulder. "You may not be a hustla, but you've got a hustla's spirit, and that can't be taught."

Jalen said nothing.

"Look, I'm sorry about Fatar. I know he's your boy, but you're old enough to know that I didn't force this on him," Kevin said.

Jalen nodded and climbed into the car.

Kevin unzipped his coat. "Those of us that choose this life know and accept the consequences. You've heard the same tired clichés I have. You either end up dead or in jail, but, for some of us, it's all we know, all we have—for the time being. I like Fatar and I believe what you said about him tonight."

Relief rolled through Jalen.

"I want you to talk to his grandmother and find out what his bail is. Take my cell number and hit me when you know. I'll put up his bail. You let Fatar know where the money came from. Tell him we know he hasn't talked to the police and he needs to keep it that way."

Jalen nodded.

"Remember what I told you before, Jalen."

Jalen tried to wrap his mind around what Kevin could mean by *told you before.*

Boom! Boom! Boom!

An addict appeared on Jalen's side of the car, knocking on the window. Jalen jumped.

"Kevin," the man said, ignoring Jalen, "ain't nobody down the way. You holding anything?"

Kevin flashed a gun. "Get da fuck outta here!"

The addict disappeared as fast as he had come.

Kevin tucked the gun under his seat. "You okay?"

Jalen nodded.

Kevin continued, "I'm not going to be doing this forever. I'm not like those fools who think this is a career. This is just a way for me to make ends meet for my family until I figure something else out. One or two more years and I'm done."

Jalen looked at Kevin, wondering whom he was trying to convince, him or himself.

Chapter 13

It was almost the end of June 1993 and the cool breeze coming in Jalen's window caused the Malcolm X and Michael Jordan posters to flap up and down. *Two graduation parties in one night? Tonight's going to be crazy!* He smiled, pulling on baggy jeans and a neatly pressed XL navy blue polo shirt.

The afternoon's graduation amounted to his family yelling and screaming his name all through the high school graduation ceremony. Envelopes stuffed with cards and money were still in his pant and jacket pockets. In less than an hour, he would take his first step into independence. Into the world. It felt eerie. Crazy. Great. Frightening. He would be leaving home in September to attend an historically Black college, Morgan State University, in Baltimore, Maryland. Ten-to-one female to male ratio. Friday to Sunday parties. Tonight would be as good of a time as any to take his first drink. Get used to the lifestyle. This warm summer night was perfect for such a celebration.

At just past nine, he headed downstairs and kissed his mom on the cheek. "I'm 'bout to get outta here, Ma. If you need to get in touch, call JC's house; that's where I'll be staying tonight."

"Have fun and no drinking, Jalen. I don't need any phone calls in the middle of the night 'bout my only son being in the hospital or worse."

Jalen snickered until he saw the serious look on her face. He walked back and pulled up a chair next to her. "Ma, you don't have to worry about me. I'm gonna be OK."

"Yeah, I did a pretty good job raising you, didn't I?" Michelle gave him a nudge in his ribs.

"Yeah, and I'm about to experience a whole new world. You know I couldn't have made it without you. Love you, Mom."

Michelle's eyes started to tear; she could barely get out her words. "I love you, too." Her nose turned red and they hugged.

Jalen hopped into his mother's car and sped toward Fairview, a miniature suburb just outside of Camden. The first party of the night was at Marquees Campbell's house, a buddy from Pennsauken High. He could see Marquees's white Colonial two-story house down the street. Though Fairview was barely outside of Camden, the change in scenery was instant. White faces and manicured front lawns, streets as clean as a living room floor. He popped the lock and walked up the street toward the sound of hip-hop coming from Marquees's house.

He smiled, anticipating the night ahead. No worries tonight. No studying. No football or basketball practice, nothing but fun. And if I'm lucky, a young lady to top off the night. Jalen stood in the doorway. The majority of the football team and cheerleaders were dancing, laughing, kissing, and drinking. A few others stretched out on the floor. Others mingled, smoking and passing weed.

"What up, Marquees?" Jalen asked as he gave up some dap to Marquees.

Marquees stood head and shoulders above him in self-confidence because the University of Wisconsin had already accepted him on a football scholarship. He'd be joining his friend, Byron Pelling, a massive, three hundred and twenty pound native of Pennsauken, who graduated last year and was already starting offensive tackle as a freshman.

"Man, can you believe it's finally over?" Marquees asked.

"Hell, yeah! Why you think I haven't stopped smiling since this morning?"

"Grab a drink and talk to some women. You know, I'ma try and run up in about two or three of 'em tonight. You know how I do." Marquees said.

Jalen laughed and whispered. "Yeah, just make sure you do it with a rubber this time. Keep those penicillin shots outta your ass."

Marquees cringed, leaned over, and grabbed his groin. "Oh, don't remind me. The drips ain't no joke."

Jalen laughed. "A'ight. I'm gettin' a drink."

Jalen made his way into the kitchen and grabbed a beer from the refrigerator. Class president and valedictorian, Tori Cruz, was talking to the class clown Kenny Butler.

"It's pre-med at Stanford or nothing," Tori said.

"Who cares about *pre-med*," Kenny replied.

Kenyatta Taylor was drunk and took the conversation into left field. "I'm headed off to L.A., the West Siiiiide, to get my acting career off, man. And, Tori how can you stand being in school the rest of ya damn life? By the time you finish I'll be accepting my first Oscar." Kenyatta held up his beer bottle, as if it were an award at his first acceptance speech.

"Well, Mr. 'I would-like-to-thank-the-Academy', remember you are allowed to bring a guest, so don't forget to invite me as your date. You always had that little hidden crush on me." Tori reminded him.

Jalen took a swig of beer and cringed. *Damn, this shit doesn't taste good at all.*

The music and the blue light drove the crowd. Jalen was on the dance floor grinding with Noemi, one of the few Puerto Rican cheerleaders, who had always had her eye on him. Tysheina entered in skintight jeans and a top that propped her chest to a new height. Her two best friends, Asia Carter and Lisa Atkins, trailed behind her. Tysheina's eyes became thin slits when she saw who had her arms around Jalen.

He almost felt like he was cheating, even though they'd broken up three weeks before the prom. The rumor that she was messing with someone else melted Jalen's ego and ended their relationship.

Lisa smiled and whispered something to Tysheina before the trio disappeared into the crowd. Tysheina broke away and wove her way through the dancers until she stood directly behind Jalen. Noemi turned her back to Jalen and began rubbing her backside on him.

Tysheina brushed a bold hand across his butt and whispered, "Does she do it like me?"

Jalen's heart leaped at the sound of her voice; he remembered all the nights he had snuck into her house while her mother was at work. When Asia spotted Tysheina and Jalen she shook her head in disappointment.

Jalen's eyes followed Tysheina to the other side of the room where Marquees was serving shots of rum.

Noemi smacked him on the chest. "If you gonna stare at her like that, you might as well go dance with her instead of me." She stormed off the floor.

Tysheina and Lisa started laughing. Heated and a bit embarrassed, Jalen strolled over to the cooler for another beer. He had danced enough for tonight. A quick check of his watch and the silver hands inched toward 11:30. He had come to this party first, knowing that the other party back in Camden wouldn't really start jumping until midnight. He made a final lap around the room ending up at Marquees's makeshift bar. He was already drunk.

"OK, ladies, it's happy hour, line up and get your shots of lemon-flavored rum. For every three girls taking a shot I'll be removing a piece of clothing. I'm headed for Madison, Wisconsin in the next couple of weeks, so let's drink up!"

Girls lined up at the bar, taking shot after shot. Marquees took off his clothes as promised. Jalen chuckled. "Marquees! Man, I have to hit another party, but I'll be back if it gets shut down by the cops or something."

Marquees winked. "A'ight, no problem. That's one less dude to compete with, but, then again, who can compete with all of this?" Marquees held his arms open as he stood there wearing a pair of basketball shorts, socks, and shower shoes.

As Jalen made his way to the door, he noticed some of the girls licking their lips; some were peeking at Marquee's shorts trying to get a take on the size of the package. Just as he reached the door, Asia and Tysheina waded through the crowd and joined him.

"Hey! You just gonna leave without saying anything, Jalen?" Asia questioned.

"It's not like that. I got another party to go to, I'll be back."

"Oh, okay then. You all set for college?" Asia asked.

"You know it. Can't wait to start. You and Omar finally decide what schools you're going to? " Jalen asked.

"Yup, I signed my letter of intent with Villanova. So I'll be running track there and Omar's going to be at St. Joe's in Philly. You know, it's kind of sad seeing all of this end. Don't you think?"

"Yeah, I feel you on that," Jalen said.

Tysheina was done listening. She wanted Jalen and shimmied past Asia in front of him. "You know, this may be the last time we see each other before we all go our separate ways to college."

Jalen could smell the rum on her breath. He had never known Tysheina to drink. It worried him. There were plenty of guys here who would be more than willing to finish her off after a few seductive words. He walked her a few feet outside, hoping the fresh air would help sober her up. Asia stood on the other side of the screen door waiting patiently for her almost drunken friend.

"You know it's too bad we're not together anymore," she whispered, lowering her hands to his thighs and pelvis. "My mom started me on the pill since I'll be going to Drexel in the fall. You could have me without a condom for a change."

She was bumping and grinding on Jalen, matching the beat and lyrics of the music inside. Although the party was full, Tysheina always managed to make him feel like they were alone. Jalen was comfortable being anywhere and doing anything with her.

He regained his composure. "I have another party to go to in Camden."

Tysheina grinned as she looked down at the bulge in his pants. "If you change your mind, come back here and *maybe* I'll have a surprise waiting for you." She kissed Jalen on the cheek, turned and walked back into the party.

"Good luck in college, Jalen. Maybe we'll run into each other when we're all grown up," Asia said followed by a wave of the hand.

Jalen returned the wave with a smile and headed for the car, but his mind was on Tysheina and what she said. *Sex . . . raw? Damn! Never had it like that*. He was throbbing with the idea of feeling her. *I'm definitely making my way back here sometime tonight.*

Jalen reached JC's at exactly midnight and headed straight to the patio where everyone was. The women were all gathered around JC, the All-American basketball player with "good hair." Jalen's mind was on Tysheina and her promise.

Students cheered and jumped up and down as JC's parents danced. They were both in their late thirties and pretty cool. JC's dad had the grill going in front of the wood patio and flipped a burger or two between dances. His mom smoked a joint while she served sodas and beer.

Jalen made sure JC's mom and his mom never crossed paths. If they had, Michelle would have a mild stroke. She would have instantly sniffed out Mrs. Collins's young carefree lifestyle. She wore the same hairstyle and painted acrylic finger nails that the young girls did.

Jalen walked up behind JC who was wearing jean shorts and a *Property of Temple University Athletics* T-shirt. "What's up, superstar?"

JC turned. "What's up, Jalen." He bumped his shoulder against Jalen's, then waved, trying to get everyone's attention. "Everybody say what up to the smartest Nigga I know."

Smartest Nigga. Definitely a better description then being called White. Too bad Sean could never see it that way. The thought saddened Jalen. He also hoped that Kevin would make good on his promise to leave the drug game. Somehow, with each passing month, as Kevin gained more money, more control—leaving didn't seem likely.

"Yo," JC said, "we celebratin' it all tonight. I'm headed to play ball at Temple. Yo ass wanna go to Maryland and learn how to build super computers. And to top it all off, guess who's back home?"

JC led Jalen back into the house, upstairs toward his bedroom. "Go ahead, open the door."

Jalen pushed the door open. A half-naked girl, with hips that begged a man to grab and hold on for dear life was on her knees in front of a man stretched out on his back on the bed. Her head bobbed, accompanied by loud slurps.

"Oh shit, welcome home, Fatar!" Jalen shouted.

Niffon Thompson, the neighborhood "jump off," grabbed her blouse as Fatar scrambled to pull up his pants. She wasn't one of the prettier girls, but her tight body and loose morals made up for it. She had been known to have a train of two to three guys from the same crew on any given night.

Fatar looked at Jalen and laughed. "Yo, man, what's up? How you gonna bust in the door while I'm trying to bust a nut? You know I been away for a while."

Fatar continued. "Ay, but for real though," he said, casting a glance at Niffon, "y'all need to get the hell out. I'll holla at y'all in a minute."

"Muthafucka, it better take you longer than that," Niffon snapped. "I didn't come up here just to give you head. I want some dick!"

"A'ight baby, calm down. You gonna get yours." Fatar nodded to the guys. "Yo, I'll holla at y'all in 'bout... um, 'bout three—" The girl groaned.

"Five minutes," he continued. She shrugged and pulled on her blouse.

"Ten—a," he said.

She paused and frowned at him.

"All right, twenty."

She grimaced. "Twenty."

Jalen and JC laughed as they headed back to the party.

Fatar came down fifteen minutes later. "Yo, smell my finger. Does it smell like fish?" he laughed, shoving his finger in their faces. They both grimaced and jumped away.

"Okay y'all, where da food at? I'm hungry as hell. I woulda been down sooner but I wanted to bust *two* nuts."

Niffon walked towards them, cutting her eyes at Fatar. "Sorry-ass muthafucka!"

Fatar chuckled. "Hey, baby, what you expect? I been locked up." He patted her butt. "It was good though. You should be proud."

She turned around, threw up her middle finger, and strolled toward the bar.

Jalen stopped laughing. "You'll never hear from her again. Now go wash your nasty ass hands before you touch the food."

It was two o'clock in the morning and the party had died down. JC's parents had commandeered a small troupe to help clean and the place looked like no one had been there. Three girls looking bored to death sat around the table listening to Jalen, Fatar, and JC reminisce about their good old days.

"Jalen, remember when we were freshman at Camden Catholic High School and you got kicked off the basketball team cause you punched that White boy who called you a Nigger?" JC asked.

"Hell yeah, I remember. That's when I knew I wasn't gonna be at that school long. I don't see how you did it. I guess being an *All-American* has some benefits, huh?"

"Then ya ass became a revolutionary and reading everything about Malcolm X, and started acting out, hoping they'd kick you out," JC joked. "Then when they didn't, you failed all your final exams, 'cause you knew your mom wouldn't pay three thousand dollars a year for you to flunk everything," Fatar chimed in.

"Hell yeah! His mom wasn't having that. She sent his ass to public school wit da quickness."

As the girls grew increasingly impatient, JC's girlfriend whispered in his ear and Jalen saw her slide his hand in between her thighs. JC's eyes widened while the fellas waited to see what he would do.

JC removed her hand. Seconds later, he said, "Lock the door when you leave; there are extra sheets in the hallway closet upstairs."

Only Jalen and Fatar remained on the patio with the women they met that night.

Fatar patted the woman's thigh that sat to his left. "Hey, won't y'all go and wait for us in the living room. I need to talk to Jalen 'bout something real quick."

The two girls looked at each other, sucked their teeth, and went inside the house.

"What's up, Fatar?"

"Ay man, I heard what you did for me when I got busted. I just wanted to thank you for what you and Kevin did. I was looking at doing some serious time 'til ya'll got me that lawyer. He got the judge to drop the second charge they tried to pin on me."

"You mean from the other alley?" Jalen asked.

"Yeah, them charges wouldn't stick 'cause where they found it was nowhere near where they caught me. Man, if I woulda gotten stuck with a public defender—"

"Man, don't thank me. I just told Kevin what I knew and he handled the rest."

"I'm thanking you anyway." He extended a fist to Jalen, who answered with a tap to the knuckles. "By the way, whatever happened to the dude that gave up his stash?" Fatar asked.

"Man, I don't know," Jalen said with a shrug. "You know I don't get involved with that. I'm a geek, not a hustler, remember?" Jalen wanted to know as little as possible. *Ignorance is bliss.*

"Come on, man, let's head back in the crib before them chicks get too mad," Fatar said.

The girls were giggling and talking until they saw Fatar and Jalen.

"Yeah, jailbird, I don't be waitin' around for nobody. Especially somebody who can't hold his nuts longer then ten minutes."

Fatar disregarded the girl's comments. "Girl, you know that was the best fifteen minutes of ya life." His gaze landed on the other girl. "You keep talkin' shit and I'll be givin' all dis good lovin' to somebody else. Ya heard?"

Jalen only shook his head. Fatar was on a losing streak with the ladies. Another strikeout and he'd be out of luck on the sex trail. Word gets around.

Chapter 14

Daddy get up! I didn't mean to hurt you, get up! Jalen was back in the house standing over his father bleeding out on the floor. Where's mom? Why isn't she in the room?

Help me. Heeeelp me. I'm dying.

I'll help you daddy. I won't let you die this time. Jalen leaned over to grab his father. Blood was still pouring out of the wound. When he turned him over the face he was expecting wasn't there. It was a face he didn't recognize, calling for help.

Help me, Jalen. Help me. I didn't mean to hurt anybody. I just didn't want to go to jail.

Instantly, Jalen realized who the person was—the runner who had gotten Fatar jail time. The young man reached for his shirt and pulled it open, two bloody bullet holes showed in his chest.

Jalen jerked forward. *Where am I? Not at home.* With the streetlight sneaking in through the window, he could see posters of Michael Jordan, Magic Johnson, and Larry Johnson as 'Grand Mama' plastered over the walls. He was in JC's guest bedroom. A warm body stirred next to him. Her black shoulder-length hair was flung everywhere. Her brown skin almost blended perfectly with the chocolate brown sheets. She definitely was not Tysheina.

He looked down and saw he still had the condom on. He carefully slipped to the edge of the bed and pulled it off, tied it into a knot and tossed it into a waste paper basket near the bed, knowing that going back to sleep would be impossible. He looked for his clothes while images of the nightmare still raced through his mind. He couldn't get Fatar's last question out of his head. *" . . . Whatever happened to the dude that gave up his stash?"*

* * *

An hour after Kevin dispersed the family under the new rules, Bucky turned the soldiers loose. They searched for Joseph, the runner who gave up the stash to the cops, in all the usual places. They turned to friends, girlfriends, and hang outs. Finally, they walked up on a sagging porch, where an older woman, with graying hair and a golden floral head rag on her head, was leaving the house.

"Hello, Ma'am, we're looking for Joseph. We're old friends of his from school. You seen him?" Bucky asked.

"No, but, if you see my son, tell him he needs to come home. Now you hooligans get away from my property before I call the police." She passed by without another word.

Bucky and Sean broke into the house, thinking Joseph's mother was covering for him. They tore up his bedroom, knocked down old basketball trophies and his pictures in his # 33 jersey. He started to knock down a picture of Joseph in an alter boy uniform.

"Look at dis," Sean said, "he used to be an alter boy, my moms used to try and get me to do dis." Soon after they charged out the rear door.

"That picture had a church banner in the background. That's the church with the shelter and soup kitchen," Bucky said.

An hour later, at Camden High Park, cars zoomed by, and leaves blew over the empty basketball court. Streetlights beamed down on blades of grass, but in the distance the sound of slaps and punches rivaled the car horns and rubber tires gliding along the asphalt.

Sean and Bucky found Joseph sleeping in the church. They took him back to the shed and beat a confession out of him. Joseph admitted freelancing in another part of town when he sold to an undercover cop. The cop told him if he gave them info on a bigger dealer, they would let him go without a charge. He told them about Kevin and where they kept the product stashed and they setup the bust on Kevin.

After his confession, Sean pulled out his .38 revolver and shot him twice in the chest. Three days later, Joseph's body was found by neighborhood kids playing basketball at the nearby court.

Chapter 15

Jalen found his jeans and quietly slid them on, still facing the bed to get a last look at the slumbering girl's body. *What was her name?* His thoughts switched to Tysheina and how she had him wrapped around her finger. He smiled just thinking about her, thinking back to the night after *the game.*

* * *

It was the first time Jalen had smiled all night after losing the basketball game. He went to Tysheina's place after his mother went to work. He looked at her and leaned in to kiss her. She leaned in to meet him. He inched closer to her, putting his hands on her thigh.

"I love touching you, Tysheina."

"Then keep touching me," she answered, as their hands explored each other's bodies.

"Baby, wait a minute," she said.

"What's wrong? You want to stop?"

"No. I want you to come with me upstairs." Jalen was excited and scared at the same time. He had never had sex. He took discreet deep breaths because he didn't want to let on that this was his first time. With every breath he took, his heartbeat amplified in his ears. He could feel his pulse in his ears, his face, his hands, his eyes, his lips.

They lay on her bed and picked up where they left off downstairs. Gradually, they undressed each other and threw the clothes on the floor. Jalen gazed at her naked body. He softly stroked her breast and kissed her nipples until she started making shallow sounds that only he could hear. He worked his hands down her side, around to her back, and finally shifted his weight just enough—making room to find the heat between her thighs. Her shallow little sounds became a full moan. She rotated her hips in a way that seemed to please her. Jalen picked up on the rhythm. Happy with his technique, she quit moving. He inserted two fingers inside of her. She made a deeper sound that said it all, deep and complete.

Tysheina reached up to feel his chest and his stomach and ventured farther down to touch and feel his hardness. She smiled and looked into his eyes as she stroked him, then spread herself wide to invite him inside her.

"You sure?" he asked.

"Yes, baby."

He leaned off the edge of the bed and grabbed his jeans finding the condom he had stashed in his pocket . . . just in case. He tore the package open with his teeth and rolled it on. After repositioning himself, he reached down and grabbed himself in search of where they both wanted him to be. His inexperience showed; after two failed attempts, Tysheina reached down and guided him in.

"Push softly," she whispered.

He felt himself gradually slide into the most perfect place he had ever been. In there was all of his dreams and fantasies. In there was excitement and joy. In there was something he never wanted to leave. In there was heaven. Jalen found the ultimate joy in life multiple times for the next hour. Until they both fell asleep, exhausted.

* * *

Just thinking about it now made him shiver. He slipped his shirt back on and eased into the bathroom. He threw water on his face, followed by a quick rinse of Listerine from the cabinet. A quick drop of his pants for a morning leak released a powerful sexual odor. He could smell the girl he had left in JC's guest room on him. He dropped his pants around his ankles and then grabbed a washcloth and some soap, turned on the faucet full blast and thoroughly washed his genitals. He didn't want to make it all the way over to Marquees's house just to get shut down because Tysheina could smell another woman on him. He bolted out the door. When he arrived at Marquees's house the entire neighborhood was silent. Marquees's front door was open. *Marquees better stop doing this, or one day he's gonna wake up and find his stereo and TV missing.*

A few stragglers were in the main area of the basement that smelled like a distillery. They were all passed out on a futon, or snoring on the floor under sheets, blankets, or coats. He didn't see Tysheina and disappointment flooded over him.

Even so, he marched on to the back toward Marquees's bedroom. A pounding, squeaking sound stole through the music that played softly on the radio. The closer he came to the door, the clearer he heard the pounding. Then he realized Marquees was pounding away on some girl. Faint sounds of their skin smacking against each other became more and more audible. He looked around the room, hoping to find Tysheina, but only found empty beer bottles and a couple snuggled together under a sheet. The smacking became louder—almost like a thunderclap.

Marquees growled, "Oh no, don't run from it! Take it! Take it!"

Jalen grinned at how cocky Marquees could be. He had heard plenty about how Marquees put it down on the nights he stayed over. It almost got them both in trouble the time his parents heard the two of them boasting about who could make their girl moan the loudest.

"I'm taking it baby! Yeah that's right, get it!" the female voice responded.

Marquees got his hands full tonight! Jalen stepped over bodies and crept closer to Marquees's room, hoping to get a glimpse.

"That's right! My sex is all that, ain't it?" the female voice panted.

Jalen's face went blank, his body went weak. He knew that voice all too well.

"Do these other chicks do it like I do? Say my name, say 'Tysheina!'"

She had never said that to *him*! He liked to hear that dirty shit, too!

"I see it all in your face Marquees," she said. "You 'bout to cum ain't you? Come on, bust up all inside me! I'm on the pill, it's okay, baby."

The rumors had been right! Jalen wanted to say something, anything, but couldn't. Anger, betrayal, disbelief, and sadness all raged inside him. He didn't know whether to cry or charge in and fight.

He did neither. He turned and quietly walked out of the house, realizing karma had slung an angry arrow in his direction. Tonight, he had been with a woman he never knew. The woman he wanted was with somebody she did know. From the sounds of it—not for the first time.

Chapter 16

The black SUV took to the highway on cruise control. Kevin leaned to one side with his left hand on the wheel. He got off at Interstate 295 North. Soon, the road narrowed and the tall trees cleared. He could see Trenton State Penitentiary, the main stop for New Jersey's worst criminals. His oldest brother, Damon was there. As a youth, Damon frequented juvenile facilities for petty crimes like assault and larceny. One day, a street fight went from a simple beat down to a man's death, and that landed him in the big boy's house for manslaughter.

Damon was the only one in the family Kevin couldn't beat in a fistfight, and the only one he respected and listened to without question. Damon had already served seven years of a twelve-year sentence. Kevin's monthly visits were special and hard to bear. He enjoyed the time they spent together, but he missed having his brother around.

Kevin stepped into a small dingy room where multiple visitors were seated. When Damon finally arrived, they exchanged smiles and sat down at the cold metal table. Kevin took notice of how all the years of weightlifting had transformed his brother's arms into miniature tree trunks. Damon was very dark complexioned in comparison to Kevin, but when you looked at the shape of their faces, you could see they were brothers.

"So, how is everything going back home?" Damon asked.

"Things are real good. Mika just had our second boy. We're still living in the city, but we finally got into a nice new house and I'm making enough to keep us going for a while."

"And how's work?"

Kevin smirked at the ongoing joke. "The store's doing alright, but we got robbed a little while back. Nothing too serious 'cause we back on track and made up for the loss. We got a new plumber to fix a leaky pipe and I had to reorganize the management."

"Hmm, you had a busy month. You give any more thought to starting a second store and getting yaself a chain?" Damon shifted his weight on the cold metal. "You got too many employees for one store."

"I thought about it, but don't think it's a good idea right now."

"Really?"

"Yeah, I think it's time to switch my game up. Making moves to a more meaningful business that doesn't have as much risk."

"Meaningful?" Damon asked. "What you talkin' 'bout?" Then he grimaced, rubbing a nervous hand through his nappy beard. "Matter of fact, I don't even wanna know. You might mess around and tell me you wanna be a Catholic priest playing with little boys' ding-a-lings."

Kevin laughed. "Hell no, nothin' like that. Nothing special, just a li'l something to make me feel good about the work I'm doing, 'na mean?"

Damon broke eye contact, focusing on another inmate to his left. Kevin turned to see what had caught his brother's attention. Another inmate sat almost under an attractive female visitor. His hand was in between her thighs; her hands were touching, grabbing, and pulling between his legs.

Kevin whispered to Damon, "It always amazes me what y'all will do to get some ass up in here."

Damon kept his gaze on the couple. "Man, when you been away from it as long as we have . . . " his voice drifted off. "Fake ass thugs be walkin' around all tough when they come in, but after a few months, they walking with a sway and calling some dude they man while cutting his hair."

"Well you keep maintaining, and I'll keep stacking ya commissary and sending you those magazines you like. Then when you get out I'll have a couple girls waiting to welcome you home in style."

"I'm getting my GED soon. Finishing what I started before Mika got pregnant." Kevin said.

"I've been taking up boxing to help kill my time in here. No disrespect and all but what's up with the GEDs and looking to start a new gig? Everything cool out there?" Damon studied him.

"Yeah, like I said, we had a minor setback, but I just want to have something more stable. You know, so when my kids go to school and I come up there for career day, I can wear a uniform and they can brag about what they daddy does for a living."

Damon looked at Kevin cross-eyed and started to speak.

"Visiting time is over," a voice yelled over a loudspeaker. "All inmates, step away from your visitors and report back to your cell."

Damon and Kevin stood. They hugged. Damon seemed disappointed, like he wanted to get to the root of what was making Kevin doubt his lifestyle. They parted with the usual salutation, "See you next month. Be strong."

Damon swaggered away, but turned back. "Ay, Kev, don't make yourself a liar. I don't wanna have to see you in here."

Kevin gave him a single nod and watched his brother disappear behind a security door, a world his brother had so well adjusted to. Maybe so well that he didn't fear it anymore. Maybe that was why Kevin sensed his brother's apprehension about him leaving the game.

He thought back to the conversation he had while driving Jalen home after he convinced them Fatar wasn't the snitch.

* * *

As they drove through the notorious areas of Camden, Jalen blurted out, "Drugs are everywhere. At almost every rundown house and old storefront on this block." Kevin turned onto another side street, thinking about his young cousin's words.

"You see these homes?" Jalen asked, pointing to an abandoned building surrounded by a semicircle of thugs hanging outside. "I bet you that used to be some family's home."

Kevin turned off that street.

"I see it on the body language of every passing addict trying to sell stolen goods just to get their next fix. Their faces look like so many people I know, or once knew. But I know they'll rob and steal from me and anyone else just to satisfy that inner demon, just like my father did."

Kevin turned onto Chestnut Street, where three women rushed the SUV, blaring open their blouses, and swaying their hips and displaying foul unkempt flesh. He sped up.

"On a good day, I see the faces of women who could have been my mother, my aunt, or grandmother. But on the bad days, the faces *are* my cousins and aunts. The same kin we both spent Christmases and Thanksgivings with, drank out of the same glass, ate from the same plate," Jalen mumbled on.

The women became small and invisible in the rear view mirror. "Family, but not family. Their own worst enemy. They leave children, wives, husbands, and parents behind. They become almost inhuman," Jalen said, as if in a trance, as if he were an old man looking back on what went wrong. Kevin gave Jalen a look. For the first time, they were having a man-to-man conversation. Jalen was no longer a child; he was a young man in high school, and feeling all of it.

"Even us poor people can look down on them—that is until they can manage to search themselves for whatever human dignity they have left to convince us they'll change."

"Then they take the few dollars we give and feed their addiction," Jalen said.

"And we swear that this is the last time we'll help them kill themselves, but we know it's a lie." Jalen stared ahead, as another corner filled with young men loomed like a large, dark storm against the sky.

As Kevin neared Jalen's house, the grip he had on the steering wheel was that of a man trying to make a heavy decision. He stopped and Jalen jumped out and ran inside.

* * *

Kevin arrived at the Camden exit of 295 South and took a left. Jalen's words had filled his thoughts all the way back to

Camden. He pulled into Haddon Avenue and rolled down his window, "Chub, come here."

Chub cut Leroy and Bucky short and ran over to the car.

"Where's Eric?"

"At the kitchen."

"Good, after your next trip to the bank I need you, Leroy, Eric, and Bucky to come to my crib. We need to talk."

"Something wrong?"

"Naw, I just been thinking over some stuff and need to let you guys know what our next move is."

"A'ight. Let me make dis drop and I'll catch up wit' you in thirty to forty minutes."

Kevin rolled up the window and pulled off.

Chapter 17

The entire crew showed up at the small brick house Kevin and Tamika called home. Tamika answered the door with their newborn, Jason, cradled in her arms.

"Hey y'all. He's downstairs."

The four teased and made faces at the baby as they came in. Downstairs, Kevin threw a left jab into an Everlast bag dangling from a chain attached to a wood beam. He had hung it in the basement years ago, using it when he needed to work things out in his head, or when someone had pissed him off enough that he just needed to pound on something. He'd hit the Everlast rather than land a weighty throw in someone's face. *POW. POW. POW.* He batted the bag.

"Take a seat," *POW. POW.* "I'll be right there." *POW. P-POW P-POW. P-POW.*

The basement was Kevin's refuge and conference room—a big rectangular kitchen table with six chairs around it occupied the back wall. Every meeting had taken place right there since that night in the park. Tamika wasn't thrilled, but she was happy about anything that would bring Kevin home. The crew sat, watching Kevin throw ferocious combinations at the bag, one crushing blow after the other.

Ding. A timer rang. Kevin froze, cracked his neck, stripped off the gloves, draped a towel around his neck, and sat at the head of the table. He downed a few gulps of bottled water and eyed the crew.

"We need to talk about our future. We're going to expand to another corner. All of the crew smiled big.

"Yeah, I thought y'all would like that."

"Damn, 'bout time. I was starting to wonder if we was gonna be working that little ass corner forever," Leroy said.

"Yeah, man. Things are good over there but we need to make as much money as we can while we can," Chub added.

"Yeah, um, I think we should expand a lil bit," Eric said.

"I don't think it's a good idea. If it ain't broke, don't fix it," Bucky said.

"Man, kill that noise! We can make more money if we work another corner," Leroy said, folding beefy arms across his massive chest. Leroy had become bolder in voicing his opinion about how things should be run. He and Kevin had always had a touch-and-go relationship, even growing up. But lately that boldness had almost landed him on the wrong side of Kevin's fist.

"Well, this is how we gonna work it," Kevin said. "We gonna vote so everybody's got a fair say. After the vote, if anyone can't roll with the decision, they can walk." Kevin's gaze leveled on Leroy. "And they won't have to worry about any beef from whoever decides to stay."

The only sound in the room was the squeaking of the chain from the heavy bag swaying from side to side from the leavings of Kevin's fist.

"One more thing," Kevin said, "I'm not voting. I'm leaving this decision up to you guys." He paused. "Y'all been taking orders from me long enough." Kevin leaned back in the chair and tapped the end of the towel across his brow. "You gotta make your own decision on this one. I'll only vote if there's a tie."

Bucky glanced sideways, but didn't say a word.

"Everybody who wanna work another corner raise ya hand," Leroy blurted out before shooting his arm in the air. Chub joined him; Bucky kept his palms flat against the table.

Eric gingerly raised his right hand. They voted three to one to expand.

Bucky shook his head. "We makin' a mistake. All we gonna do is bring more heat on us. Gettin' rich quick only gets you jail time." Then he looked up at Kevin. "But I'll respect the decision and roll with it."

Leroy bared his teeth in a broad smile. "Hell yeah, this is what I'm talking 'bout. Time to make some real money up in this bitch. As a matter of fact, I been checking out this spot in East Camden."

Kevin watched him, waiting for all his plans to spill. Plans he was sure Leroy had pieced together prior to tonight.

"I got this chick in East Camden I mess wit' when my girl ain't actin' right. And she was telling me these Puerto Rican cats be hustling out there around the clock, all day every day, all month."

Bucky perked up. "All month? Nobody hustles all month nonstop."

Leroy grinned. "Dem rice and beans-eating muthafuckas do." Leroy paused, as if to let the information sink in. "Them mida midas round there hustle like dey addicts. I saw it myself."

Kevin leaned back, watching closely, listening to every word.

"When Tasha had our baby last month, she was in the hospital for two weeks straight 'cause Leroy Jr. was premature. She didn't wanna leave da hospital. So I stayed wit' dis chick for a couple days after visiting hours, and man, I'm telling you. I saw them moving product like it was the first of the month and y'all know Jr. was born on da twenty-third. So if it's like that at the *end* of the month, you can imagine how da rest of the month is when peeps get they checks from the state—"

"With a flow like that, somebody gotta be running it and they gotta have soldiers," Bucky said.

Leroy nodded, unfolding his hands so he could press a single finger on the table. "You right 'bout dat, some Puerto Rican kid is running things out there and he got a li'l crew. But this the strongest we ever been and we got soldiers, too." He eyed the fellas at the table. "So let's go take dat shit. Sean can body half those muthafuckas by hiself."

"Yeah, that fool is crazy like that," Bucky agreed. "Like I said, just cause I don't agree with it, don't mean I'm not down to roll wit' y'all. So let's make it happen."

Kevin finally broke his silence. "Sounds like you been putting some serious thought into this, cousin. You been plotting on dis corner for a while, huh?"

"Naw, it ain't like that. Jus something I fell ass backwards into, 'na mean?"

"Yeah, I know exactly what you mean," Kevin said as he stared directly into Leroy's eyes. "Okay, no more talk."

Everyone went silent, looking to Kevin for direction.

"We gonna bump dem fools and take they corner, hold it down and hustle both," Kevin said.

"We done here." Kevin walked them to the door, watching as they got into their cars.

The phone rang. "Kevin, Sergeant Banks is on the phone." Tamika said.

The last of the cars disappeared before Kevin picked up the phone. "Yes."

"Hello, Mr. English, this is just a reminder that your written exam for the Camden Police Department will be the last Saturday of next month," Sergeant Banks said. "That gives you another four weeks to get the results of your GED exam. You'll need to bring proof of passing your exam to qualify for the next academy training class."

Kevin's gaze fell on pictures of Tamika and his two boys. "I'm expecting the results this week. I'll be there to take the exam. Thanks for the call."

Kevin leaned back on the sofa. The crew would look at him differently if he landed on the police force and Leroy would definitely lead the charge against him.

Tamika strolled in, searched Kevin's eyes for a moment, then cuddled up next to him, pulling him in for a kiss. Slowly, he opened to her, allowing his hands to roam her lush body for a moment and sweep away the issues that plagued him.

She pulled away, placing a single hand to his face. "Everything okay, baby?"

"Yeah, everything's fine. Nothing for you to worry about," he said, twisting his lips to kiss her hand. "Everything's just fine."

But Kevin knew his world had just become that much harder to navigate.

Chapter 18

Even a week later, the last "family" meeting was still heavy on Kevin's mind. He sat in the den running the plan through his mind, over and over, in different forms. After Leroy had laid his cards on the table, Kevin knew that one corner wouldn't be enough. If everything turned out the way he wanted, Bucky could split the responsibility of the first corner with Eric. Leroy and Chub could run the new corner in East Camden. Deep down, Kevin had always been impressed with Bucky, but couldn't show him too much favor since he wasn't blood.

Leroy believed that only blood family members should make the real money and outsiders do the dirty work. That way, if things went sour, no blood family member would do time. The bulk of the money would stay in the family. Kevin knew, though, that Bucky wasn't your average mule.

Leroy would be the only problem. He wouldn't take a split. He'd want it all. Greed was a deadly sin that had filled the prisons with Blacks, Whites, and Latinos. The fire in Leroy's eyes said it all, one corner would never be enough, two would just whet his appetite. Having the entire area under his control would be more to his liking. Throw Sean into the mix, and there would be bloodshed. Kevin needed to bow out without causing any ripples, turn the reins over to the most levelheaded, and move quietly into the Police Academy. Change his life.

All day he wrestled with the plan of easing out, without breaking up the family or going to jail. That night when Tamika and the boys were asleep, Kevin got up and called Bucky. "Y'all ready?"

"I been ready for the past twenty minutes, but the rest of them running late."

"Bucky, round them fools up and get over here. Now!"

"A'ight."

Kevin paced the floor. *The only one on time is not blood. After tonight, take your money and go. The rest will be their problem.* This would be the final meeting before taking the East Camden corner.

Twenty minutes past 1 o'clock that morning, the crews arrived at Kevin's house. Black jeans, sweats, and hooded sweatshirts paraded past him. Eric, Chub, Leroy, Fatar, Sean, Bucky, and a new soldier named Norris stood around the table, waiting. Kevin leaned back in the chair and looked at all seven, making eye contact to try and gauge their state of mind.

"Whoever's not ready to do this needs to walk, now, and don't come back," Kevin said.

No one moved.

Kevin got up, threw on a black hooded sweatshirt, and grabbed a duffle bag. The crew followed him outside and split up into two Black SUVs.

Chapter 19

The two trucks cruised in the crisp night air. "The corner" stood on the intersection of 40th and Federal Street. It ran along a hill right after Woodrow Wilson High School. A park was its backdrop while addicts scurried by getting high or looking for their next fix. Stray cats screamed in the trashcans.

Weapons snapped and clicked as the crew loaded up. At a distant corner, the two SUVs split. Kevin, Bucky, Eric, and Fatar stayed on Federal Street. Leroy, Chub, Sean, and the soldier Norris turned right.

Kevin's SUV sat at the light that turned red and then green again. They waited.

Ring! Ring! Kevin answered his cell phone.

"We at the other end of 40th street," Chub said.

Kevin looked up at the light and watched as it went from red to green. "A'ight. We rolling."

Fatar accelerated, watching the speedometer to make sure he stayed within the thirty miles an hour.

"One Mississippi, Two Mississippi, Three Mississippi," Norris counted before hitting the accelerator in the other SUV.

Six "corner boys" stood on the intersection, some with their backs against the wall of an abandoned row house while two others smoked cigarettes, one facing the direction of Federal Street traffic. On the opposite corner, a stocky Puerto Rican, with a shaved head, wearing a red, white, and blue T-shirt emblazoned with the Puerto Rican flag on it, surveyed the flow of traffic.

"That's Federico; if we don't get anyone else, we have to get him," Kevin reminded the passengers.

An array of agreeable grunts cut loose. Half way up the block, Fatar turned off his headlights. Norris motored simultaneously on 40th Street, and cut off his lights. Kevin's SUV approached the corner and slowed to fifteen miles an hour. Then shots rang out. Empty shell casings ejected in rapid succession. The addicts scattered, then Frederico and his workers fled without a single return fire.

Norris and his team roared up 40th street. Passengers in his SUV fired repeatedly out the window. Two people running hit the pavement. Kevin assumed it was Frederico's guys. Norris plowed into a runner. Leroy and Sean took aim and fired shots without remorse, their bullets targeting whoever survived the first onslaught.

Frederico sprinted up the street. His light skin and loud shirt made him an easy target. Leroy yelled to Sean, "That's Frederico, get him!"

Sean fired a shotgun. Frederico reached down and grabbed his leg. He tried to keep running, but a limp set in. After a half block, Frederico collapsed onto the pavement.

Sean punched Norris in the shoulder. "Stop the fucking car! He's still alive."

Norris punched the brake.

Sean jumped out, pulled the .38 from his back, and ran over to Frederico.

"Monte Gon . . . Puto!" Frederico cursed before turning to face Sean. "Who da hell are you, puto?" Frederico asked.

"Death." Sean said, blasting him twice in the chest, then fired one last shot between Frederico's eyes.

The two cars tore off in opposite directions, leaving four dead and sirens screaming on opposite ends of the street.

Chapter 20

Kevin jogged around the next turn, heading toward the last straightaway of the New Jersey Police Academy training facility track. He was soaked in sweat, breathing heavily, and lightheaded after struggling the last mile of the run. The other trainees ran in silence, except for the occasional profanity when their bodies attacked them with fatigue and cramps, warning them of exhaustion. The New Jersey Police Academy's five-mile morning run was nobody's pleasant jog. It helped that Kevin had so much on his mind that he always got lost in thought. *I hope she has everything she needs til I get home. She's got money. I'll call her tonight to make sure.*

His thoughts turned to his crew. Chub, Eric, Leroy, and Bucky. This was the first time he wasn't involved in every move they made. *They'll be a'ight. I taught them what they need to know. They know what they're doing.*

His two mile jog, calisthenics, and hitting that bag everyday for the past few months hadn't prepared him for these "drop on request" runs, obstacle courses, self-defense, and heartless training officers. He never had anyone outright insult and belittle him like the training officers did. Days of training in the rain, followed by classrooms, eating bland slop they called food, and no Tamika. Going home was going to feel like heaven. But it would be a while before that happened.

A training sergeant blurted through a bullhorn.

"You trainees are going to need stamina, strength, and conditioning to keep up with New Jersey's criminal element. They're motivated to stay one step ahead of you wannabe, some-day-hope-to-be police officers."

There was no *wannabe* for Kevin. He basked in the fact that he ranked at the top five percent of his class. His classmates had come to rely on him when they needed a partner for physical training and studying.

"Kevin, get out in front and lead these pampered momma's boys and prom queens to the finish line," the sergeant said.

Excitement rushed through Kevin's veins. Working hard, being able to properly provide for his family without worrying about his life on the streets, was a beautiful thing. The Academy's disciplined routine reminded Kevin of his routine back home.

Beep, beep, beep!
"Kevin, get up and turn off the alarm clock," Tamika groaned still half asleep. It was six a.m., time for Kevin's morning jog and work out.

He slid out of bed and dropped to the floor. "One, two, three, four, five . . . thirty-five, thirty-six . . . forty-nine, fifty!"

Fifty push-ups, seventy-five sit-ups, three rounds on the heavy bag, a two-mile run around the Camden High School track and Kevin was back at his house.

"Baby. I made you pancakes, eggs, and bacon. I'm going back to bed for another half hour before the kids wake up," Tamika said pecking Kevin on the lips.

"Thanks, babe. Love you." Kevin said.

"Love you too, baby."

After eating, he went downstairs and sat at his table, studying for his GED test. Training his mind was just as important as training his body. Without the GED, the academy wouldn't accept him no matter how physically fit he was. Hours later, he was in his crew's "kitchen," watching Eric and Leroy cook the product they would soon be selling on the streets. He whispered the process to Bucky. How to "step on" coke to get more product by mixing it with baking soda. After cooking it, "weighing it wet."

Finally, they hit the streets. Kevin watched the flow of traffic on the corner from the pizzeria across the street. Soon, kids about the same age as Bucky were sneaking sales to Kevin's clientele. Kevin schooled Bucky some more.

"Bucky. You see that? That youngin down there is taking money out of our pockets. That can't happen. Send a runner down there; tell him he needs to move his thing off this block. If he don't listen, then ya'll move him. You feel me?"

"I'm on it," Bucky answered.

As Kevin ran the last few steps, he got excited because a break in the routine was coming up. Today would be the first firearm training session.

"Trainees, step up here in alphabetical order," the firing range instructors yelled.

The trainers talked through an hour session on gun safety, then took their position in front of the group. "Trainees, step up to your assigned shooting range and take firing positions. On my command, steady yourself, aim your weapon, and fire until your weapon's empty. Is that understood?"

"Sir, yes, sir." they all answered.

"Ready. Aim. Fire!" Gunfire rang out slowly at first. Then as the crew got used to the kick of the weapons, guns discharged rapidly.

"Trainees, holster your weapon and stand at ease for evaluation and grading." The instructors retrieved the shooting targets and examined the scoring. Training Officer Sergeant Andrew Falconi checked Kevin's target, then eyed him with admiration. Or was it suspicion.

"That's pretty good shooting, Trainee English. Looks like all your shots hit in the kill zone. Your fellow trainees barely connected with half." Falconi turned to the rest of the class. "The rest of you may have to spend extra time in here to get up to speed with Trainee English."

By the end of the firearm training session, the other trainees had improved, but none matched Kevin. One of his classmates, Francis Harris, a man with freckled complexion and shaggy brows, whispered to another trainee. "I guess so, Camden babies come out the womb carrying guns."

89

Later that night, in the mess hall, trainee Rashon Irvin sat next to Kevin. "'Sup Kevin, I wanted to give you props for your marksmanship today. Only half of my shots hit the target, man. Bottom of the totem pole for me. I was hoping you'll give me a few tips."

"You gonna get stuck behind a desk if somebody don't help," Kevin said.

They laughed.

"Yeah, sure man, I'll help you, but I get dibs on your dessert at dinner. Cool?"

"Aww, come on bruh, you gonna take away the only vice the state of New Jersey provides?" he asked.

"Hey, this meatloaf, rice, and soggy vegetables is like cardboard. See, my girl can lay down some sautéed boneless chicken breast with Spanish rice and string beans. Some homemade ice tea's waiting to wash it down. And some good loving too. Whew! Stick a fork in me 'cause I'm done." Kevin elbowed him.

"Yeah, man, my mom can throw down too." Rashon paused and gave Kevin a side look. "Um, don't know if I need to be handing out the 411 on—" He paused again and then shrugged. "Just watch out for Francis. He was hating on you at the shooting range."

"I'm not sweating it. I'm not here for him." Kevin answered.

"Yeah, I feel you on that one," Rashon said. "But it's crazy guys like that who'll probably graduate and work in a city where the majority of the people he's supposed to protect and serve look like us. Feel me?"

"Yea," Kevin said.

"Not the kind that grew up around Blacks and Latinos."

"He didn't call me out my name or something did he?" Kevin asked.

Naw, he ain't crazy, but, after you lit the place up, he said he wasn't surprised because babies in Camden come out the womb with guns."

"I got you. Thanks."

"Being from Newark and all, I know how dudes like to group us in some negative bullshit." Rashon said.

"Yeah. Let's get outta here. I'll have him kissing my ass when I graduate top of this class. But ay, we got a deal on the desert thing or not?" Kevin asked.

"Yeah man, I got you."

Around two o'clock the following morning, the creaking sound of an old worn mattress made Kevin's head whip around. All those nights being on edge kept him aware even when both eyes were shut. A dark calm had settled over the trainee dormitory. Bunk beds on both sides of the room created a makeshift center aisle bordered by footlockers at the foot of each bed.

Francis walked down the center aisle toward Kevin. Kevin saw the pale figure pass him and go into the bathroom. Kevin crawled out of bed and toward the bathroom. He stood outside the threshold with his left hand over the light switch, glancing around the room, pressing his back to the cold wall, listening for footsteps, trying to regulate his breathing. Every dragging footstep counted. When Francis crossed the threshold, Kevin slammed a right into his gut. It was a solid blow, quick, hard and almost noiseless. Francis chocked, bent over, and gasped. A swift left hook to the jaw and he went down, unfurling like a lion under a tree. Kevin knew he was unconscious. He had rendered and observed unconscious before.

He left the body on the floor, then flipped off the light to conceal his getaway. He crawled quietly back to his bunk, smiling. *Yup, still got it.*

Later, Kevin woke up from hearing Francis stumble around in the dark. He crashed into bunks. Kevin said nothing, but a few other trainees growled in their sleep. He tripped over a footlocker, grunted and hopped back to his bunk.

Kevin smiled broadly in the darkness.

Chapter 21

Back in Baltimore, the seasons were changing and the once barren trees were budding. Birds had returned from the south, chirping and making nests. The spring semester of 1995 on the Morgan State University campus was no different. Jalen stared out the window of his lecture hall. He looked past the statue of Fredrick Douglass to admire the assortment of benches modeled by the campus's Greek and non-Greek organizations. He was trying desperately to stay awake as he looked up at the wall clock reading 7:30 p.m. His gaze switched to his wristwatch reading 7:40 p.m. He had set it ten minutes fast to be sure he would never be late. *Just twenty more minutes and its back to the room to rest a few hours. Stay awake; you have an exam on this next week.*

Professor Ginesh shook him.

"Is everything OK, Mr. Carthane? This is the second time this week you've been sleeping in my classroom."

Jalen widened his eyes and wanted to stretch, but dared not. "I'm sorry, Professor Ginesh. I just started this new job, so I haven't been getting much rest lately. It won't happen again."

* * *

Beep. Beep. Beep. Beep. Jalen's alarm clock woke him the next time. He reached over and hit the off switch, then reached for his room phone and dialed a four number room extension with his eyes still closed. He called one number after the other and left the same message. "We got an hour. Come to my room and we'll leave from here."

Boom. Boom. B-Boom. Tap. Tap. Tap. Jalen heard the knock and got out of bed and stumbled to the door. A male friend walked in and they nodded at each other, Jalen was still half asleep. Twenty minutes later, eight other young men tapped out "the coast is clear" knock on the door. They all wore black hooded sweatshirts, carrying book bags packed to capacity. They checked each other's clothing to make sure everyone matched from head to toe.

"Invictus. Begin," the shortest of the young men said.

They recited in precise unison.

"Out of the night that covers me
black as the pit from pole to pole
I thank whatever gods may be
for my unconquerable soul
In the fell clutch of circumstance
I have not winced nor cried aloud
Under the bludgeoning of chance
My head is bloody but unbowed
Beyond this place of wrath and tears,
Looms but the horror of the shade
and yet the menace of the years finds,
and shall find, me unafraid.
It matters not how straight the gate,
how charged with punishments the scroll
I am the master of my fate,
I am the captain of my soul.
Invictus, by Ernest Henley"

Finally, they had finished ten poems in the same fashion. Jalen looked at his watch. *10:45 p.m.* Forty-two minutes before their meeting.

The bell tower at the heart of the university's campus chimed twelve times while a mass of students huddled outside talking, waiting, and anticipating. It had been rumored that one of the fraternities would be *crossing* a line tonight. It was only speculation since the membership process was secret.

A large, dark-skinned brother of the hosting fraternity demanded the crowd's attention.

The rest of his brothers chimed in as their call flooded the night air, forcing utter silence. A commotion began off in the distance. Nine men lined up so closely it was difficult to distinguish where one began and the other ended. Two other fraternity brothers yelled orders as they marched violently toward the crowd.

"You got to bop to Omeeeega, got to bop to Omeeeega, got to bop to bop to bop to bop to, bop to Omeeeega...." the young men roared.

The crowd started yelling and cheering as the line marched forward with stomping feet until they stood front and center before the crowd, their hoods tied tightly and their faces buried in the back of each other's necks.

"Remove your hoods! Take them off! Take them off!" The dark-skinned brother commanded. This would be the first time the students had the opportunity to see the nine men's faces as new members of the fraternity. The crowd erupted in acknowledgment of the students they recognized.

"I see you, Steve!"

"I see you, Dante!"

"Okay, Jeremy!"

"There's Danny!"

"That's Jerome and Jalen!"

"I see you Errick!"

"Isn't that Mal and Hassan from the band?"

The nine men started reciting the poems that they had spent weeks perfecting.

"Spaces!" the dark-skinned brother commanded.

The nine men reached out to grab the belt of the person in front of him and rapidly stomped in place. This exercise created the space needed between them to perform a marching exhibition. Jalen began to sing in a deep baritone voice.

"Allllll of my looooove, my peace and happiness.

I'm gonna give to Omeeega."

The remaining eight of his brothers chimed in perfect harmony.

"Alllll of my loooooove, my love, my love, my peace and happiness.

I'm gonna give to Omeeega."

The crowd exploded but their voices didn't drown out the unified enthusiasm of the new Omega men.

At the end of the exhibition, the dark-skinned brother addressed the crowd. "At this time, we would like the students of Morgan State University to welcome the newest members of Omega Psi Phi Fraternity, Inc., *The Never Ending Nine.*"

The crowd cheered and the fraternity's brothers rushed the new members, hugged them, and issued the secret handshake. These were Jalen's new brothers. The brothers he wished he had always known, been close to, bonded with. Frat Brothers. A flashing thought compared them to his cousins—that world-wide difference, or were they that different after all? Both were the only brothers he had ever known.

Chapter 22

"What the hell happened to you, Trainee Harris?"

Kevin peered out the corner of his eye to enjoy the moment.

"Sir, I'm not sure, sir, I fell last night, sir, I . . . I think," Francis said.

"You dumb shit! What the hell you mean you think?" Sergeant Falconi said.

The class stopped shooting and turned toward the two men.

"How do you THINK you fell? What the hell kind of answer is that? Either you fell or you didn't. I bet one of the other trainees kicked the shit out of you for biting his cock or something? Or did one of the female trainees whip your ass for trying to steal some pussy? Is that it, Trainee Harris?"

"Sir, no, sir."

Trainee Rashon Irvin snickered.

"And what the hell are you laughing at? What the hell are ALL of you looking at? Did I tell you to stop firing? Continue with your training. NOW!"

"Sir, yes, sir!" they all yelled back.

"Are you gonna answer me or not, Trainee Harris?"

"It happened in the dorms, sir, and I'm not sure, sir, I think I fell, sir."

Falconi saw the confusion in Francis's eyes; he wasn't lying. He walked away. "Get back to your training, Trainee Harris!"

"Sir, yes, sir."

Kevin exhaled in relief. Good thing he knocked him unconscious with the second blow.

Chapter 23

The weight room was the only place for solitude, the only place to get rid of built up anger and frustration. Kevin's regular workouts at the gym provided him with the only familiarity of the home he had left three months ago. Now, he looked forward to going back to Camden and starting his new career. He had left his home in the Centerville section of Camden as a criminal, but would return as an officer. How ironic. The jokes his cousins and other guys still in the hustle usually aimed at "pigs" would now come his way.

Sergeant Falconi walked into the free-weight area of the gym where Kevin was working out. "Trainee English, can I join you?" He stood by the bench press.

Kevin jumped up. "Sir, yes, sir."

"You know, Trainee English," he picked up a twenty-pound dumbbell and began speaking in a dry tone. "I have to admit, when I first set eyes on you, I figured you for the usual cocky street kid that slipped through our test screening thanks to Affirmative Action." He lifted the steel barbell.

Kevin's jaw clenched automatically, but he held his tongue, lifting his own forty-pound weight.

"Now I realize I had you all wrong." Seconds ticked by as the sergeant's gaze flickered over his shoulder hoping to draw some emotion out of Kevin. "You're pretty smart, almost making it through training with none of us the wiser." A toothy grin split his thin lips. "And you still have them fooled, but not me." He placed the weight on the floor.

Falconi lifted his gaze to meet Kevin eye-to-eye. "You know, a few months ago, all I knew about you was what I saw everyday

97

during training, and what your file contained . . . GED score, physical training scores, psychological profile assessment. You even beat the lie detector." He picked up the weight again and breathed in deeply.

"But then you slipped up."

Kevin rested his weight in mid-air. "Sir, I'm not following this conversation. I—"

"Do you watch videos, Trainee English?"

Before Kevin could answer, Falconi continued, "Me? I love videos." His muscle plumped under his skin. "I love them so much that sometimes I watch the surveillance tapes of our facilities when I'm bored. We have cameras all over the place just to keep an eye on you all." He gazed in Kevin's eyes. "Are you following the conversation now, Mr. English?"

Kevin's mind raced as he breathed in real deep and hoisted the weight above his head.

"I see you're not in the talking mood today." Falconi paced a few feet in front of the bench. "After seeing Mr. Harris's bruised face, I figured *something* must have happened that was worth me getting some popcorn, beer, and making it a Blockbuster night."

Another trainee strolled in. Falconi waved him back. "And boy, am I glad I did," he said, turning full face to Kevin again. "Because, if I hadn't, I wouldn't have seen you." Falconi favored him with a sly grin. "You have a pretty good left hook, and turning off the light was pretty smart, too. But you can't hide from Massa."

Kevin's insides boiled, but he didn't utter a word. *Let's see what he's got first.*

"After my movie, I did a little checking to see what else I could find out about you. Guess what I found, English?" He dropped his weights on the floor and sat up, not pretending to exercise anymore. "You and your girlfriend own three houses in Camden." He held up three fingers. "I asked myself, how does a guy with only a GED and wife that works as a nurse at Cooper Hospital own three houses, two of which are rentals. So I had a friend of mine at the Camden precinct check on your two 'rental' houses. Come to find out, you're running a pretty successful drug business that the police know nothing about."

Anger raged like a spreading flame in Kevin. The hairs on the back of his neck raised and a sneer formed at the corner of his mouth. "Sir, I don't know anything about any drug business, sir. Me and my girlfriend just got the houses to bring in a little extra money."

The sergeant took two steps closer to Kevin's bench. Kevin stood, and the two stood almost toe-to-toe. Falconi was in his face. "Look, you piece of high yellow shit, don't feed me that cookie cutter bullshit. I might not be able to prove you're involved, but then again I don't have to."

Kevin's eyes searched Falconi.

"All I have to do is accuse you and your training, those drug houses, the house your girlfriend and children live in will be gone."

Kevin's anger grew hotter and almost uncontrollable because he knew he was telling the truth. His head felt like it was about to explode.

Falconi took a step back, dropped his hand and made a complete turn back to Kevin. "And you know what pisses me off the most? It's seeing you Black bastards making money doing God knows what, driving around in your fancy cars, wearing your fancy clothes and jewelry—" He leaned forward, poking a finger in Kevin's chest. "And I'm stuck here scraping to get by, hoping for some damn pension at the end of my career. You sons of bitches make more in one month than I do training sorry-ass people like you in a year."

Falconi took a deep breath and waved his balled fist at Kevin. "Then, to top it all off, you have the audacity to come to my training facility and take the place of someone who really deserves to be here." He shook his head wearily. "Well, I got news for you. From now on, I'm not waiting for my pension. From this day forward, we are officially partners. I get a cut of whatever you make selling drugs, 'renting' houses—or whatever the hell your Black ass does."

Kevin inhaled a sharp, angry breath.

"Because if you don't," Falconi said coldly, "I'll wash you out of this academy. Then I'll shut down both of those fake 'rentals' and indict your monkey ass for conspiracy to sell narcotics. When I'm done, the next time you see your sons, they'll be arrested and meeting you in prison."

Kevin tried to keep the scowl from his face.

"I know all this may have come at you a little fast and you may need some time to process it. So just to show you I'm not a bad guy, I'll give you a full day to think about it."

Kevin saw his hands choking Falconi until every breath left his body.

"You have until lights out tomorrow. If I don't hear from you by then, it'll be movie night for the instructors and closing time for your drug houses." Falconi stormed out.

Kevin dropped down on the bench, shaking, realizing that one night of revenge had cost more than he cared to count.

Chapter 24

Kevin lay on his bunk, listening to the snores of his fellow trainees and the hum of the cooling system. He mentally kicked himself for being so dumb. *If I had just left Harris alone, there would have been no bruise, no tape of me hitting him, and things would be normal.* Well, as normal as his life could ever be at the moment.

The next morning when all trainees emptied into the mess hall, even before breakfast, one of them ran up to Kevin and tapped him on the shoulder. "Sergeant Falconi wants you in his office. Right now."

Hmm, he's early. Kevin kept his calm veneer as he found his way through the aisles of the cafeteria and moved toward Falconi's office at the end of a hall. He faced Falconi whose feet were propped up on the edge of a brown wooden desk. At the sight of Kevin, he rose up and lit a cigar. A videotape sat near his nameplate like a trophy. A smile parted his lips. "Have a seat, Trainee English."

Falconi glared at Kevin. "So do you have a new business partner or a new enemy?"

Kevin leaned back in the brown wood chair. He knew he had been temporarily trapped. "Partner."

Falconi's smile widened.

Kevin took a long, slow breath, thinking how he would get even one day. "There are some things you should know, though. I'm not in the game anymore. That's why I'm here training."

The man's smile disappeared like a dying ember. "That would be sweet and admirable if it wasn't a pile of shit!"

"Sir, it's the truth. Why would I bother with training here if I was still hustling the streets? The two never mix."

Falconi went silent again, inhaling a lungful of smoke.

"All the money I make is legit. I don't want to end my training, so I have a way that we can both be happy."

Falconi exhaled. "I'm listening."

"I'll give you the money I make on one of the houses," Kevin said smoothly. "That's an extra thousand a month in pocket, tax free. In return, you forget about the tape, let me finish my training. I become a police officer, and you don't make any calls to your *friend*."

The sergeant looked at Kevin a long moment. "That's a nice offer, Kevin, but . . . No! You don't tell me what you'll give me. I tell you what I want and you say yes."

Kevin sat back in his chair and rubbed sweaty hands on his pants legs.

"I want the rent from both houses. That means I get two thousand a month, and you get to keep your dirty little drug dealing secret. Okay, homie?" Falconi mocked.

Kevin resisted the urge to smack the smug look off Falconi's face right then. Instead, he nodded.

As Kevin turned toward the door, Falconi asked, "Don't you want the tape?"

Kevin turned back. "What for? I know you made copies. But I also know that if you release it, you don't get your two thousand a month. *Partner.*"

Falconi leaned back in the chair and grinned. "See, I told you, you're smart."

Kevin closed the door, except for a crack less than an inch. His limited view still found Falconi, picking up the phone, pressing his back to the wall.

"Hey little brother, he decided he'd better play ball." A hearty chuckle followed. "You were right about him going straight, but I still made a sweet deal for us. He's going to hand over a thousand. That's five hundred for both of us for sitting on our asses."

Kevin seethed. *The bastard's cheatin' his own brother?*

"Look, you just listen to big brother and we'll milk this monkey for everything he's got, then you'll get credit when we bust his ass. Next thing you know you'll make sergeant. All from being assigned this shitty detail in Camden." Another nasty laugh.

"Yes, I thought you'd like the sound of that."

At that moment, Kevin knew that his time as a police officer would be limited by the sergeant's greed.

Chapter 25

Though the Camden streets had doubled the family's income, it also landed Sean in jail. His rage caused him to beat an addict he felt disrespected him as the cops were driving by. Sean then punched and floored the arresting officer, who in return wrestled him to the ground, handcuffed him, and returned the beating on their way back to the precinct. The cop and his partner booked him for resisting arrest and assaulting an officer. Then the judge shipped him off to jail for a five-year minimum sentence.

Since the family started running the two corners, Eric took a backseat and let Bucky have his run of the house. Competition disappeared because of their rough reputation. Occasionally, a knucklehead would take a few customers, but it never lasted long. Bucky would turn a couple soldiers loose to run off the freelancer.

East Camden was still dark when the clock read 5:30 in the morning. Leroy was up and had just finished counting the money. The phone rang. It seemed too early to be good news.

"Hey, I'm coming by with the new package."

"Ah, it's you. When?"

"In thirty. Gotta go to the 'bank' first," Chub said.

As promised, Chub showed up with two soldiers, Fatar and Norris.

"Today was good," Leroy bragged to Chub as he handed over the sixty-five hundred in fives, tens, and twenty-dollar bills.

Chub wrote the amount down on a note pad, then handed over a large plastic bag with the new bundles of product. Leroy glanced at the pad. "What the hell? How they only make just over thirty four hundred today?"

Chub's head whipped around as he snatched the pad from Leroy.

Leroy glared. "We damn near doubling their sales." He leaned closer. "But we ain't g'tting' paid double. This fifty-fifty shit's got to go, Chub."

"Stop worrying 'bout dat! We all got plenty of money and no worries. You just worry 'bout hiding side chicks from your wife," Chub said.

"Don't worry 'bout my women," Leroy snapped. "You need to worry about our money." He ran his hands through the bundled packages to get an idea of what he had. "We had to get two soldiers to replace Sean's crazy ass and we stacking his commissary with dough. And don't forget dis rent money to Kevin we gotta pay." Leroy said.

"I know, but—"

"He left the game to be a damn cop! Dat shit ain't right, Chub. Just 'cause Eric's family, you letting both dem niggas slide. We clocking more dough and getting more heat after droppin' them bodies taking this spot." Leroy tied the bag and handed it to a runner. "This shit ain't easy and—I ain't waitin' til Kevin get back to call a meetin' either!"

Chub nodded, angry with himself for leaving the pad out for his brother to see. He had made the drops for almost two years and had always kept track of how much money they made. For a while now, he had known East Camden was bringing in more money than the other houses, but he wasn't greedy like his brother.

The problem wasn't that Leroy didn't make enough money. It was that he spent it all on renting hotel rooms, clothes, jewelry, and the women he juggled between his wife and children. Further, his wife, Tasha, didn't work and she liked spending Leroy's money just as fast as he brought it in. She felt entitled ever since she had his first child. Now that they had three kids, she was even lazier. Even when she caught him cheating, she reminded him she wasn't gonna leave him as long as he was taking care of her. In turn, he reminded her that no one was jumping to take care of a high school dropout with that many kids and no job.

"I'll call the meeting for tomorrow, just calm ya ass down," Chub reassured his brother.

Chub turned and headed to his SUV. When he reached the car, he glanced at Norris and Fatar, then dialed Kevin's cell phone. The call went straight to voicemail. "Kev', this is Chub. I need to holla at you, so hit me back. It's important."

At the Police Academy, Kevin never had access to his phone to check his messages. Chub hoped he would check them tonight. He knew he had to talk to Kevin before the meeting. He needed to get his help in diffusing his brother's craziness before they all paid for it.

The following day, Leroy, Eric, and Bucky met Chub at his house in Camden. The green and white row house screamed "bachelor pad." There were no decorations, artwork, or food in the refrigerator. The dining room set he purchased two years ago had the original plastic cover on the seat cushions.

Chub only bought what he needed. He didn't have a steady girl or children. If he needed affection, he would invite over a neighborhood girl, but he made it clear that their arrangement was not a permanent one. He got the attention he needed and sometimes the girl did, too, but, in case she didn't, he always gave her a few dollars to buy herself something nice. Each girl was treated exactly the same way.

With the exception of his family, he pretty much kept to himself. He paid close attention to his mother, Janet Smalls. She had a bedroom upstairs, was an alcoholic, and couldn't keep steady work. He moved her in to make sure she had a place to live. Most times, she sat quietly upstairs.

Now, all of the cousins piled inside and Bucky led them to the basement like a single row of ducks. Chub took his place at the head of the table. Leroy flashed a mocking grin.

"Look, my little brother's a carbon copy of Kevin. I taught you well, young buck," he said.

Leroy's smart comment broke Chub's concentration. Kevin still hadn't returned his call, so it was all on him now.

"The reason we here is 'cause, well, for almost a year now, we've had two corners," Chub said, eyeing each man at the table, one by one. "And, after moving our work off corners and in the houses we drew less heat from the cops and brought in more cash than ever."

Nods and murmurs drifted about.

"As y'all know, I collect money from both houses and deposit them in our 'bank.' Business is so good that I had to get more safes to hold the extra cash. We got three now. For the last few months, the house in East Camden's been bringing in more money then the first. It'll probably double the first house by the end of this year."

Leroy rocked back and forth on the back legs of his chair. Finally, his bronze lips opened and he spoke. "On the real, I don't think we should keep splittin' the profits evenly." Chub's heart was pumping fast. The split made perfect business sense, but Chub sensed his brother's greed.

"Salaries should be level with the amount your house brings in, not both houses combined," Chub continued.

Bucky leaned forward. "What did Kevin say about all this?"

"Man, *to hell* with Kevin! He's a cop now, remember?" Leroy said. "He's only around to collect our rent money. *We* make all the decisions and I say we go ahead with what Chub is saying."

Chub glanced at his brother again, before looking at the expectant faces around the tables. "I tried calling Kevin, but couldn't get in contact with him. We on our own for this one. So, as usual, we gonna vote and majority rules."

"Fine, let's put it to a vote," Bucky said.

"All those in favor of salaries and profit based on the house you work raise your hand," Chub said.

Leroy's hand shot up along with Chub. Leroy stared at Eric and he raised his hand.

Bucky jerked forward. "What the hell you doing? You're voting to cut us out of the money from the second house *we* helped to take, remember?"

Eric shrugged and put his head down. "No, I'm not."

Leroy grinned.

"See, me and Leroy talked about it earlier today," Eric said. "I'm gonna work the house in East Camden with him and Chub. I'm tired of worryin' about new packages, paying runners, *cooking.* You gettin' a promotion, Bucky. You get the spot all to yourself."

"What the hell—?"

"See, at the other house, I'll still be making the same. Maybe a li'l more if business keeps getting better like Chub said."

Chub had no idea about Leroy's conversation with Eric. His brother had set him up. Leroy got what he wanted and if Kevin was here he'd be pissed.

Chapter 26

Summer arrived, with full sunshine and feathery white clouds floating in the occasional breeze that blew across the open field. The New Jersey Police Academy graduates were seated in their uniform blues, smiling. Graduation was over and Kevin was taking pictures with classmates, probably for the last time before being assigned to duty.

"Hey! Officer Rashon Irving. I guess you finally learned how to shoot straight, or did they feel sorry for you and assign you to meter maid duty?" Kevin yelled to Rashon while taking a group photo.

"Yeah, I can aim just fine. You'll see when you develop these pictures. I cut your head off in every photo. I didn't want your high-yellow glare to ruin all the shots."

Kevin's family waited while he took his last pictures and talked with his training officers. He strolled across the summer-green lawn toward his family. His mother, Rhondella, reached out and gave him a long, lingering hug. Tamika grinned as she held the children. Their oldest son, Ronald, was trying to break her grip, but Tamika held him back. Jalen and his mother, Chub in three-piece suit, along with the other cousins, stood to the side, gloating.

Eric was happy but still timid around Kevin after the demotion little over a year ago. He just shook his hand and hugged him. Kevin greeted Jalen, who hadn't really been around since he went to college. He had put on some weight and his facial hair was clean shaven, except for the thin mustache he had cut to perfection. He wore a blue business suit and Omega Psi Phi fraternity pin on the left lapel.

"Congratulations, Kevin. We're all proud of you, man," he offered a hand that turned into a bear hug.

Kevin rushed over and picked up both his boys, one in each arm. He mauled them, and then kissed them on the cheek. "You guys been taking care of your mom?"

The oldest son, wearing a short version of a light blue and white suit yelled, "Yea, I put out the trash every week."

The younger son, Jason, nodded and seemed embarrassed.

Eric intervened. "How long before you climb to Chief of Police?"

"Yeah, *pig*. People back home gonna have a field day when you jump outta a squad car pointing ya flashlight and gun," Leroy laughed.

Kevin smiled and pointed to his silver badge. "If you act up, you gonna see my night stick."

"Careful, cousin," Jalen said grabbing his mother's video camera. "You have to make sure nobody's taping before you whip out the night stick."

Everyone laughed as they headed toward the parking lot. Before Kevin could get into the driver's seat, Sergeant Falconi walked up. "Officer English, I request an opportunity to meet the family before you depart."

Kevin cringed at the sound of his voice. "Sir, of course you may, sir."

Falconi didn't wait for the introduction. "Everyone I am Sergeant Falconi, one of Officer English's training officers. It's a pleasure to finally meet all of you."

Everyone smiled, except Leroy, who instinctively whipped on his sunglasses. Kevin introduced each of the family members.

Falconi shook each one's hand. "I have to say it was a *pleasure* training Kevin and his class." Falconi winked at Kevin before he walked away. Kevin felt trapped, subdued, and silently humiliated like a black man being lynched from a tree. His shoulders tensed and he drove off in silence. How he wanted to kill Falconi! Heat rose up in his body, and his mind swirled with anger.

When Kevin's caravan drove into Camden's city limits, it was mid-afternoon. The music was already kicking into high gear.

Chub hazed Jalen into serving the chilled beer to all family members of drinking age. Baked chicken, macaroni and cheese, collard greens, candied yams, and corn bread spread along a rectangular wood table. The delicious smell sent Kevin's stomach growling. He piled food on his plate and the radio played the latest hip-hop and R&B hits from Power 99FM.

Kevin wanted to forget Falconi. He'd deal with him later. "Now that training is over, I'll be assigned to a precinct in the next couple of weeks," he said smiling down at Tamika.

She smiled back.

"I'll probably be right here in Camden," Kevin said.

Everyone laughed as someone rang the doorbell. Jalen walked over and pulled the door open. Bucky charged in.

"I popped by to congratulate Kevin," Bucky held up an envelope.

Jalen grinned. "So where's mine?"

"Man, you didn't graduate from no academy. You ain't even graduated from college yet, and you here asking for a handout."

Jalen laughed, leading him past Kevin's sons to the marble dining room table. The moment Kevin saw Bucky, he stood and led him to the living room.

"What's up, Five-O? Life treating you good?" Bucky teased.

"I don't know, you tell me. You looking like you back in high school. Face all shaved. State issue bowl cut."

Bucky passed him a white envelope. "Congratulations, man. Good things are gonna happen for you."

Kevin opened the envelope and thumbed through the modest stack of bills. Surprise showed on his face as he counted. "You early? You still got a couple weeks. And you're overpaying me? I'm guessing it's about three grand in here."

"You guessed right. That's ya rent for our house and an extra two thousand for ya graduation."

Kevin smiled. "Thanks, man, come get something to eat."

Tamika walked in and cuddled her head against Kevin's shoulder. "You hungry, Bucky? We got plenty of food."

"Thanks, but I gotta go," he said, eyeing the food hungrily. "I got some things to take care of." With that said, he disappeared through the screen door as quickly as he entered.

111

Later that night, Chub got a call that prompted him to leave the room. He talked less than a minute, then hung up the phone and returned to the party. He walked over and whispered to Eric and Leroy. They nodded.

"Kev, we gotta go," Chub said.

"Something wrong?" Kevin asked.

"Nothing special, same ole, same ole. You know how it is. You can't leave them alone for too long before they think the smallest thing is gonna bring the world to an end. But ay, enjoy your homecoming, man. We'll catch up a li'l later… flatfoot."

Kevin smiled and hugged each of his cousins.

Jalen stood up next. "Ma, I have to go too. I got something going on tonight."

"Well, can you drop me and your aunt off at home?" Michelle asked.

"Y'all ready now?"

"Hmm, she must be really something for you to be rushing us like that."

"It ain't even like that, ma," Jalen said with a sheepish grin. "Why you putting me on blast?"

Finally, everyone departed and Kevin was sitting on the couch with his family. Tamika took the kids upstairs and tucked them in for the night. When she returned, she reached down to pick up a toy. Kevin put out his hand to stop her. "You can do that tomorrow. Right now, we need to be about more important things."

He stood and wrapped his massive arms around her hips and lifted her off her feet. She wrapped her legs around his waist. They kissed passionately.

"I missed you so much, Mika."

"Don't tell me baby. Show me."

Kevin lifted her to the wall, supported her with one arm, and pulled her shirt over her head with the other. He pulled down the straps of her bra and exposed her breasts and devoured them.

She moaned and shivered.

Tamika reached down and unbuttoned her fitted jeans; Kevin released her long enough to remove his. He grabbed two handfuls of her backside, lifted her up the wall so he could lose his face in her thighs. She scraped at the ceiling with one hand and the back of his head with the other. Fluid began pouring out of her as he lowered her to the floor and drove himself into the dark, warm, wet place he knew so well. They remained that way until they were satisfied, exhausted, and content.

Chapter 27

At the end of the month, Kevin placed a call to Chub. "What's up? You got that for me?"

"Yeah man, you know I gotcha."

"A'ight, when you coming through?"

"Lata tonight, cool?"

"Yeah, one."

"One."

Kevin hung up, angered that the money Chub would place in his hand wouldn't find his own pocket, but that of Falconi. All the work it took to get those houses, all of Tamika's overtime would result in a payoff for someone else. It made Kevin's blood boil all over again. His muscles tighten until they hurt. But that wasn't the end. He had a pressing feeling that the sergeant was going to set the dogs loose on him after he'd been juiced for everything he was worth.

This shit's not gonna fly. I have to do something—and fast.

Chub arrived at Kevin's house around eleven o'clock that night. Tamika let him in. "You know where he's at. Go on downstairs."

"'Sup Kev," Chub said, strolling to a spot near the punching bag. "I can't stay too long. Here's the loot we owe you."

"Thanks, man. Bucky showed ya'll up the other week. Paying earlier and with extra. If I didn't know any better I'd think Bucky made a power move while I been gone and he running the family." Kevin shot him a tested smile.

Chub broke eye contact with Kevin and went silent.

"Naw man, nothing like that. You know Bucky always been on point like that but . . . um . . . ay, I need to get back to the house. Things are real busy over there."

Kevin sized Chub up while he held the money and caught his breath. Chub pounded fists with Kevin.

"Ay, is everything cool?"

Chub just stared at him.

"You know with business and the family." Chub began biting his bottom lip, casting an uneasy glance at the punching bag swaying back and forth.

Kevin wasn't used to this type of behavior from Chub. "You wanna holla at me while you're here?" Kevin threw him a lifeline. "I know I'm a cop now, but you can still talk to me 'bout stuff. Whatever we discuss is between us. We was family before I went to the Academy and we still family after it. Feel me?"

Chub paused, scanned the badge, gun, and academy diploma. "Naw, everything's cool. Business is good," he dodged Kevin's eyes. "Only drama since you left was Sean getting locked up, but you already know 'bout dat silly shit he did." Chub turned toward the door. "But ay, I need to get back. I'll holla at you lata."

Kevin was unsettled. He felt like he was in exile of a kingdom he created. His friends weren't the only ones that had to get used to him wearing a badge.

Chapter 28

Christmas was only one week away. There was no snow-storm in the forecast, but the cold was bitter. Everyone had traded in their Jordans and wife beater tank-tops for Timberland boots and full-length, oversized, North Face winter coats with fur hoods. Kevin patrolled the streets of Camden with his new partner, Officer Brendon Freeman, who was also his training officer.

"Time's flown by since we started," Kevin said.

"Yeah, it was like that for me when I first started, but I didn't have to draw my weapon as quick as you did." Freeman seemed like he wanted to snicker.

"Yeah, I see the squad's never gonna let me live that one down," Kevin said.

"Well, English, you've made it kinda hard for us to forget," Freeman chuckled. "Imagine a rookie 'accidentally' shooting the family dog while clearing a house after a burglary was reported. The old lady damn near had a heart attack after you shot Fluffy."

Kevin's embarrassment always came back full force when anyone mentioned that accident. He looked straight ahead, though. No laughter, no defense. He just gazed straight at the road. Part of their patrol was driving past his old corner on Haddon Avenue. Addicts went in and out of the alley leading up to the house he rented to Bucky like it was a revolving door.

The police were none the wiser, or didn't care, as long as no one loitered on the corner anymore. Kevin thought deeply on the addict traffic getting higher every month. He could only imagine what it was like at the second house. Falconi's bribes ran through his mind, and the fact that his cousins could afford to increase his salary. *I need to raise their rent.*

Night had fallen over Camden, quiet and dark. It felt like impending danger. The cold numbed his feet and fingers. Lights from warm windows spoke to him of what heaven must be like. Just then, he saw Chub and his usual two soldiers cutting around the corner to the Haddon Avenue house, probably to make a pickup.

* * *

Chub dialed his cell phone.

"Yeah?" Bucky answered.

"Ay Bucky, I'm about to roll through. You ready for me?" Chub asked.

"Yeah, we straight over here. See you when you get here."

When Chub arrived, Bucky had already counted the money, separated it according to denomination, banded it, and placed it on the table. Chub walked up to the front door and headed straight for the kitchen where they served customers from an open window.

"Ay Chub, sorry for not telling you before you got here, but we gonna need two thousand worth of product to last us until tomorrow morning. We'll be out in a couple of hours," Bucky said.

Chub counted the cash—just under forty-five hundred. "What the hell you doing out here? Buying it yaself and smoking it? You been pulling in numbers like this for a few months now."

"Things running a lot smoother since our *transition,*" Bucky answered as he gazed out the window where another teenager, maybe thirteen, was serving customers.

"Plus I keep a small stash of some product that's not 'stepped on.' If the people we serve bring new business our way, I break 'em off with some real good shit. You know, give them a little incentive to bring in new clientele. Pretty soon I'ma have these fiends taking buses from all over Camden to buy our shit." Chub marveled at his ingenuity. "Plus, since we don't have much competition, I don't need as many soldiers, so I only keep one on the roof, one in the house with me, and two outside—just in case," Bucky said.

"A'ight Bucky, I see ya work. We might have to think about adopting ya ass and making you *real* family," Chub said.

Bucky said nothing.

"Anyway, I'll bring your two thousand worth once I drop off this money."

As Chub got back in the car, he looked at his note pad and double-checked his numbers. *Damn, just like I thought. Since Eric started working at our house, Bucky is bringing in more cash.*

He flipped the page, then looked at the second house's numbers. They had maintained their usual earnings, but with a new man on board, it was cutting the usual profit.

Leroy and Eric thought they got over on Bucky to make more money and Bucky ended up with a sweeter deal. Damn, that's poetic justice. Chub headed for the "bank".

He'd keep that bit of information to himself. If Leroy heard about it he would set off the same thing all over again. And with Kevin home now, there would be no way to hide it. *I can't let Kev know I got played by Leroy.*

"Yo, Chub. Everything alright, man?" Norris asked. "You kinda quiet."

"Everything is cool. I'm just getting things together to make this drop." Chub started stuffing brown paper bags with the money in the pockets of his fatigue cargo pants. They drove across town in silence and arrived in thirteen minutes flat. Chub and Fatar piled out. Norris fumbled with his Black 'n Mild cigar. Chub walked up to the door and slid his key into the lock.

Shots rang out. *Pop! Pop! Pop!*

Chub jumped, broke the key in the lock and turned around just in time to see Fatar's body fall toward and finally on top of him.

"You shot him before he unlocked the door, fool," an overweight man yelled, coming closer with the speed of light.

Chub, frozen with fear stared up at a Glock semi-automatic handgun and met the face of the young gunman with a muddy-red complexion and a cap pulled low on his head.

T-Tat! T-T-Tat! Chub's bladder gave up its secrets and he closed his eyes thinking those shots signaled his death but he was wrong. The shots came from Norris, who had jumped from the SUV spraying the two men with an Uzi 9MM. The men scrambled for cover, only returning fire after Chub pulled himself from under Fatar. Chub crawled away, drew his gun and began to shoot. Bullets sent the would be robbers running. One of Norris's shots tore through a shoulder, the other into the gut. Seeing that, Chub sprinted down the block opposite of the men, letting loose the remaining ammunition from his gun. The would be robber dropped to the ground, writhing. The other dropped a few feet behind him.

Norris hopped back in the SUV and sped down the block. Near the turn at the end of Park Boulevard, Chub hopped in, checked himself for bullet wounds, and let out a sigh of relief. He remembered the money from the houses. The bags of money were still in the cargo pockets but were now soaked in urine.

Chub glanced over his shoulder. "I think we got away. Head back to our house in East Camden. We need to get the others and move the bank. Somebody's been plotting on us."

"Phew! What da hell's that smell!" Norris said.

* * *

Meanwhile, Bucky stood at ease with his hands clasped behind his back, watching over the young teenager serving the customers.

"I'll be back in a li'l while. I need to hit the bathroom." The boy nodded and went back to work.

Bucky thundered up the wooden stairs and into the bathroom. He lined the toilet seat with paper, rested his gun on the floor, pulled down his pants and sat down. He sat there staring out the window to the brick wall of the house next door. Then suddenly, he heard parts of a voice from downstairs. "Bucky, we g'tting' jacked!"

Pop! Pop! Pop!
Tat, T-T-Tat! Boom! Click-Click, Boom!

Bucky jerked up from the toilet, yanked his pants up, and crouched next to the wall. He lifted the lid off the tank of the toilet, and reached in, taking out two very large plastic bags. One contained a Mack-10 semi-automatic gun. He stuffed the other bag into his pocket, grabbed his gun, and ran downstairs. He tossed his handgun to the server who crawled along the floor under the window.

"Hey, stay here," Bucky ordered. "And if anybody comes through that window, blow their fuckin' head off." He glanced out the window and saw his men trading shots, but he couldn't make out with whom. He jumped out the window and joined them.

"Bucky! Where the hell you been? They came outta nowhere! There's three of them still out there."

One of his men pointed to the high grass and weeds on one side of the alley, then to an abandoned house on the other side. "That's where they ran."

Crouched, Bucky scanned that area instructing his troops in strained whispers. "When I tell you, run toward those weeds, keep shooting until whoever is over there stops moving. I'll get the two on the left."

He reached into his pocket and pulled out the plastic bag. In it were a lighter and four illegally made M-80s he held over from the Fourth of July. He lit and threw one in each direction. **Boom! Boom!** With the explosion, car alarms went off. Smoke dimmed the whole area.

"Go now!" Bucky ordered.

They ran forward, spraying bullets as they ran. When the smoke cleared, the three would be robbers were stretched out in the alley—riddled with bullets. Sirens screamed in the distance. The two soldiers dashed out of the alley. Bucky dropped the remaining M-80s on the ground and broke into a sprint, heading back toward the house. He was just a few feet from the house when the red, amber, and blue flashing lights pierced the darkness of the alleyway.

"I have to flush the drugs and get out with the money!"

Bucky leaped onto the window ledge, holding on for dear life, then pulled himself through. He came face to face with his Berretta in the shaking hands of the thirteen year old.

"No—"

Bop!

The bullet tore through Bucky's left cheek, sending him falling backward to the ground. Hearing the noise, the thirteen year old opened his eyes, inched toward the window and looked out. Bucky lay unconscious, stretched on his back, the Mack-10 beside him. The kid tossed the gun and jumped out the window and sprinted into the alley, and onto the street.

The moment he stepped out of the alley into the street, a speeding police cruiser just off the edge of the curb met him. The cruiser slammed its brakes but not in time. The young boy crashed the windshield and ricocheted into the air above the cruiser. He landed onto the asphalt. Other police officers jumped out of the cars and surrounded him. The blank expression on his face confirmed he was dead.

They stomped into the alley, found the remaining dead bodies, guns, and continued to look for witnesses or survivors. They blocked off the area with yellow tape that read: *Police Line. Do Not Cross.*

Bucky lay outside, barely breathing. Drugs and money still inside.

Chapter 29

Bucky strolled the prison yard alone with a white gauze bandage taped to his face. The police had found him with the Mack-10 beside him, his fingerprints pressed all over it. The cops sent him to the hospital for a quick patch up and then the law hurled him into court before the blood could dry. He was tried and sentenced on two counts of murder for killing the would be robbers found in the alley. The drugs and money found in the house were pinned on him also.

At twenty-three years old Bucky faced the reality that he would die in prison. He leaned on a fence and looked up at the faded winter sun and wondered what he would look like when he was 80. Something sad and regretful ran through his mind. How could he have done it any different? His little brother was only four, as cute as life, and when Bucky tickled him, his laughter made his day. He needed an operation for Sickle Cell. He knew it would be impossible for him to finance a bone marrow transplant for his only little brother now.

Bucky kept running the District Attorney's interrogation over in his mind. He would never forget the prosecutor's name. Wilford Desilva. "Mr. Wilford DeSilva," he kept reminding Bucky when he addressed him as "Wilford DeSilva."

"Alphonso 'Bucky' Trent, you know you're facing multiple counts—from possession and distribution of narcotics to murder. You're about to spend the rest of your life in prison. How's it feel knowing that you're going to die in there an old man *or woman*, once those bulls get a hold of your pretty ass?"

"You can't talk to my client with that kind of intimidation," his Public Defender, Mike Schwartz, said.

Desilva's angry eyes ignored Schwartz. "The inmates are so hard up they won't even mind that hole in your face. From what I hear it's better to die early in there."

Bucky looked up and his jaw tightened.

"I understand you keeping silent. Code of the streets and all that. Right? But, sooner or later, you need to decide what's best for you and this is the only time you have to do it. I can offer you a deal that will cut your time in exchange for information on who's running the house."

Bucky eyeballed the prosecutor and released a nonchalant breath between his full lips. "Send me back to my cell. You gonna make me late for chow."

The prosecutor shook his head. "So be it."

* * *

The same night of the murders and attempted robbery, Chub and Norris made it back to the East Camden house to let everyone know what had happened to Fatar. They had to wait a few days until homicide completed its investigation of the crime scene before they could go back and relocate the "bank" to the East Camden house.

Fatar's murder brought a lot of attention to the area. Citizens became more concerned with their neighborhood. Some started Neighborhood Watch programs and notified police of suspicious activity. The pressure was moving way up the ladder toward the chief of police. Governor Whitman, accompanied by Secret Service agents, attended the City Hall protest to denounce illegal drug activities running rampant in Camden.

The mayor publicly expressed her disappointment in the chief and reaffirmed her dedication to provide the citizens with the protection and law enforcement to which they were entitled. The media found out Kevin owned the house and started writing articles on police corruption. The headlines read "*Camden's dirty little secret.*"

Kevin had been called in for questioning, and was dreading it.

"Officer English. Have a seat." Two other officers in blue and gray suits joined the chief. The officer in the grey suit leaned on a file cabinet reading out of a yellow manila folder; the other stood behind Kevin and began the questioning.

"Officer English, my name is Detective William Cooper and that's my partner Detective Peter Dunbar. We are with Internal Affairs and have been assigned to investigate your involvement in the shootout that has dominated the media this week."

Kevin nodded, his voice almost a weak whisper. "Yes, sir."

"We're going to get right to the point. We know you legitimately purchased the home where police found three dead bodies, guns, and more than a thousand dollars in crack cocaine. Our question is, did you know anything about what was going on there?"

Kevin wiped sweaty palms on his pants legs and took a deep breath before answering.

Never tell on yourself, if they're going to catch you make them earn it.

"Sir, no, I didn't know. I'm a law enforcement officer. It would be against my oath and unethical for me to turn a blind eye to activity like that."

Lieutenant Dunbar slapped the folder shut and joined the questioning. "Did you make them fill out an application? Request references? Or perform a background check, or verify source of income?"

"Sir, no I—"

"Of course you didn't. So where did you think they got their money to pay your rent? Is it safe to say you knew but didn't want to know?"

"Sir, I placed an ad in the paper and Mr. Trent responded with cash for the first and last months' rent and a security deposit. In hindsight, I realize I should have been more thorough in questioning his income and background. I've taken that as a life's lesson, but I assure you, the activities that went on in the house did so without my knowledge." Kevin hoped he had convinced them because he, for sure, hadn't convinced himself.

"Well, for your sake, I hope you're telling the truth, because if you're not, we'll find out." Detective Dunbar moved closer to Kevin, placed both hands on his shoulders from behind and whispered in his ear. "And, when we do, I'm going to crucify your ass to the wall, as if you were Jesus Christ himself."

Now it was the captain's turn. "Until further notice, you are assigned to desk duty pending the results of this investigation. You're dismissed, Officer English, and I use that term, '*Officer*' loosely."

Kevin rose, saluted the officers, and left the office. When he turned around, he saw the three of them still discussing what he thought was about him. His knees shook.

When Kevin set foot in his front door at home that night, he was worn out. He felt the pressure of a thousand pounds on his shoulders. His flesh felt like it was tearing loose from his bones. Tamika handed him the phone. "Baby, your partner is on the phone. He said it's important."

Kevin shook as he took the phone.

"Kevin, we need to talk," Officer Freeman said. "I got pulled into the captain's office by Internal Affairs this afternoon and they started asking me all kinds of questions about you."

"Like what?" *Feel him out.*

"They're saying the captain has orders from the Police Chief to assemble a special drug task force with the DEA to find out if there are any more of these drug houses in your name. Some people around here are saying you may even be involved."

Kevin's heart sank and he could feel his pulse throbbing in his throat. "All I can say to you, Freeman, is that the Internal Affairs investigation is a misplaced suspicion."

"Um, usually where there's smoke, there is fire."

"Hey, you've ridden with me for months. How could I hide something like that from an entire department?" *Don't tell on yourself.*

"I hear you, man, but I have to be honest with you. I requested to be removed as your training officer. I can't afford anything like this on my file."

"What? On a rumor?"

"How would it look like if I've been field training you for all these months and not know about something as serious as that? You know how it is."

Kevin understood. When a street corner got hot, the hustlers found somewhere else to work until it cooled down. Except, this time, *he* was hot instead of a corner.

"Yeah, man, I know how it is. Don't worry 'bout it. I'll be on desk duty for a while anyway, so you'll probably get reassigned before I get back on the streets. I appreciate you being straight up with me." Kevin hung up the phone.

Tamika sashayed by Kevin. "Baby, is everything okay?"

Kevin stood there with his back to her for a second before he responded. "Yeah, babe, things are okay. I'm just catching a little heat from the job over the house we rented to Bucky, but it's gonna be alright. We didn't do anything wrong. It'll blow over."

"But what about the other house?"

"I'm gonna talk to Chub and them. Tell them to lay low and watch their backs for a little, till the heat dies down."

"They better listen. I'm not losing you to prison, Kevin. Not after all the work we put into this."

Kevin turned to see her eyes welling up with tears. He walked over and gave her a reassuring hug, but he knew he couldn't fool her. He felt her heart racing. He knew that she knew everything just as quickly as he felt it. He had to make it better for his family. He owed his life to making it better. He was going to make it better.

He went to sleep and woke with his mind still racing. When he arrived for his shift at the precinct that morning, Kevin was greeted by stares, whispers, and side conversations. He headed to his desk to see what busy work they had given him, but another officer occupied his desk. His papers and files were scattered all over.

"Um, excuse me, but this is my desk," Kevin said.

"Are you Officer Kevin English?" the man with dark hair and green eyes said.

"Yes, I am."

"The Captain moved you to a desk near the supply room down the hall. Sorry, man."

Kevin straightened his shoulders and walked to his new desk. On the way, he passed a meeting room where he overheard the captain speaking. "Officer Falconi, would you mind running that by me again?"

"Sir, of course not, sir. I said I have pertinent information that is vital to the new joint task force and I would like to volunteer myself and that information." *Now he's gonna turn me in to fast track his career.* Kevin slowed. "Captain, I have a lead on the location of another drug house and I would like the opportunity to head up that team in the raid."

"I assure you, officer, if the information you possess is fruitful, you have my permission to head the raid and your name will be duly noted in our records. The media will be able to use that credit as it sees fit."

Kevin felt lightheaded. *All of this couldn't be happening. Didn't I leave the game?*

"Officer Falconi, let's finish this discussion in my office."

Kevin quickly ducked out of sight. When the coast was clear he dragged back to his desk and pushed the boxes aside with his knee, then squeezed sideways past the water cooler. He plopped down, heavy with the burden. Looking up, he watched Grant and Falconi disappear into the captain's office.

I have to warn Chub, Eric, and Leroy. Damn, why didn't they get Bucky a decent lawyer? Wouldn't have been like that if I was still around. Everything's falling apart.

Falconi rushed from the captain's office, grabbing a few more officers. He heard two officers walking toward his desk but they could not see him because of the vending machines.

"Let's grab something real quick because we might not get a chance to eat if we get the search warrants."

"What search warrants?" another officer asked.

"The Captain just sent a surveillance team to scope out another suspected drug house that might be connected to some rookie cop here. If we get some photos showing illegal activity, we get the warrants and then a team will raid the place."

Kevin leaned back in his seat to further conceal his presence. Their footsteps beat heavy against the tile. His heart beat so fast he thought he might faint. Then the sound of footsteps faded and Kevin was left alone to ponder his fate.

I can't believe it. It might happen today. I've got to warn them. Now. If they get busted we're all headed upstate! Kevin reached in his jacket pocket for his cell phone, but he couldn't find it. *Damn, left it home. Can't use the department phones. Pay phones are across the street.* Kevin slipped out of the precinct.

"Hello?"

"Listen to my voice. You know who this is but don't use any names. Shut the house down! Police and DEA are watching you right now!"

"What? What you mean—?"

"*Listen*, no time to explain. Just shut it down!"

"Aight, I'm out." Chub hug up.

Kevin stood at the phone booth pondering what he had just done before returning to the precinct; he could do nothing but wait and see what happened. After an entire day as an outcast, and watching police officers run in and out of the precinct, Kevin rushed home. He hoped his warning hadn't fallen upon deaf ears.

Tamika met him at the door. "Kevin! Chub and Leroy have been calling here for the past two hours. They said they need to see you as soon as you get back." Tamika was frazzled. "What's going on, Kevin? Are you in some kind of trouble?"

"No, Mika. I can't explain right now. I need to find Chub first. I'll talk to you about it when I get back. Where's my cell?"

Tamika just stared at him refusing to answer.

"Mika, where's my phone?"

She slowly turned, walked into the kitchen, and opened the drawer where she had stashed it.

Kevin grabbed it and saw he had multiple missed calls from Chub and Leroy. The phone went off again while it was in his hands.

"Where ya'll at? Uh huh. Be right there." Kevin dashed out the door without saying a word to Tamika. He arrived at Chub's house in minutes and pounded on the door.

Eric yanked the door open. "Everybody's downstairs waiting."

"'Bout time you got here, cousin!" Leroy snapped.

"Shut up, Leroy, he was at work and got here as quick as he could," Eric shouted.

"Chub, what happened? Did you shut it down in time?"

"Yeah *we* did," Chub said, eyeing Eric. "Woulda been done a lot sooner if somebody wasn't bullshittin' *as usual*."

Kevin looked at Eric, who put his head down and sat real quiet.

"Okay, fill me in. What's the damage?" Kevin asked.

Leroy jumped in and focused his attack on Eric. "First off, dumbass over there didn't answer his phone, 'cause he was upstairs sexing some chick. Me and Chub had to come back to the house from Lawnside and found these fools sitting around chillin', business as usual, wit' a plain ass Ford Taurus parked up the block. Don't nobody in this city drive American cars except Po-Po. If his dumb ass had been doing his job, we wouldn't a needed you to drop dime." Leroy was fuming and squirming in his seat.

"Leroy, chill ,man. Nobody got caught up, so we good," Chub said. "After we kicked Eric's chick out, we started clearing the house. Dumping drugs down the toilet, tossing guns up on the roof, but then we had to get all that money out without them noticing. We didn't have any trash bags or anything to put it in, so I told them to just pop the trunk of the SUV and we'd put the whole safe in there."

"What?" Kevin said.

"I know, but we didn't have no choice. We didn't know when they was planning on rolling in, and ain't no way in hell we can explain having over three hundred thousand dollars in cash. So that's what we did," Chub said.

"Me, Leroy, and Eric left with the first safe out in my truck but that tipped the cops in the Taurus. We left Norris behind to load the other two safes and he said as soon as we pulled off cops were everywhere. Norris got away and said they swarmed the house and got the other two safes, but they didn't find no drugs or weapons. The people they caught will get their walking papers soon 'cause they not saying nothin' after what happened to our last snitch," Chub said.

"Well, I guess it could have been a whole lot worse," Kevin said. He felt a little better knowing the whole story but he knew he wasn't out of the woods yet. Sooner or later they will find out the house belonged to him. *I'm fucked!*

* * *

Kevin's shift began at eight the next morning. After fighting with Tamika all night, he was exhausted. The moment he stepped across the threshold, Grant called him into his office. Kevin stomped in and took his seat. Both Internal Affairs detectives were there, along with Officer Falconi, with his thin-sliced lips smirking.

Here we go.

Pictures of Leroy, Chub, and Eric along with a few of their men were displayed on a tack board next to Falconi. Some he recognized and some he didn't.

"Mr. English, I'm sure you know why you're here," Captain Grant said.

He looks as bad as I do today, either from the lack of sleep or rage. "Sir, no I don't, sir."

"Really? Well, let's start here. Do you know the men on the board behind me?"

No law against having cousins. "Sir, yes I know a few of them. Three of them are my cousins."

"Your cousins? Well, well," the captain teased. "Finally, we're getting some truth out of you. So that means you also know they're suspected of drug distribution out of yet *another* house you own?"

"No, sir, I didn't know that," Kevin said smoothly.

The captain stood and shouted, "You lying sack of shit! Yes you do! You tipped them off, didn't you?" The color in his face quickly matched the red in his eyes. "You told them we were coming."

"No, sir, I didn't even know. How could I, sir?"

"You're a liar and a disgrace to the badge and uniform." Spit shot out of the captain's mouth as he struggled to contain himself. "We can't prove you or your family is involved—yet.

But we will. And when we do, all of you will be sharing a cell block in Rahway."

The other officers remained silent and observed as a formality.

"As of today, Mr. English, you're no longer a law enforcement officer for the City of Camden. You're done here. Turn in your badge and your gun and get the hell out of my office and my building."

Kevin stood up, looked at each of the officers, and slowly turned in his weapon and badge. *All the time it took to get here— the early mornings and late nights. Putting up with abuse from the training officers, being away from my family. They were all so proud when I graduated. He's taking all of that away from me! Just like that.* Kevin headed for the door, the last of his efforts to go straight and legit.

"And be forewarned," the captain added, "when we do catch you, I'm gonna be there to personally cuff you and applaud in the courtroom when they convict your ass."

The officers didn't even wait until he left before placing Kevin's picture on the top of the pyramid, right above Chub. He closed the door behind him. On the precinct floor, his fellow officers stared at him like he was a traitor. Falconi had done exactly as he promised.

Now, dishonored and disgraced, Kevin still had a promise to keep to Tamika, his children, and himself.

Chapter 30

Kevin's entire world had collapsed in less than two days, so he couldn't go straight home. This was the first time he experienced a loss of such magnitude. He still needed to take care of his woman and two children, but now he wasn't sure how he could make that happen. He wasn't about to, nor did he want to, return to his old lifestyle. He promised his family that he would stay clean. He had to talk to his cousins again, right now. After heading to a local bar and throwing down five shots of cognac, he whipped out his cell phone.

"Eric, round up everyone and meet me at your place. I'll be there in an hour."

"Why, what's up?"

"Damage control." He flipped the phone shut.

An hour later, he arrived at Chub's house and his Aunt Rachael opened the door. She was obviously soused. "Heeellllo, Kevin."

"Hey, Aunt Rachael. Chub downstairs?"

"Yeah, baby, he down there. Go on down while I finish my drink. Want one?" she asked, landing in a heap on the sofa.

Kevin grabbed the Johnny Walker Red Label by the neck and poured a mouthful and gulped it down while heading downstairs, bottle in hand. Kevin heard Leroy's voice blaring from the top of the stairs. "We lost like two hundred grand. *Everything* in those two safes." His fury turned on Kevin. "And look at dis muthafucka!"

Kevin set his neck in a slant of contention.

"Yea. You'd think having you on the force woulda kept us from being raided."

"So I'm to stop every raid they plan?" Kevin shouted.

"Po-Po got away with *two* safes full of our fuckin money!" Leroy shouted back.

Chub tried to reason with Leroy. "Kev's the one that tipped us off, man." He bit at the remaining white of his fingernails.

"How the hell we been operating all these years, then soon's he turn *pig* we get robbed and raided?" Leroy asked.

Kevin looked at his cousin, the alcohol revving up his anger, but he told himself to be cool. One night of revenge had already brought him on a straight path to hell.

"Well? Say something!" Leroy yelled.

Kevin said nothing.

Leroy lunged at Kevin. "You fucking *bitch*!"

Kevin dropped the bottle and threw a lighting quick jab and two combinations. The fight lasted only a few seconds. Kevin wrestled him to the floor, placed a standard police chokehold on his neck. "You crazy? I'm the reason you got anything. The reason you're not in jail."

Leroy started to say something, but Kevin tightened the chokehold. "Naw, you were sloppy and that's why I've been fired."

Leroy's body went limp. Eric and Chub grabbed Kevin's shoulders and pulled him off.

Leroy floundered around the floor, regaining his breath.

"See? He don't even fight like us no more. He fights like a cop," Leroy said between gasps. He pulled himself from the floor and started ambling toward the door. "I'm through with y'all. Break me off my share. Do whatever the hell you want to do."

"Go on give him his money," Kevin said, "and we'll sit back and watch how far he gets on his own."

Chapter 31

That spring, Jalen was at the tail end of his senior year. He'd hit the ground running. He had earned a spot on the National Dean's List, became president of his university's chapter of Omega Psi Phi Fraternity, Inc., and appointed Executive Board Business Manager by the Student Government Association President. His life was open to greatness.

That balmy spring night, he celebrated his appointment with Nicole Henry, the newly elected Miss Morgan State University—cheap Andre' champagne in stemmed plastic glasses and Chinese take out on the only two plates he owned set the mood.

Ring, ring, ring, ring.

"Who is this?" Jalen asked.

"It's your mother."

"Uh, ma, hold on for a second."

Jalen jumped from in between the beautiful university ambassador's thighs and found a place on the side of his bed. She muffled her laughter while the two played tug a war with the navy blue sheet they shared, as if his mother was actually in the room instead of on the phone.

"Uh, hey, ma. What's up?"

"Nothing much. I decided to give you a call and catch up. Everything alright?"

"Yeah, things are good down here. I was just celebrating being appointed to the Student Government's Executive Board when you called."

"Oh, that's nice. You're having a get together at your apartment?"

"Yeah, something like that. Just a small group of friends." Jalen sneaked a peek at Nicole. She was lying next to him with her eyes closed, her back arched and hand between her thighs.

"Uh, Oh God!" Nicole purred and sent Jalen an invitation. He got up and walked into the living room to protect himself from Nicole's mischief.

"Jalen? Did you hear what I said?" his mother asked.

"Huh? Um yeah . . . I mean, no. Can you say it again? I had to switch ears."

"I said your cousin Kevin lost his job on the police force."

"What? He just started. How did that happen?" Jalen asked.

"I'm not sure. I don't get into people's business like that. If he wanted me to know, he'd have told me. I'm sorry for having to tell you this over the phone, but Fatar's grandmother called the house looking for you."

"Is Fatar in trouble again? I haven't talked to him since the last time I came home."

"Jalen. Uh . . . "

Jalen could sense her hesitation.

"Fatar was murdered."

"W-When—How did it happen?"

"Happened last year—"

"Last year! And you're telling me now?"

"Jalen, I'm sorry, but it happened when you went on your spring break to Miami Beach. I guess I just kept putting it off till I forgot."

"Hey ma, I'm gonna call you later. I need to go right now."

Jalen hung up and called Kevin's cell. The number was disconnected. He called the cell phones of his other cousins and got the same response. *What the hell's going on up there?*

He walked over to his refrigerator and caught a glimpse of the offer letter from a software company in Bethesda, Maryland. After last year's summer internship, they offered him an entry-level position at forty-eight thousand, pending his graduation. Somehow, it now felt as though it meant he had abandoned his family.

He decided right then and there against it and tossed the letter into the trash. He remained in the kitchen a minute while a single tear fell from his eye. The young woman he left in his bedroom had been forgotten. She didn't matter anymore. His job offer didn't matter anymore. Everyone that mattered was back home and he needed to get there as quickly as he could.

* * *

Kevin was walking on unfamiliar territory and the strain was evident on his face. He sat at the dinner table and Tamika's body language disturbed him. She shifted in the chair.

"Kevin, I need some money. The plumber is coming tomorrow to snake our drain since the toilet keeps overflowing and I need to go to the supermarket."

Kevin answered without looking up from the plate of spaghetti. "I'll get you the money for the plumber after I eat but don't you have enough money for the market?"

"No, I had to use everything I had to pay the mortgage *and* both our car notes."

Kevin raised his eyes just enough to see if she was being sincere or malicious. Tamika didn't back down.

"This isn't easy for me, you know. Our money has been tight ever since I was dismissed from the force and they seized the two rental properties. So I don't need you throwing money shortages in my face. These temporary jobs aren't enough work, but there are only a few options for someone with a GED. I swear it feels like the past couple of years made things worse, not better."

"I'm not throwing anything in your face, Kevin. I know what you're going through because I'm going through it with you. But that don't make the stopped-up toilet go away. And we still need food, toilet paper, Kotex, toothpaste, and shit like that, and, if I don't have the money, who else am I gonna ask?" she snapped.

"Who you think you cussing at, Mika?"

The children sat in the corner at their multi-colored plastic miniature table, staring at their parents. Episodes like this had become more frequent. Kevin jumped up and rushed to the basement, reappearing moments later with a thousand dollars in wrinkled twenty-dollar bills.

"Here, pay the plumber and get whatever you *need* for the house. Times ain't like they used to be, Mika. Money like that isn't just lying around anymore. We gonna have to tighten our belts to stay afloat."

Kevin practiced what he preached. He managed to keep a modest amount of money stashed away in a safe in his basement. In total, his rainy-day savings had equaled a little more than $30,000. But with two growing boys, a mortgage, car payments, and a wife to take care of, funds were dwindling faster than ice in hot water. They were down to $10,000.

Toward the end of the school year, Kevin found some steady work as a janitor at Camden High School. His paycheck was barely enough to cover the house's utility bills. It was especially hard when the neighborhood kids saw him in his janitor's uniform and sporting worn-down work boots tattooed with stains. For years, they only saw him driving nice cars and wearing the newest styles and flawless footwear. He was worse off than before the drugs started. But Kevin never once complained or felt sorry for himself. When he kissed Tamika and the kids goodbye every morning, it reminded him why he was doing it.

Chapter 32

The spring of '99, Jalen said goodbye to Morgan State University. He packed whatever was left of his apartment into his car and jumped onto I-95, heading home. An hour and a half later, he drove over Camden's city limits. When Jalen left Camden four years ago, everything he knew was balled up into the city that raised him. Coming back made him realize how naive he had been about what lay beyond his city—the Morgan State University scene, the world.

His classmates, a mere one hundred miles away, looked like him and the people he grew up with, but their speech, personalities, swagger, and personal style covered an entire spectrum of things he didn't know existed with African Americans. He was grateful to his mother and family for the opportunity to experience it, but at the same time, saddened that not all his buddies in Camden got a chance to experience it.

Camden still had young men sporting baggy jeans falling off their asses the way he used to wear them. Young women squeezed into clothes two sizes too small. He and his University Alumni had left all that behind. He no longer feared the street ridicule: "You talk and act White." University classmates congregated on the 'Bridge' and compared grade point averages and ridiculed those on academic probation. Jalen quickly decided the level he wore his pants should parallel his self-worth, self-esteem, and intellect. He no longer wore sagging jeans. Beautiful women he shared classes with traded in their three-inch sandals, mini skirts, and freshly pressed hair for gray sweat suits, tennis shoes, and a ponytail because getting to their eight o'clock class after pulling an all nighter was more important than fashion.

A huge "Welcome Home" sign and his entire family met him on the front porch. His mother was flanked by her sisters Rhondella, Rachael, and Janet. Kevin, Eric and Chub stood on the sideline, giving him the once over. Leroy floated around, grabbing food off the table. The only one missing was Sean.

Unknown to Jalen, this was the first time Leroy and Kevin had been in the same room together since Kevin choked him in Chub's basement. Jalen wanted to talk to Kevin, but put it off until later. He would piece together everything that happened in the past few years and figure a way to make it right again.

"Welcome home, college grad," Michelle yelled to Jalen, holding out her arms.

The smell of soul food was delightful. Cases of beer sitting on the floor said he was among friends and family.

"What's up, big man? You didn't leave any babies down there in Maryland, did you?" Kevin teased.

Jalen laughed. "Not that I know of."

"Come on inside. We hungry. Ya mom wouldn't let us eat 'til you got here," Chub said, chucking Jalen's shoulder.

He pushed through the orange and blue balloons, his university's colors. The aroma and sight of cherry cheese and carrot cakes made Jalen's mouth water. "I'm getting a plate right now!"

Now he was inside, looking around. "Mom, when did you get hardwood floors? This looks like the Boston Garden."

"If you had come home more often, you would have known."

"Are you up here for good, Jalen?" Eric asked.

"Yeah, I'm gonna look for work in Jersey or Philly and then get a place of my own. Until then, I'll be living at home again."

Michelle was happy that he was home with her, even if it was for only a little while.

"What's your degree in, anyway, Jalen?" His Aunt Rhondella asked.

"Electrical Engineering."

The same month, Jalen began his career with a Process Automation Company in Philadelphia, making more money *legally* than any man in his family had ever made. That was a good feeling.

Chapter 33

Kevin could see something was wrong when he pulled up in the Camden High School employee parking lot. It was empty. *Where's everybody?*

Voices came from in front of the school. When he reached the large cascading steps, a circle of adults were holding picket signs and chanting:

"What do we want?"

"A coooontract!"

"When do we want it?"

"Now!"

What the hell? A strike? I can't believe they actually did it. Kevin walked closer to the picket line. "You guys can't be serious!"

"Yes, we are," one responded. "We haven't gotten our new contract and our current contract is about to expire."

"It's the first day of school," Kevin said.

"Striking at the beginning of the school year is the best time to do it. The district will feel the most pressure this time of the year."

"What about the kids? What about employees like me? If the school's closed, the kids don't come, then they don't need me, and I don't get paid!"

"Hey, sorry brotha, but we're not getting paid while we're on strike either. The district just might get its butt off the bench if we keep at this a few weeks."

"A few weeks?" Kevin yelled.

A small group formed a circle. "What do we want?"

"A coooontract!"

"When do we want it?"

"Now!"

Kevin slowly turned from the crowd and headed back to his car. *Now what?*

Before he headed home, he spoke with his supervisor, who in turn contacted their management. Unfortunately, since Kevin had only been employed a little over two months he was not eligible for unemployment insurance that would have paid half of his salary while he waited out the strike.

It seemed to Kevin like hours while he drove home. He didn't know how to tell Tamika the latest bad news, so he walked slowly trying to think how to say it. What could possibly make it sound better?

"Mika, I'm home," Kevin yelled as he crossed the entrance.

"Kevin? What are you doing home so early?" Tamika asked as she eased down the steps in one of his T-shirts and spandex pants. She seemed bigger with the pregnancy of their third baby than either of the older two.

"Stay up there. I'll come up. Didn't the doctor tell you to take it easy?"

Tamika turned to go back upstairs and Kevin joined her. She laid on the king size bed and propped her feet on the pillows. Her ankles were swollen.

Neither of them spoke immediately, but they were thinking the same thing.

For the last month, Tamika's mother had been giving her a break by watching the children during her difficult pregnancy. Money was already tight when the doctor made Tamika stop working last month. Kevin was down to his last $5000 stashed in the safe. He decided right then what to say and do.

"The teachers at the school decided to go on strike today."

"Oh God, not now," Tamika said. She pulled herself up grunting, looking at Kevin helplessly. "Baby, I know with your pride, you'll never consider borrowing money, but this is getting really serious. I talked to my parents and they said we can move in with them and rent out this house until we get back on our feet."

Kevin leaned over and kissed her on the forehead, got up and started to leave the bedroom.

"Kevin where—"

"I need a little time to figure some things out," Kevin headed downstairs, through the living room, and clunked down to the basement. When he hit the landing, he walked in and placed his cellphone next to the timer on the neat little desk, set it for ten minutes, slipped on his gloves, and started slugging the bag. *What can I do?* The only thing he ever did well besides hustlin' was being a cop. Flashes of the faces he hated most shot in and out of his head—Captain Grant, Sergeant Falconi, Francis Harris, and Leroy.

After ten minutes, the timer sounded. Kevin stepped away from the bag. His hands ached and his forehead dripped with sweat, but his mind was clear. He grabbed his cellphone, walked outside, and sat on his front step.

After a quick phone call, he went back into the house, into the basement, opened his safe, took the last of his money, dropped it in a brown paper bag, and headed for his car. He popped in a CD and it seemed as though the CD was speaking directly to him:

"Somebody's pulling me close to the ground,
I ain't panicked, I been here before . . .
OK I'M RELOADED!"

A chill ran down Kevin's spine. He peeled off, stereo speakers blaring, and looked back.

Just before turning off his street Tamika looked down from the upstairs window. He imagined the sadness in her eyes. He had a foreboding feeling too. *I'm breaking a promise I made to my family and God. What will His punishment be?*

Twenty minutes later, he pulled into a secluded public park and dimmed his lights. He placed both hands on the steering wheel, and rested his head on it. *God, what am I doing? Why am I here again?*

A black SUV flashed its lights and Kevin jerked upright. He stepped out of his SUV and walked over to meet a small White male, Anthony Phillips and a larger man with beady eyes called Flaco.

"Kevin, I almost shit myself when I saw your number show up on my phone. It's been a while. How are you, man?" Anthony asked.

"Everything is everything, Tony. I see you still got Flaco shadowing you." Kevin flashed a look behind him, and all around the darkness of the park.

"Yeah, well a person can't be too careful these days. Time Magazine labeled Camden as one of the poorest cities in America. Not to mention you guys have been ranked in the top five of the country's most dangerous city category for some time now. Those kind of statistics can make a little White guy like me nervous."

Kevin shuffled, but tried not to. It made him angry as hell to be categorized, but…

"Sorry to hear about your misfortune, but I'm glad you came to me in your time of need." Anthony said, cracking a smile.

"Yeah, it's been a li'l rough lately. Not too many prospects out there for steady work and with another kid on the way my hand's being forced."

"Yeah, I see what you mean," Anthony said. "People were saying you were out for good."

"That's why I need you to hook me up with something till I figure out my next move."

Anthony smiled and nodded. Kevin reached into his jacket. Flaco pulled out a .44 caliber semi-automatic hand gun.

Kevin threw his hands in the air. "Yo! Take it easy. I'm just getting my money." He never took his eyes off the two as he slowly pulled out the brown bag.

Anthony laughed. "My fault, Kevin."

"After all the business we've done together?" Kevin asked. He tossed the money to Flaco.

Anthony nodded to Flaco. "Get what Mr. English needs."

Flaco headed to Tony's big, tan SUV and ran back with a plastic-wrapped brick of cocaine. He handed it to Kevin.

"Wait up, Tony," Kevin called after them. "I only gave you $5 K and you're giving me a whole brick?"

Anthony and Flaco turned around. "Look, Kevin, we've been doing business for years now. I know you're good for it," he said with an evil grin. "That cute little girlfriend of yours is used to money floating around like dust, trust me *I* know. At least yours still works. My wife hasn't worked in years."

Kevin said nothing.

"Just settle up with me in two weeks for the rest," Anthony said.

Kevin stuck the cocaine under his North Face coat, shook Anthony's hand, and headed for his car.

"Remember, Kevin, two weeks," Anthony called. "Don't make me regret this random act of kindness."

Kevin looked at them and even contemplated backing out of the deal, but he remained his course and drove home.

He was surprised to find Tamika waiting on the couch. He positioned his arm to conceal the bulge in his coat. "Shouldn't you be upstairs resting?" he asked.

"The doctor said I should rest, but he didn't say where I had to rest. Where have you been?"

Kevin was taken aback. All the years they had been together, she had never questioned his whereabouts. "I had to do something," he said, heading straight for the basement.

Tamika wasn't letting him get away so fast. "Why you in such a hurry, Kevin? What you got to hide?"

"What's with all the questions, Mika? You having trust issues?"

"I've always trusted you, but I just want you to show me some respect by not lying to me and show me what's makin' that bulge in your jacket."

Kevin stopped abruptly, turned toward her, and pulled out the brick of cocaine. Tamika gasped and shook her head, then looked into Kevin's eyes. "What about your promise to me, Kevin?"

"Mika, I don't have a choice right now. We have no money coming in, four mouths to feed and one more on the way, a mortgage, car notes, and you can't work. Right now, this is my only option and I'm gonna use it."

Tamika didn't answer. Kevin took off trotting down the stairs. He placed the brick into the safe, closed the door, dropped into a chair at the table, took in a deep breath, and stared at the empty space before him. *Now that I have the product, where do I move it?*

Taking two stairs at a time, Kevin rushed back in the living room. Tamika had retreated back upstairs. He continued outside and jumped into his car, throttled the engine and sped off. He scanned neighborhoods, blocks, and abandoned buildings for places he could start over. He checked out the corner store where he worked before he started hustling. He rolled by slowly, and noticed that the building and neighborhood were both decaying.

An addict ran up to his car. "Hey man, you got anything? I got a few dollars for you."

Kevin didn't blink. Addicts were like mushrooms, popping out of nowhere at the oddest places and times.

"Naw, man, I ain't holdin nothing. Find somebody else to get what you need."

"Somebody else?" he asked. "Man, ain't nobody else. The last crew got shutdown. It's a drought around here. You sure you ain't got nothing?"

Kevin drove off and did a few laps around the neighborhood. The addict was right. Only a few people roamed aimlessly in the streets. Addicts with no supplier.

Ground zero.

Chapter 34

Chop. Chop. Chop.
Flick. Flick.
Ssss.
Chop. Chop. Chop.
Flick. Flick.
Ssss.
Chop. Chop. Chop.
Flick. Flick.
Ssss.
Ring! Ring! Ring!
"Hello?"
"Ay, Chub. You and Eric ready?" Kevin asked in a stale and raspy voice.
"Yeah, we'll be there in a few."
"A'ight, one."
"One."
Chop. Chop. Chop.
Flick. Flick.
Ssss.
Kevin felt like he was in a time warp. It had been a while since he had to cook and package the product. The process rivaled men and women in the Detroit car assembly lines. He wondered if past hustlers had developed carpal tunnel syndrome from this type of work.

So many hours adding to days, adding to weeks, and adding to months of chopping the cooked coke into smaller rocks, then putting the rocks into small plastic baggies followed by finger flicking the bags to make sure all of it fell to the bottom. He did it so much the nail of his middle finger felt like it was going to fall off. But it had to be done. Otherwise, the product might burn when he used the hot clothing iron to melt the top of the baggy shut.

After a seven-hour shift of chopping and flicking, Kevin sat down, contemplating what he had to do. His next move. He still had time to dump the whole thing, but his pride wouldn't allow him the option of not taking care of his family.

Ding-dong!

Chub stood in front of the peephole. Eric stood beside him.

"Hold up," Kevin called. He grabbed his coat, gun, and a $1000 worth of what he had been packaging all night and headed outside. The three men jumped into Chub's truck like old times. They rode with Kevin in the back seat, skimming over the plans. In his head, he repeated every detail of getting back into the game, just as he had done to himself ad nauseam last night.

Kevin scratched his unshaved face and rubbed his bloodshot eyes. "Y'all know I couldn't have done this without y'all."

"Come on, man. We family. You know we got ya back," Chub said.

Eric nodded. "Yeah, cousin, we'll always ride with you."

Kevin, Chub, and Eric parked on a corner off of Sixth Street, checking the flow.

"Been a while since we had to carry weapons, cash, *and* product, Kevin," Chub said.

"We starting from scratch for real. We better find some youngins quick to do this for us," Eric added.

"I feel you. It'll happen soon enough. First, we gotta make our presence known," Kevin said.

An hour later, they'd made sales to a few addicts. By the next day, word got around and the flow of addicts began to rise. By the end of the second week, Kevin had the money he needed for Anthony.

Kevin gave Eric and Chub a heads up. "Ay, I gotta go do that thing. I'll be back."

* * *

Kevin hopped into his car and made a few turns, and then glanced in the rear view mirror. A green Grand Jeep Cherokee had been trailing him for a few blocks but he didn't want his nerves to get the best of him.

"Okay, who the hell are you and why you following me?" he muttered, picking up speed. He had stashed the cash behind the front passenger seat along with his gun. Kevin stopped at a red light. The Jeep pulled up behind him. Slightly tinted windows made it difficult to see who was driving.

Window tint on a Jeep? You're not the cops. I'm being paranoid. Kevin reached out to change the radio station. The Jeep hit his rear bumper.

"What da hell?"

Kevin didn't get out. He waited at the light to see what the other driver would do. The Jeep sped up and angled across the road, blocking his car. The front and rear passenger side windows of the Jeep rolled down. The front passenger pointed a handgun and the rear passenger aimed a sawed off shotgun.

"Play time's ova!" the man with the shotgun yelled. "Hand over your cash and whatever else you got."

Kevin's mind was racing. The one wielding the shotgun hopped out of the Jeep and ran around to the front passenger side jumping into Kevin's car. He checked Kevin's neck and wrist for jewelry and patted his pockets for cash.

"I know you got more than this bullshit. He trashed the gum and change from his pockets. Where da cash at, nigga? We watched you just leave ya corner. Come up off it."

"I stashed it, just take it easy. You got it. Ain't nothing I can do," Kevin told him.

"That's right, where you stash it at?"

"It's in a bag right behind your seat," Kevin said.

The gunman took a quick peek over the headrest and saw the bag. "This gonna be easier then I thought." He reached around the seat, grabbed the bag, and pulled it onto his lap, keeping his gun and eye on Kevin. He used his free hand to open and check the bag, then howled in victory.

Kevin chose that split second to chop the gunman on the strategic spot on his Adam's apple. The blow was quick, sharp, powerful, and precise just like he was taught at the Academy. He yanked the shotgun barrel with his left hand, pointed it toward the Jeep, and squeezed the gunman's trigger finger while he gasped for air.

The gunman in the Jeep slumped from sight. *Must a caught him.* The gun's recoil forced the butt of the gun into the face of Kevin's hostage. The moneybag fell to the floor and the hostage leaned against the door, unconscious. Kevin started driving, turning the wheel back and forth forcing his car to partially climb the sidewalk until he was free. He reached over, opened the passenger door, and used the shotgun butt to push the robber to the sidewalk. The gun went off, hitting the man in the back as he tumbled out. Kevin dropped the gun and punched the accelerator, speeding down back streets.

He passed a parked police cruiser that instantly gave chase. Kevin reached behind the passenger seat, grabbed his gun, and tossed it out the window after swinging around a corner. He lost the cruiser momentarily so that the officer didn't see him toss the gun.

Kevin floored his SUV and dipped around making three sharp turns around corners. He still couldn't shake the squad car. He led the cruiser at high speed until he got far enough away from the gun, then skidded to the side and stopped.

"Turn off the engine and step away from the vehicle," rolled out of the cruiser speaker.

Kevin did exactly what the officer requested.

The African American officer walked up with his gun drawn. "Turn around and place your hands behind your head. Drop to your knees."

Another patrol car pulled in and joined the arrest. "Look who we have here," the first officer said, pushing in close. "Kevin English. A lot of people at the station are gonna be happy to see you in handcuffs."

They searched his car and found the robber's sawed-off shotgun and the bag of money. "Wow, this is a nice chunk of change, Kevin. You mind telling us where it came from?"

Kevin gazed out at rubber necking drivers. "I have the right to remain silent. If I choose to give up that right, anything I say can and will be used against me in a court of law. I have the right to an attorney . . . "

The two officers laughed heartily as Kevin recited his own Miranda rights.

Chapter 35

After Kevin's arraignment on the first of October, he was escorted from the county jail to the Hall of Justice on Martin Luther King Avenue for the third time. The judge denied bail, and Kevin didn't look forward to the back and forth shuffling to his hearings. Kevin stood next to his lawyer, William Poindexter II, the criminal defense attorney from Columbia University School of Law, who had represented his Aunt Michelle. Like Johnny Cochran, he was registered to practice law in more than one state. Jalen paid his retainer. Tamika and the children sat a few feet behind him. When Poindexter stood to full height, he was an imposing six feet three inches tall, a prince in a tailored navy blue suit and matching tie that hung neatly from a pristine white shirt. His opposition stood from chair and presented its case to charge Kevin.

"Your Honor, Mr. English was fired from the Camden Police Department, resisted arrest, and is under investigation about his ties to drug distribution. It all seems so coincidental that he is involved in a shootout that left one person dead. Furthermore—" the prosecutor said.

"A career criminal is dead, Your Honor," Poindexter corrected. "My client has never been charged or convicted of any criminal activity up until this point."

"Defense counsel, you are out of order. Please show the prosecution the respect he deserves."

"You're absolutely right, your Honor. My apologies."

The prosecutor continued. "Your Honor, we only have still photos shots, so we cannot see in real time what actually happened at the intersection, so we can not completely release

Mr. English of any responsibilities of wrong doing. We are asking the court to deny the defense counsel's attempt to dismiss this case and provide the city of Camden and its citizens the due process it deserves." The prosecution took his seat and awaited his opposition's response.

"Defense counsel you may present at this time." the judge announced.

"Your Honor, I would like to take this time to inform the court that my client, Kevin English, was only resisting arrest because he was the victim of a vicious car-jacker, who managed to elude police. Under such circumstances, he had no choice but to shoot at two of the assailants, or be shot while trying to wrestle away their weapon," Poindexter began.

"Luckily for my client, the city of Camden had just installed cameras to catch speeding motorists at the intersection of that street. We have two photos of the would-be carjackers aiming firearms at my client. A third photo shows my client attempting to escape after injuring one of the assailants who, by the way, has a long criminal history."

"Will the bailiff hand me the photographs?" the judge said.

Poindexter handed a packet of photographs to the bailiff. "Your Honor, prosecution made a very valid point about these *still* photos. We are unable to see completely what did occur in real-time so it would be fair to conclude that if this case was taken to trial it would be impossible to charge Mr. English with any wrong doings beyond a reasonable doubt. Based on that fact realized by both legal Counsel I move for an immediate dismissal unless the prosecution has evidence to prove anything to the contrary."

"That's a very good observation, Counsel." the judge added before Poindexter expressed his point.

"Your Honor, the only charges that have been determined beyond a reasonable doubt is that Mr. English discharged an illegal, unregistered firearm within city limits and resisted arrest," Poindexter said.

The prosecutor's face turned red and his lips tightened.

"Understood, Counselor. It is the ruling of this court that the charge of manslaughter be dismissed and the charges of illegally discharging a firearm within city limits and resisting arrest be upheld. I don't see the need to schedule a sentencing hearing and further clog the court docket with this matter. Mr. English, you are hereby placed on house arrest for six months, followed by three years probation. This Court is adjourned."

The prosecuting attorney threw his notepad and other materials into his briefcase and charged out of the courtroom without a word. Poindexter smiled as he shook Kevin's hand before sending him home with his family.

Fortunately for Kevin, the money the police found in his car never made it to the police evidence locker, or into the police report. There would have been no way he could have explained fifteen thousand dollars in small bills in any court. His good luck equaled his misfortune, because not only was he a week late paying Anthony, he had no money to pay him.

Chapter 36

Early the next morning, the house phone chimed.

"Kevin you want me to answer the phone?" Tamika yelled from downstairs.

Kevin sat upright, wide-awake, checking the caller identification. It read "Restricted." He only knew of one person who called him from a restricted number. "No. I got it." Kevin scratched at his anklet that monitored his every step. *House arrest is a bitch.*

"Kevin, have you forgotten about me?"

"Naw, Tony. I ran into a problem last week."

"Yeah, Yeah, Yeah, I heard that shit before." Anthony brushed off his excuse. "All I need to know is: do you have it?"

"Uh, yeah I got it."

"Good, then you need to meet me at our usual place and hand it over before Flaco gets angry with you. You do remember Flaco, don't you, Kevin?"

"Man, I'm on house arrest! I can't just pick up and go whenever I feel like it."

"I don't give a damn what you're on. Come to our place at four o'clock sharp!"

Kevin sat in silence. He thought of calling Chub and Eric, but they were working the new corner on their own and he didn't want to interfere. Finally, he dialed from his cell phone. He had no choice. "I need cash to cover what I owe Tony."

"If we give you everything we got right now, it'll leave us short of what *we* owe Tony," Chub answered.

"I know, but I can't put him off any longer," Kevin said. "If I go there with something, I'm sure I can talk him into giving me some extra time to make the rest back."

"Man I don't know," Chub said, "If we was in his shoes, we wouldn't be trying to hear no 'I need extra time shit' from whoever owed us money."

"Man, I ain't got no choice. If we don't pay, he's gonna send Flaco our way and we don't need that distraction right now. At least this way it don't seem like we ducking him and we can still make good on what we owe later. Just come to the crib and give me what we got." Kevin hung up.

Kevin was on the phone with his parole officer when Chub showed up. "Mr. Bishop, I need to take my wife for a maternity checkup. I should be done in a hour. Can I make this run? I'll call you as soon as I'm done."

Kevin could hear his parole officer shuffling papers, maybe searching his conscience as compared to the rules of the law.

"Mr. English, you have exactly one hour, whether that appointment's over or not. You are to return to your home immediately and call me, or you will be in violation of your probation and I will send you straight to jail."

"No problem, sir."

Chub handed him a brown bag of money. Kevin took it and dialed Anthony to let him know he was on his way. He rushed out and jumped in his SUV and took off. When he arrived in the park, Anthony's SUV was already there.

Kevin got out of his car. "My fault about last week, Anthony, but it couldn't be helped, you know?" Kevin pulled up his pants leg, displaying his black box ankle bracelet.

"I don't give two shits about that. Just give me my money."

Kevin handed over the brown paper bag to Flaco. "That's another thing. I don't have quite everything we owe you. The cops jacked me for the money when I was on my way to meet you."

Anthony snapped his head toward Flaco.

"Looks like only about half of it," Flaco said.

"We'll be able to get you the rest by the end of this week."

Anthony nodded in Kevin's direction, turned his back, and started to walk to his car.

Kevin started to follow Anthony. "I'm serious we'll get you the money by—"

Pop! Pop!

Kevin's eyes widened as the lead bore a hole through him. He fell to his knees and landed face down in the grass near the side of the SUV. Flaco stood over him, kicking him, baiting his body to respond. When Kevin didn't move, Flaco ran to the SUV and drove away.

An hour later, two officers tracked Kevin from his leg monitor when he didn't return home. The first officer spoke into his shoulder mounted two-way radio.

"This is Bravo 346. We have a 187 at Camden High Park. Victim is believed to be Kevin English. Multiple gunshot wounds to the back."

The second officer scanned the area, then walked over to Kevin. He placed his index and middle finger along the side of Kevin's neck. "No, wait! He still has a faint pulse! Get an ambulance, quick!"

The first officer dispatched again. "Dispatch, this is Bravo 346 again. We need an ambulance at our location. Victim is still alive."

Chapter 37

The paramedics whizzed Kevin into the Cooper Hospital Trauma Center emergency room, where nurses scrambled around and the smell of sterile air lingered.

* * *

Tamika wasn't far behind. "Kevin English! Do you have Kevin English in here?"

"They just took him from the ER up to surgery. If you'll have a seat, the doctor should be down momentarily," the nurse said.

"But, he's my husba—my boyfriend. I need to see him now."

"Sorry, but until he's out of surgery, you can't. Please have a seat." Tamika struggled her pregnant body to a chair in the corner and eased herself down with her right hand bracing her back.

About an hour later, a doctor walked into the waiting area. "Is someone named Tamika English here?"

Tamika pushed herself up out of the chair. "Doctor, how is he? Can I see him? How bad is it?"

"You are his wife?"

"Uh—Yes."

"Well, he was brought in with two gunshot wounds to his back. One of the bullets hit a rib; the second went into his lower back but missed any vital organs. He lost a lot of blood because the police said he was lying in the park for a while before he was discovered. We were able to remove the bullets; he's stable, but we need to monitor him in Intensive Care until he is fully conscious."

"Thank you, Doctor. I appreciate you for taking care of Kevin. When can I see him?"

"I'm not sure, maybe an hour or two. Someone will come for you when he wakes." The doctor walked away.

Every fifteen minutes, Tamika checked with the desk. Finally the nurse came from behind the counter and told her Kevin was in Room 308. She wasted no time before struggling down the hall and barging into the room. Kevin was lying on his side. A nurse was checking his vitals. "Kevin? Baby? Are you OK?"

"He's still groggy from the anesthetic. He'll probably be this way another hour or so. Why don't you make yourself comfortable in the lounge? I'll come for you as soon as he's awake," the nurse said.

Tamika walked reluctantly into the lounge. Chub, Eric, and Kevin's mother walked in there also.

When she saw Chub and Eric, rage grabbed her. "What the hell happened to Kevin? Why is he in the hospital with bullet holes in his back? Answer me, or get the hell out of here and stay away from him. It's your fault he's in here in the first place," she snapped. "I swear to you if you ever come around him again, I'll murder both of you myself."

Kevin's mother pulled Tamika into a smaller room to the side. "Calm down, Tamika. You're pregnant and we don't want you going into early labor," Kevin's mother ushered Tamika toward the couch in the sparsely furnished, dimly-lit room.

"I know, Ms. English, but when I think about what just happened to Kevin . . . I don't know what I would do without him." Tamika looked around. "Get me outta this room. It looks like a place you go and wait for someone to die."

It was a quarter to seven that evening when they got back to the main waiting room. Tamika saw Jalen standing to the side of the reception desk. Kevin's doctor came down to the waiting room just behind them. "Kevin is awake, so two family members at a time can visit him—"

Tamika charged through the door. The doctor held up his hand. "Let her have her moment alone. Then two at a time and only for a few minutes. Right now, the most important thing is rest."

"That's my child," Rhondella said, walking out.

"Kevin? Hey, baby. You had us so scared," Tamika said between sobs.

"Yeah, baby, you gave us all a bit of a scare. I don't know what happened, but you need to start thinking about your family and what this would have done to us if you hadn't a made it," Rhondella added.

Kevin stared. Tamika reached over and kissed him on his dry, cracked lips.

A nursed opened the door. "OK. That's enough for now. We need to move the next group in before visiting hours are over."

Eric, Chub, and Jalen walked in as Tamika and Rhondella walked out.

"Hey, Kev, don't worry about anything," Chub said. "We're going to take care of everything. Money for Mika, the kids, your mom, whatever you need, man. And if who I think did this to you, just say the word and I'll take care of it tonight!"

Kevin gave the slightest headshake.

"We can't let something like this just fly," Chub pleaded.

Kevin gazed forward. Then his lips alone said, "No."

Chub and Eric walked out leaving Jalen alone with Kevin.

Jalen pulled up a chair next to the bed. "You've got to think what you'll do when you get out of the hospital, cousin."

Kevin continued his gaze.

"Think of how you're gonna take care of your family."

Kevin's eye swelled up with tears. This was the first time Jalen had ever seen Kevin beaten.

"Don't worry, cousin, I got your back. I'll make sure you won't ever have to worry about our family again."

Kevin eyes intensified.

"I'm gonna look after you like you looked after me over the years."

His heart monitor's alarm shrieked. Kevin shook his head as rapidly as he could.

"Look, you're shot up and facing jail time for violating parole. How do you know whoever did this won't come after Tamika and the kids next?"

Kevin shook his head more and a tear fell down his face.

"Right now its not about want, its about necessity. So I'm going to fix it once and for all. I won't carrying a gun, but I can carry a business. You back me with Eric and Chub and the rest will fall in line."

Kevin's stare became a resolve. "Tell them I'll be running the business until you get back on your feet. See, I've been flirting with an idea of making some extra money on the side for myself, but if I throw your money into the mix, we can all make out and you guys can leave the streets behind you."

A near smile opened his eyes.

The idea was just something Jalen had been bouncing around in his head. "It's completely legal. No angles." Jalen stood, placed a hand on Kevin's shoulder and walked outside. He joined Eric and Chub in the waiting room. He told them what he told Kevin. They cut their eyes at him and cocked their heads.

"They musta got his morphine drip way too high or he would never listened to no shit like that," Chub said.

"Yeah, man, no disrespect, but you don't have no kinda street credibility," Eric added.

"I know, and I'm not looking for any. That's what ya'll do, and business is what I do. I can make all of you some real money. *Clean* money!" Jalen searched their eyes. "Besides, if you don't, one by one, you're all gonna end up in that bed." He nodded toward Kevin.

"Chub, if something happens to you, who'll take care of your mom? Eric, when you can't do this anymore, you gonna give up your lavish lifestyle?"

Silence hung around the stark white wall, the slow ticking clock, the distant sounds of people talking in the hallway.

"You guys give me a month and I'll show you how to work these streets like a Fortune 500 company."

"Fortune what company?" Eric questioned.

"Like Microsoft and Bill Gates. You know the richest man in the *world*. If I don't deliver, I'll walk away, no questions asked."

Chapter 38

The whole family waited for Kevin's arrival home. It had been almost a month of medication and therapy, and the day had come. The ambulance brought him home and delivered him in a wheelchair. In his eyes were circles of regret and apprehension. How would he feed his family from a bed? How would he take care of Mika? How would his children judge him as a father? He refused to be just another man who made babies he couldn't take care of. He was not a dead beat. He was a man of integrity. He always took care of his family; otherwise what was the use of living? There was only one hope. Only one. He took Chub's hand and pressed a small piece of paper in it. On it was the scribbling of a man who had been shot, but was too determined to allow that to hinder his wishes to be met.

Chub took the note and walked away from the family. Eric read it over his shoulder. They both looked at Jalen. He noticed and walked over and read too. All three of them just shuffled around the space without saying anything. Their usual laughter with the family was absent.

After six days, Jalen plunged into Chubs basement where Eric and Chub were already waiting.

"Who shot Kevin?" Jalen asked sternly.

"We don't know for sure but when we last talked to him, he was on his way to pay Tony," Chub said.

"Who's Tony?" Jalen asked.

"Anthony Phillips. Kevin's connect for the coke. He only had about half of what we owed him. I think Tony shot him cuz he was short on the money," Chub said.

"Set up a meeting with Tony as soon as possible to settle the debt. Tell him I'm your new source of income, so he knows to expect me," Jalen said.

"Expect you? I thought you said no street—just business?"

"That's right, this meeting will be all business. Tell him we'll all be there. How much coke did you get last time?"

"A brick, but Kev only paid five-thousand, we still owe fifteen," Chub said.

"Tell him we have cash for two more bricks plus what Kevin owed him. Let's see if that grabs his attention."

"We don't have enough cash for two bricks and what we owe. Besides, he'll probably think it's a trap because he shot Kevin," Chub said.

"Don't worry. I have the money, just set up the meeting. Set him at ease and tell him that we just want to square things away and make sure there's no bad blood between us," Jalen said.

"He's not gonna come alone. He got this big country white boy named Flaco to watch out for him," Chub said.

"Flaco? What the hell kinda name is that? Anyway, don't you worry about Flaco, Anthony is the brains, right?"

"Yeah."

"Then he'll follow Anthony's lead," Jalen said.

Days later, Chub called Jalen's cell phone while he was at work. "Hey, this is Chub. The meeting is set up for tomorrow night at ten. In the same park where they found Kevin."

"Okay. Meet me tonight, 7 p.m. at your house. I need to go over a few details. I need to know how these meetings normally go."

As soon as the clock struck 3 p.m., Jalen rushed out of work early. He slowly navigated the rush hour traffic of I-76 east toward Center City. He exited the expressway, made a quick turn, and was on Broad Street. He pulled to the side, near Alleghany Hospital, and was met by an old college friend in a white laboratory coat, her hands shoved in her pockets. He rolled down the window.

"What's up lady, how you been?" Jalen smiled as he popped the locks.

"I'm fine. A bit overworked, but fine." She stepped inside the car. "You mind telling me why you need this? I don't need any trouble."

"I could have ordered it myself, except I needed it before morning. You won't get in trouble. I promise."

She handed him a 16 oz. brown bottle. "I just don't want anything to happen to you before we can go out," she said.

Jalen leaned and smacked her lips before she hopped out. He put the bottle into a small cardboard box that he sat next to him. In twenty minutes, he parked outside of Chub's home. Chub was pacing at the front door, waiting for him.

"You're going to be a new face to him, so expect him to ask questions, but you shouldn't ask him too many. If you do, you'll come off like a cop. He'll probably have Flaco pat you down for guns and a wire so don't get nervous; just let them check you, get it over with, and make the deal. Don't expect Tony to handle the money or drugs. He doesn't get his hands dirty with either; he has Flaco for that," Chub warned.

* * *

The following evening Jalen sat quietly in the back of Chub's SUV feeling the bass from the amplified box compete with the pounding of his heart. Chub was playing Notorious B.I.G.'s latest—"Life After Death" CD. He stared out the window at the clear evening sky analyzing Biggy Small's explanation to the world of what 'beef' meant to urban Americans.

He could see every star in the universe tonight. Everything outside of him was peaceful and tranquil, unlike where he was heading.

"Hey Chub, crack your windows it's hot in here," Jalen said. They traded looks and Chub cracked the window, and cold air flowed through.

"You a'ight, Jalen?" Chub asked.

"Yeah, I'm fine, just a little warm in here."

When Chub pulled into the park, Jalen placed the lid of the Wawa coffee cup back in the cardboard cup holder. Chub cut the switch and Jalen grabbed the gym bag with the money in it.

"Hey, Eric can you open the door for me when you get out? I spilled some coffee back here and I don't want to get it all over Chub's door." Chub shot him a mean look, inspecting the back of his car.

"Don't worry, man, it didn't mess up your ride. It mostly spilled on my gloves," Jalen said.

"Eric, let this fool out. I'm not trying to have him messin up my whip."

They stepped out of the SUV and met Anthony and Flaco midway between their cars. The parking lights shined dimly from both cars. It was in the middle of winter, brisk enough to wear an overcoat, but Jalen was the only one wearing gloves and a scarf. He shook hands quickly and firmly with Anthony, then Flaco. Anthony snatched his hand back. "How the hell did you get your gloves wet?"

"I spilled a cup of coffee. Thought I dried them, but—Sorry, about that."

Anthony eyed him keenly. "Well, enough of the small talk." Anthony snapped his fingers at Flaco and pointed toward Jalen. Flaco patted all of them down roughly, almost a jailhouse frisk.

Jalen raised his arms and let Flaco pat from head to toe—in his shirt collar and coat. He pressed the gloves, unfolded his scarf from around his neck, checking for anything that looked suspicious. He nodded to Anthony. "He's clean."

"So, you took over Kevin's debt? You look like you'll do a better job of paying me back. I liked Kevin, but if you don't pay the debt, you pay the consequences. That's the nature of the game."

"That's why we're here. To take violence out of our future," Jalen said. "Now can we get this over with so we can all be on our way?"

Anthony grinned. "Straight to the point."

"Exactly. And I don't like the way your gorilla is looking at me."

Flaco cut his eyes at Jalen and clenched his fist.

Anthony laughed.

Jalen threw the gym bag to Flaco.

"That's forty thousand for two bricks, plus another fifteen grand that Kevin owed you. Fifty-five thousand in all."

Flaco searched through the bag and nodded to Anthony. "Damn, did you spill a cup or a gallon of coffee? The bag's wet, too."

"Flaco, go and bring back what they need and be quiet."

Flaco huffed and walked to Anthony's truck, placed the money in the back, and brought back a smaller gym bag to Jalen. Jalen handed the bag to Chub. Chub ruffled through the bag and nodded at Jalen. Jalen turned to Anthony. "You know, I could save you another trip out here in a month or two."

Anthony looked at him and laughed. "You plan on moving that much weight in two months?"

"Yup, and I'll need the same amount next time, but like I said I can save you the trip if you have more on you now. I don't have the money for the extra, but, when the month is up, I'll pay. If I don't, you can kill me. I bet Flaco would like that," Jalen said. He could feel Chub and Eric's confusion but they remained calm.

Anthony looked Jalen in his eyes. "This is how Kevin got into trouble, you know, but I've always been a fan of ambition, and who could say no to a deal like that?"

"Only a fool," Jalen said.

Anthony laughed. "You got balls. Chub and Eric, see what happens when you add new blood to the mix? Where you been hiding this guy?"

Anthony nodded to Flaco, who was headed back to the truck. Shortly, he brought back another bag.

"I was keeping this for another customer, but it's yours now. You have two weeks not a month to get me my money," Anthony said.

Jalen nodded and he signaled for Eric and Chub to get ready to leave, as Anthony said, "I'll tell you like I told Kevin. If you don't have my money in a couple weeks, I won't hesitate to do what's necessary to get it."

"You'll get what we owe you. You got my word on that," Jalen said, as the trio headed for the SUV. Anthony and Flaco departed and as Jalen got closer to the SUV he made another request. "Eric, can you get the door for me again?" Eric cut his eyes. "Who da fuck you think you are? The president or some shit?"

"It's not like that, trust me I'll explain when we get in the car. I just *need* you to open the door."

Eric opened the door and the three hopped into the SUV. Jalen watched as Anthony and Flaco pulled out of the park.

"What was the sense in the two extra bricks Jalen?"

"How we s'pose to pay?" Chub scolded.

Jalen threw them a look of disgust. When Anthony was out of sight, Jalen carefully removed one of his gloves and dropped it into the box behind Chub's seat.

Chub was yelling now. "How the hell we gonna move these extra keys in one, two weeks?"

"We can't, but that's not a problem, because we'll have all the time in the world to move them."

"What the fuck you talking about? See, I knew this was stupid. You don't have a clue about what we do," Eric said.

Jalen looked him in the eyes. "When the time comes for Anthony and Flaco to collect, they'll already be six feet under— cyanide poisoning."

Chub and Eric shot shocked stares at each other. Then they looked at Jalen.

"Look back here," Jalen said.

Chub and Eric looked toward the back-seat floor, where Jalen was carefully placing the coffee cup and its holder in the cardboard box behind Chub, a brown bottle was in clear view. Jalen picked it up and pointed to the label: "*CYANOGEN CHLORIDE.*"

"That's why I needed to know how these meetings operate and why I had Eric let me in and out of the car. I didn't want to contaminate your car. I wasn't sure how I was gonna pull it off until you told me about Anthony and his habits…you know, never handles the money. I laced the bag with it for Flaco. It didn't hurt that he touched my gloves when he patted me down either. They're both dying right now and they don't even know it. In the meantime, we have four keys for the price of two." Jalen turned back to disposing the gloves. The slight breeze blowing through the trees diminished their voices. His two cousins watched him remove the last glove.

"But what about you? Ain't you gonna get sick too?" Eric asked.

Jalen removed the last glove, dropped it inside the box and held out his hands revealing the two layers of white plastic surgical gloves he had on to protect himself. He then carefully peeled them off and tossed them in the box with the rest of the evidence.

"Why didn't you tell us anything?" Chub asked.

"The less you knew the better. Now, can we go home? I'm a bit nervous about sitting in a car with enough coke to send me to prison for the rest of my life."

Eric and Chub sat there for a moment pondering what their younger cousin had just done. Jalen directed them to drive by Cooper Hospital, where they found the contaminated dumpster for the hospital and dropped off the box. They looked at each other and then turned to Jalen.

"Welcome to the family."

"Welcome to our *new* family," Jalen corrected.

Chapter 39

Even the early morning sunshine the following weekend looked cold as it glimmered through the kitchen's icy windows. Jalen prowled around in the kitchen, pouring orange juice, drinking it, and flicking toast in the toaster. The click of the toast popping up made him jumpy. He chomped, still walking. Chub and Eric waited at the tiny breakfast table, touching nothing. While the local news played in the background, Chub leaned over to Eric. "Man, that poisoning shit was genius, but I still don't know what Kevin was thinking when he let Jalen start off like this."

Eric nodded and scratched his stubby beard. "Well, that's what we came here to talk about. And if things don't start to make sense real soon, then we just fill Kevin in tonight."

"For the time being, we gonna give Jalen some slack and see what he does with it," Chub said, sitting back in his chair. "If he starts to hang himself, then we'll step in, period."

Jalen stopped the circling and eating and walked over to them. "You guys getting nervous on me already?"

Mouths hung open, Eric and Chub turned around in surprise.

"I understand your skepticism," Jalen said.

"Our skepta—what?" Eric said.

"I see why you think I'm not up for this."

"Oh, okay," Eric said.

"We just stole a lot of product from one of the main suppliers in this city."

"Exactly!" Eric said. "So what we gonna do now? We only got one corner, and only me and Chub to work it."

"Who said anything about going to a corner?" Jalen's arms folded across his chest.

Silence hung in the air.

"Why would I let you go back to the 'corner boy' lifestyle that got Kevin shot and Fatar killed, Chub?" Jalen shook his head, eyeing them. "This family is done with corners!"

Eric jumped up. "What! So what you take all this coke for? We gonna give it away like we Robin Hood or something?"

"No. We *are* going to sell it, just not on any corner." *Especially not a corner in Camden . . .* "We got the coke from the burbs, so we gonna take it right back to the burbs."

"Okay, yo ass has *officially* gone crazy," Chub blurted out.

"Hear me out," Jalen said. "You think that Blacks and Latinos are the only ones who like to get high? If you do, you've went dumb watching too much TV. White people like to get high, too. Their communities just don't get flooded with drugs like ours. And they got businesses to go to and companies to hire them when they get cleaned up. So we're going to make a move to put the money we make off this stuff and put it to some good use for a change."

The two men leaned forward, their eyes blinking. Jalen pulled out a road map of South Jersey from his back pocket. "We're going to have to be smarter now. That's why we're saying goodbye to corners." Jalen touched each of his cousin's shoulders. "Besides, the suburbs don't have corners. We'd have to setup shop on somebody's manicured Kentucky Bluegrass lawn."

He spread the map on the table, tapping his fingers on the page. "If you change the market and group you sell to, then you have to change the selling method and tactics."

"I thought Aunt Michelle sent you to school for Engineering, not Business?" Chub asked.

"Electrical Engineering is just a method of routing component parts in the right direction for the highest yield of energy for the entire entity," Jalen responded.

Both Eric and Chub's faces went blank before returning their eyes back to the map.

I can't believe it. I actually have their attention. " This is how it's gonna work. You know how you've been out hustling and some white kids pull up trying to get some weed or coke?" Jalen asked.

"Hell yeah. We rob they asses or we sell 'em some bullshit 'cause they not coming back complaining," Chub answered.

"And when you drive down Broadway at night where the prostitutes are, you always see a few white chicks all strung out selling their ass, right?" Jalen asked.

"Hell yeah, they quick to give up some head for a couple hits," Eric boasted.

"Exactly, and I guarantee you she wasn't born and raised here in Camden. She grew up in the same suburb them white kids come from that y'all robbed or beat with oregano instead of weed. Before she became a crack head she was one of those kids looking for weed. Weed led to pills, pills led to coke, and then somebody put a pipe in her mouth and it was a wrap."

"Uh, huh," Eric and Chub said in unison.

"Welcome to Camden, where the crack is abundant."

"Dis guy better stop with all these big ass words. Da shit confusing enough," Eric said grinning.

"And that's the plan. We going to use those white girls to lead us back to the people they got high with before they found the pipe. *That's* our new clientele."

Eric's eyebrows raised and he tilted his head in approval. "But how we gonna sell it if we don't have corners? The cops will have our asses arrested in them suburbs in a few days. Just being seen in the neighborhood is enough to get us a couple years."

"We take it *indoors* like we did with the houses Kevin was renting to you guys," Jalen said. "The only difference is that we won't squat there permanently like you all did."

"Ah," Eric said.

"What we're going to do is use the white girls to get in good with their people and we'll throw a party. Let 'em get a taste of what we've got and sell out of their houses, apartments, condos as extra insurance. If they want coke, we give 'em coke. If they want crack we'll give 'em crack. They won't drop dime cause its in their house. If they do, the cops will take their crib."

Eric glanced back at the television for a hot second; Chub's eyes stayed glued to the map.

"We move the parties from house to house and in different suburbs. We never stay put more than a couple days," he said sternly. "Move it fast and cheap since we got all that extra coke for free and we still come out on top. When we run out, that's it. No re-ups."

Eric gasped and opened his mouth to speak.

Jalen raised his hand. "No re-ups!" We take the dough and Kevin and I go to work on a real-estate angle I've got my eye on. You don't have to hustle the street to get rich in America. This country gave birth to dumb ass inventions like the beer hat, the pet rock and the damn Chia Pet. Those damn things made their inventors millionaires. Now it's our turn."

"Oh shit. Tony's picture is on TV," Eric said, pointing at the screen over Jalen's shoulder.

Chub scooped up the remote, pointing it toward the set to turn up the volume.

"We have a second mysterious death . . . " the newscaster began. "Today, a successful local businessman, Anthony Phillips, died while on family vacation with his wife and two children. This followed another death discovered yesterday when a local high school football star Emanuel "Flaco" Flacolli, was found dead in the basement of his mother's home. Initial tests suggest that both deaths, seem to have been caused by poisoning . . . "

Jalen took the remote from Chub and switched off the TV.

Chapter 40

Jalen pulled out of the driveway through McDonalds and made a left onto Haddon Avenue just a few blocks from City Hall. Another left onto Market Street, and he had arrived. He found a parking space to finish his double cheeseburger and orange soda. When he finished, he got out of the car, placed three quarters in the parking meter, and walked the couple of blocks to City Hall.

For the past month Eric and Chub had been throwing their "parties" on a regular basis. Money was piling in, so now Jalen had to stay true to his word and put together a way for them to leave the streets behind them. Jalen had only seen his cousin Charles a few times between the time he helped him and his mother move to Camden. A lot had changed since then, though. Jalen had pledged the same fraternity Charles did when he was an undergraduate at Rutgers University, and this would be the first time they had seen each other since Jalen became a member.

Jalen remembered the day Charles drove him and his mother into Camden, how he boasted about knowing all the high-ranking officials in the city. Jalen had figured how to make that pay off. Make it the perfect opportunity for the family. Charles was currently the chairman of the Housing and Redevelopment Planning Committee. Rumor had it that the city had big redevelopment plans, but Jalen wanted to hear that directly from the source.

After going through the metal detectors and taking the elevator to the third floor, he walked over to room 318 and tapped on the door. "What's up, Charles? The city's keeping you busy, I see."

Charles gave him a toothy grin and ran a hand across his graying beard. "You know it is, young bruh. How's work and the women treating you?"

"They're both making me crazy." Jalen said before taking the seat Charles offered him. "Charles, I know you're a busy man and all, but I wanted to pick your brain on some noise I've been hearing about the city doing some redevelopment work."

Charles got up and closed the door, then turned to Jalen. "What noise?"

"About Camden making a comeback. Big plans to put the city back on the map."

Charles took a few moments, like all good politicians do, before sliding into his large swivel chair. "It's been a few years in the making, but finally we're going to start seeing some results from all the meetings and lobbying. Yea, we will be redeveloping a few strategic sections."

Jalen leaned forward. "Can you be a little more specific?"

Charles swiveled around to face the window. The view of the waterfront and the banks of the Schuylkill River loomed in the distance. "Well, allegedly, it will be based around the Waterfront, Aquarium, and Entertainment Center," he said. "All the surrounding properties near that area will more than double in value. The development will gradually span out from there. So, pretty much every piece of property along the river bed will be prime."

"So everything between the waterfront and downtown, right?" Jalen asked.

Charles nodded. "If I wasn't a civil servant, I would piece together what money I could and buy up as many of the abandoned and dilapidated houses as possible." He pointed out of the window in the direction of some old storefronts and duplexes. "Some are going for twenty to twenty-five thousand because the city has a grip on homes that people lost for property taxes or foreclosure." He turned to face Jalen again. "Then I'd sit on them until the city began to buy out the owners at about sixty to seventy thousand a piece." He shrugged. "But that's just me."

Jalen understood his point and changed subjects. "Okay, so you're for which team this year in the Super Bowl?" Jalen asked.

"Man, I don't even watch football anymore," Charles said, chuckling. "I'm a baseball man myself. I caught a few ball games at the new Campbell Soup baseball field. You know we got a team now, the Camden River sharks."

"Yeah, I heard about them," Jalen said. "That's part of the redevelopment?"

Charles winked at him. "You got it." He flipped his wrist, looking at his watch. "But, hey, young blood, I have a meeting with the mayor in about ten minutes."

Jalen stood. "I won't keep you then."

"Hey."

Jalen watched as Charles scribbled on a notepad.

"Here's Hector Velasquez's number. He works here, too. Right down the hall. He'll be able to get you some specific information about our plans and targeted areas. The pickings might be few to none, but he'll have a listing of all the properties that are available to the public. Stop by and see him before you leave. Tell him I sent you so he doesn't brush you off."

Jalen exchanged their fraternity's secret handshake, thanked Charles, and jaunted out.

A half hour later, after Jalen met with Hector Velasquez, he made his way down the steps of City Hall. The music blasting from an all-black Jeep Cherokee was strong enough to feel it vibrating through his body. He froze when the vehicle slowed down, then stopped in front of him.

The window rolled down.

Leroy poked his big head out of the window. "What up, little cousin? What you doing coming outta City Hall? Thinking bout running for mayor?"

Jalen chuckled and looked to see who was driving. Someone he didn't know was chauffeuring Leroy around.

"Where you headed?" Leroy asked.

"To my car a couple blocks down. Why, what's up?" Jalen asked.

"You don't have to walk," Leroy said, popping the locks. "Get in. Besides there's something I wanna talk to you about, *Mr. Professor.*"

This time the stranger chuckled. An uneasy feeling settled in Jalen's gut. He peered at both men before getting in the back seat. The driver pulled off slowly. "Chub tells me you're running things since Kevin's been laid up in the hospital."

Jalen shrugged. "Naw, I'm not running it. I'm just lending my brain out until Kevin's back on his feet. *Kevin's* still got the throne."

Leroy turned in the passenger seat, to get a better look at his cousin. "So, you're putting that college brain to work over there. Things in the city are a little dry after what happened to Anthony. People scramblin' round to make new connects."

Jalen knew Leroy was just stroking his ego, wanting him to drop his guard so he could come at him with whatever angle he had. He scanned his cousin's crooked smile, but Leroy stared Jalen back.

"Brooklyn, there's his car. You can stop right there," Leroy said to the driver.

Brooklyn? Thought he looked like he was from NY.

Brooklyn pulled into a spot near the jet-black Nissan Maxima.

"You know I got my own corner now? Brooklyn and me working out some things in Pollock Town," Leroy bragged. "Business over there's good and we got a few toys to show for it."

Leroy lifted his shirt sleeve and a new diamond studded watch sparkled. He then touched the gold and diamond necklace draping so far down his chest that Jalen couldn't see the charm.

"But you know business could always be better," Leroy added. "If I had a lieutenant to help make my business run a little smoother, you know, we'd be doing big things over there." Then he shrugged. "But I'm just a street thug. Ain't got them college degrees like you."

Leroy and Brooklyn looked at each other and laughed.

"A'ight, stop with all the bullshit and tell me what you want," Jalen said.

The laughter ended just as quickly as it began. "A'ight cousin, it's like dis. Kevin's on da way out and my crew on the way up. So, won't you stop fuckin 'round wit Kevin and head over to my camp and make some real dough. You know, lace me on the business side like you doing for Kevin."

Jalen already knew what Leroy wanted. His obnoxious cousin wasn't known for tact. The whole time he was talking, Jalen's attention was focused on the area of land that Hector Velasquez had shown him before he left his office. Originally there had been more than three hundred lots for sale; now only eight remained. Before Jalen left Velasquez's office he expressed an interest in four of the lots and Hector provided him with the paperwork. The total was approximately eighty thousand dollars.

The more real estate we own, the better our chances of staying off the corners. We'll need more than four lots.

"So what you think, *Mr. Professor?*" Leroy asked.

"You know I'm working with Kevin," Jalen said.

"Come on, man. Why da hell everybody on Kevin's sack?" Leroy said, slamming his hand on the dashboard. "He not gonna be doing this shit much longer after he got lit up the way he did—."

"But that doesn't mean I can't help both of you out," Jalen said.

Brooklyn and Leroy exchanged looks. Leroy leaned forward while Jalen kept talking.

"I mean it's not like I'm out there working the streets," Jalen said. "I'll give you the same deal I'm giving Kevin as long as you break me off a respectable salary."

Leroy looked out the front window, as if to contemplate the offer. He jerked around to Jalen. "Fine wid me. If our profits increase for a few months, then we can even work out some *extra* loot for you."

"Cool. I'll call you later tonight," Jalen said, and he stepped onto the sidewalk.

Brooklyn floored the SUV with the music blasting, Leroy giving him a chastising glance.

Jalen jumped into his car and pulled out the copy of the map Velasquez had given him. He took a pen from his inside coat pocket and circled the remaining four properties that he couldn't afford. Now, in a matter of minutes, the whole world had changed. All of their lives just got better. Like a lightning flash. He was now employed by Leroy, and would soon have enough cash for all eight properties.

Chapter 41

Three weeks later, Jalen pulled up to Leroy's beige aluminum sided town house in Sicklerville, New Jersey, twenty minutes outside of Camden. He rang the doorbell and Leroy's wife, Tasha, answered holding Leroy Jr. and her belly swollen with another pregnancy. She turned to head upstairs while Jalen took an uninvited seat on the couch.

"Leroy! Leroy!" Tasha yelled. "I know you hear me calling you. Jalen's waiting for you downstairs, and I need some money to finish Christmas shopping." She paused. "You hear me talking to you?"

Leroy remained strangely silent.

"Jalen, you can come upstairs," Tasha said. "His lazy ass is still in the bed."

Jalen climbed the steps and found Leroy with a white sheet wrapped around him. His eyes cracked open just enough to see his wife standing over him, hands on her hips, neck swaying from side to side, raining down attitude and verbal abuse that made Leroy duck farther under the covers.

Jalen grinned. It was obvious the greedy woman had run through the Christmas money. Seemed the "big man" was avoiding her by staying in bed, trying to think of a way not to give in without an argument. Three little girls marched up the stairs. They were her best allies. They shook and nudged their father.

"Come on, daddy. Momma's going shopping for our presents—and yours too." The baby squealed. "My new Barbie, daddy," Lisa, the oldest daughter said.

"And the yellow corvette for me, daddy?"

Leroy opened his eyes and grimaced, giving the girls a sarcastic, "Good morning."

"Ew, daddy your breath stinks. You was drinking again."

Leroy cast a sly glance at his wife who glared at him. "Out drinking again with one of ya boys or one of ya bitches?"

Jalen leaned against the door as the girls giggled.

Leroy crawled out of bed shrugging. He kicked his way through piles of clothes and shoes, and headed to the bathroom. As he stood at the toilet, Tasha laid their son down on the bed and walked in after her husband. The sound of her smacking him could be heard all the way in the hall. "Damn! What the hell you doing? You got my piss spraying all over on the wall. Now you gonna have to clean it up!"

"I ain't cleanin nothin'. If you can't piss straight dats your problem."

Jalen stood there, shaking his head.

"Don't start yo shit this morning, I ain't in the mood. Leave me alone and let me piss in peace."

"I'll leave when your hung over ass gives me some money to finish shopping."

"Money?" Leroy yelled. "What happened to the two thousand I gave you a few days ago?"

"What you think? I spent it. I got the girls, my mom, your mom, you, and your brother gifts."

"That sounds like everyone to me. What you need more money for?"

Tasha sighed, and shook her head. "I only got you one gift and I didn't get your cousins anything and I still haven't gotten anything for myself."

Leroy shook his head. "Fuck that. You ain't gettin' another dime."

Another smack sounded against his flesh. "Money, Nigga, give me some money!"

Leroy sounded like a dragon. Then the immediate sound of a clap of thunder. A yell, and a force hit the door and slammed it shut.

"Bitch, didn't I tell you I wasn't in the mood for your shit today? Don't think 'cause you pregnant I won't check yo ass."

Jalen jumped to the door with the girls on his heels. They banged on the door as the scuffling noise grew louder.

"Leroy! Cut that shit out. The kids are out here, man." Jalen turned the knob a few times trying to force it open, but Tasha's body held it shut.

"Daddy, don't hit mommy, you gonna hurt the baby," Lisa said. "You said you wouldn't hit her no more."

Jalen's heart hurt for the little girl whose brown slanted eyes filled with tears and worry. He had felt this moment before, many years ago and the pain never completely disappeared. He heard the desperation in her voice and the helplessness of it.

"Ya'll go downstairs," Tasha yelled through the door. "Everything's okay, we're not fighting."

The children instantly turned away as if they knew the routine. Jalen stayed at the door listening for his chance to burst in there and stop the fight. *This Nigga ain't shit!*

"Please baby, I didn't mean it like that," Tasha whimpered. "I just wanted to get the rest of the shopping done, that's all. I'm sorry! Don't hit me. You might hurt the baby." Then everything went silent.

Jalen slowly and quietly turned the doorknob so he wouldn't startle them. The door swung open easily. He froze. Leroy stood near the sink, while Tasha sat on the toilet, head bobbing back and forth in front of Leroy's naked body. The white sheet had fallen down around his ankles and feet. The argument was over.

Jalen turned away disgusted and took the children into the living room. Twenty minutes later, Tasha walked downstairs with Leroy Jr. propped on her hip, sporting a wide smile, *and* a hand full of money. Mission accomplished—only a few bruises for her trouble. *Dumb. Just fucking dumb.*

"Y'all ready to go to the mall now," she asked the girls.

The girls' faces lit up. "Yes, mommy," they answered in unison.

Seconds later, they filed out of the door, one by one, except Lisa.

"Lisa, lock the door behind us," her mother said.

Lisa turned her back to the door, pulled out a small kitchen knife and placed it on a table near the front entrance. Her once tear-filled eyes locked with Jalen, as his heartbeat quickened. He closed his eyes and old memories flooded his brain. It had been so long since he thought about that night his mother gambled her freedom for his. Up until now, he had done everything to repay her. He'd stayed out of jail. He graduated from both high school and college with honors, pledged a historically respected fraternity and managed a respected career.

But that all had changed now. He was sitting in the living room of his cousin, a known drug dealer who had just beat his pregnant wife, and instead of calling the police like he had done for his mother, he was waiting for him to come downstairs so he could conspire with him on how to maximize his potential earnings dealing drugs. *Have I really accomplished anything? Has my father's tainted spirit continued to live through me and I'm just realizing it?*

His eyes shot open as Lisa slammed the door shut to join her battered mother on their latest shopping spree.

Chapter 42

The Monday morning air was filled with the condensation floating from the mouths of everyone holding a conversation near Jalen as he walked toward City Hall. Constituents and the politicians representing them all filed in and out of the building. Jalen wondered if any of them had any idea what he was planning. He arrived at Velasquez's office and knocked on the glass pane door. He saw Velasquez's thick head of spiked black hair. His face was clean-shaven and a protruding gut forced the navy blue jacket open. The secretary led him in.

Jalen walked up to his desk and placed a folder before him. Velasquez reviewed the documents for the four properties they had previously discussed plus an additional four, thanks to Leroy's advance. That brought the total to eight. Velasquez slid the documents back into the folder and placed it on the side of his desk. "Everything looks in order. I see you're not messing around."

"I take my future very seriously."

"You know, when we first met, I didn't take *you* seriously. I thought that would be the last time I would see you." He cocked his head and mused. "But I stand corrected. It's good to see a young man taking an interest in real estate at such an early age. It's just too bad there aren't any more small lots available. You could have carved yourself a nice little niche in this city if we had been introduced a little sooner."

Jalen shrugged. "Yeah, well what can you do? If it's all gone, it's all gone." He got up to leave.

Velasquez leaned back in his chair and placed both hands on top of his head. "Well, it may not *all* be gone. I said all the *small* lots are gone."

"So, are there more available or not?" Jalen asked.

"That depends."

"On what?"

"How much extra capital you have to play with. I mean you just spent a pretty good amount of money on eight lots. I'd assume you've been saving for some time to make this type of investment."

"How about you tell me what you have to offer and I'll count my own money."

"Well, the eight lots you bought come from a group of properties the city anticipates making known to the general public. It's mandatory we put it out there. But there are larger plots that the average Joe can't afford. We keep those for major developers and real estate tycoons to fight over."

"Keep talking," Jalen said.

"Since you seem to be a *junior* developer in the making and the city of Camden likes to encourage minority business, we might be able to work something out. That is, if you can accumulate the funds. "

Accumulate the funds? He knows this money isn't clean. "Go on," Jalen said.

"Developers and real estate tycoons basically bid for the rights of larger plots, like apartment buildings, parking lots, or just flat pieces of land they have money to build on. My job is to work directly with those people and let them know what's available and negotiate the asking price."

"And you have one of these larger plots available for an aspiring developer such as myself?"

"Perhaps. I can show you what I have. And if you see something that interests you and it's in your price range, I could be convinced to keep it off the other developers' radar."

"And I'm assuming there's a fee associated with that assistance."

"Hey, you said that, not me. But I have heard of finder's fees associated with these types of transactions, somewhere around the fifteen percent range. I mean that's what agents get for putting together deals for professional athletes," Velasquez said, smiling.

"Agents get ten percent," Jalen corrected him. "But I understand, it's something like a consulting fee. In cash, of course?"

"You said it, not me." Velasquez repeatedly swayed side to side in his chair.

Jalen looked at him for a moment, weighing the money he had coming in, balancing the possibilities of the new opportunity. "How do you know I won't turn you in and get you booted out of City Hall, blackmail you?"

Velasquez smiled. "You may not have guessed it, but I come from the same streets that raised you. Matter of fact, I still live not too far from where you and your family grew up."

My family?

"My stepson recognized you the last time you were here. He remembers when you first moved into the neighborhood when the two of you were much younger."

Jalen racked his brain. *What's he talking about?*

Velasquez pointed in the direction of his stepson's desk. "That little nuisance used to run the streets until I married his mother and exposed him to military-style discipline." Velasquez pointed to a plaque honoring his stepson's service as a Marine. I even got him a job working here. He told me a little about your family." Velasquez rested the side of his face on his thumb and index finger. "So, let's just say I'm not worried about your integrity, especially considering we both have dirty laundry."

He knows the money's dirty.

"Now don't worry. I'm not here to judge you or anyone you're associated with. I'm just hoping to appeal to your entrepreneurial side, so we both can make out well here. City officials are under the microscope to ensure we don't make any sudden purchases based on the information we have access to. If I bought those eight lots, I'd be front page of the Courier Post tomorrow morning. But that doesn't mean I can't make some quiet money on the side with you."

So that's his angle. Just dangle the opportunity in my face and see if I bite. "Give me a couple days to think it over." Jalen stood and shook Velasquez's chubby hand and headed directly into the hallway. There, he noticed a Puerto Rican guy about his age, standing over a desk filled with papers and files. *He doesn't look familiar.*

Jalen walked over and stood in front of his entry-level desk.

He looked up at Jalen. "Can I help you?"

"Um, maybe. I'm Jalen Carthane, and—"

"You don't remember me, do you?" His smile was as wide as his face.

"Sorry, I can't say I do," Jalen said. Then suddenly, it hit him. The square jaw. The flat nose and straight black hair in a ponytail. "You were part of the welcoming committee when I first came to Camden."

The scar on the side of Jalen's eye started itching again. He was the kid, now grown up, that stopped the others from beating him to death. "So you're the Good Samaritan?" Jalen said. Rafael came from behind the desk to greet him.

Chapter 43

The snow had melted and spring leaves sprouted. Five months had passed since the incident and Kevin could function on his own, walk without a cane, and dress without Tamika's help. Now he was rough-housing with his boys, as the doctor had given him permission. To Kevin, those short spurts of playtime were worth every agonizing second of rehabilitation.

Trips to the quaint Cherry Hill Rehabilitation Facility off of Route 70-East were arranged by Tamika's health insurance. Four days a week, his physical therapist caused buckets of sweat to pour out of his pours due to muscle-fatiguing exercise: walking, standing from a seated position, bending over. The first few days were grueling, as pain etched its name on his insides with every move he made. Kevin realized how many of the simplest tasks involved every muscle in his back.

Today was another milestone. He took the road trip to Trenton State Penitentiary. He could see Damon's head from the first turn on the road. He was waiting on the bench at the bus stop with a plastic trash bag thrown over his shoulder. The sky was cold and blue, the wind almost still, a metaphor to the calm of Kevin's heart. Joy swelled in Kevin's chest. Damon was being released from prison. Free.

Kevin eased out of his car and hugged him as he handed him a bag with a brand new pair of white Nike sneakers and a black and red sweat suit that barely covered his penitentiary fed body.

"Hey man, I thought I was gonna have to catch the bus home after you didn't visit me the past few months."

Kevin laughed.

"What happened to you? You look thinner," Damon said.

"Come on, let me get you home. A lot's changed since the last time I was here. I thought I'd wait until you got out to tell you."

Damon looked curious, but didn't say a word while the two walked to the parking lot. A minute later, they piled into Kevin's SUV and he drove back toward the highway.

"Jalen's made his way into the family now," Kevin said.

Damon jerked forward. "Who? Jalen? College boy Jalen? What the hell was you thinking?" he said.

"It's not what you're thinkin' man. He's working on somethin' to get us off the streets. He's not a soldier or anything like that," Kevin explained. "We just putting all his business sense from college to good use."

"So how'd all this happen?"

Kevin hesitated. "Flaco shot me and left me in the park for dead, and—"

"Shot? What the fuck? I know y'all took care uh that shit, right? Right?"

"I didn't do anything," Kevin said. "I was laid up in the hospital." Kevin felt a knot tightening in his throat, as he felt the helplessness of those days come rushing back, a time when his whole world had been torn down.

"So Chub took care of it. Cool, but what the fuck does this have to do with college boy getting mixed up in dis?" Damon asked.

"After I was shot, Jalen came to the hospital and told me about a plan he had to make himself some extra money. He actually thought of a way to use our money to get us off the streets," Kevin explained.

"Thought how to use our money?" Damon paused.

"Now, don't get me wrong, I was dead set against that shit too. And maybe the trauma and drugs helped me listen a little bit more than I would have under normal circumstances—"

"Man, I don't give a fuck if ya ass was *chasing the dragon*, him being down with us ain't neva gonna be right wit me. He barely been in fights growing up, you think he would throw down and blast faggot ass Flaco if he was there when you got shot?" Damon yelled.

"It ain't about that. The kid's smart and what he said made sense," Kevin said.

"It ain't about dat?' Tell them niggas up in the pen '*it ain't about dat*'," Damon shot back.

"Look, I'm vouching for him. I wasn't too sure myself until . . ." Kevin pulled onto 295 South, heading back to Camden.

"Until what, nigga?" Damon demanded.

"Until he handled both Anthony and Flaco for trying to kill me. After that, I didn't need to know any more. I don't know what happened to him between the day we bailed him out of that fight in middle school and now, but he can take care of himself."

Damon turned and looked at Kevin. "Jalen caught two bodies straight out the gate?"

Kevin nodded. "He don't have full run of things. We keep him focused on the business and he's been doing a good job. We're not even on corners anymore." Kevin chuckled again and shook his head. "You know, he got us slinging coke and rock to white folk out in the suburbs?"

"What! Are y'all crazy?"

"Naw, man. We all thought the same thing, but talk to Eric and Chub; they'll cosign it. They been out in Lawnside, Collingswood, Voorhees, and Cherry Hill throwing *parties* and these white folk are in there getting high and buying bundles of stuff at a time, instead of one or two bullshit bags like the addicts in Camden. Some of them are buying so much they might be slinging themselves, but why should I care as long as their money's right."

"I'll be damned!"

"That shit is more than right. That shit is long too. After every party's over, we bounce. We sell out and never go back. Then we take that money and buy houses in the city."

Damon seemed dumbfounded.

"Trust me, Damon, if we pull this thing off, we'll be set, and Sean's ride home from jail will be the last ride back home from the penitentiary for any of us."

Damon tore his gaze from the window. "Look, I been away for a while and you been running your own thing, so I have to trust your judgment. If what you're saying is true, then I can't argue with it."

"It's under control. By the end of it all, we'll probably end up working for Jalen's ass, getting a check cut for doing nothing," Kevin said.

"Really? I guess we'll just have to keep an eye out for our little genius 'til whatever you two got cooking comes through," Damon said.

"It's cool wit you then?"

"Yeah, like you said, I hope Sean'll be the last one coming home and none a us will have to go through what I did the past few years."

Kevin didn't want him to talk about it. He didn't want to hear anything about it from his brother.

"That place turns men into animals. The things we have to do in there to survive . . . I wouldn't wish that on the guys that shot you."

Kevin looked at his brother, as if Damon was trying to tell him something, something he didn't want to know. The two had always been straight up with one another, and if he had something to say, he would eventually come out with it. Maybe one day when he felt stronger.

Chapter 44

The next year moved like stet. The summer of 2000 to the following summer all merged into one. Sean was released from prison and now lived in Eric's spare bedroom until he could find work and his own place. Now he walked out of the two-bedroom apartment in tan khakis, a white button-up shirt, and the black wing-tipped shoes that he and Jalen found on sale last week.

Jalen held back his laughter as Sean got in the car, on his way to his third job interview that week. Minutes later, Jalen guided his car into a black gravel parking lot in front of a silver, gray, and blue diner.

"Alright, Sean. I'll wait for you at the counter until you finish your interview. You want me to order something for you, too?"

"Naw, I'm good. I had some cereal this morning."

"Cool, well good luck." Jalen pounded Sean's fist with his own and they walked inside. Jalen walked off to take a seat at the counter and picked up a menu. Sean spoke with the hostess.

Jalen placed his order, while a tall, bald, brown-skinned man escorted Sean, along with his application, to an empty booth at the back of the eatery.

"Excuse me, Miss. Can I sit in that booth?" Jalen asked, pointing to the area where Sean was filling out his application.

"Mr. Bartrum, how are you?" the manager asked.

"I'm fine, how are you?" Sean returned.

Way to go, Sean. Sounding like a white boy!

"Great, thanks for asking," the man said, smiling. "I see you're applying for the dishwasher's job. Now, I'm going to be honest with you. It's hard work and only pays minimum wage, but it's an *honest* living and there's room for growth."

"Anything's better than nothing in this economy," Sean answered.

In this economy? You've been hanging around me too long.

"Well, let's see what else we have here, Mr. Bartrum." The manager browsed the application. "Your application seems complete and umm—"

Jalen's heart sank.

"I see you did some time in prison."

Jalen signaled the waitress to hurry up with his order.

"Do you mind if I ask why?"

Sean hesitated. "I was convicted for aggravated assault and a very minor drug possession." His voice wavered.

The man's eyebrows raised and the smile faded. "Uh huh? I see," he said. "Well, I have a couple more people to interview, but I will be sure to let you know by the end of the week. Thank you for your time, Mr. Bartrum."

Jalen knew Sean wouldn't be getting that job. The manager of the diner stood and shook Sean's hand, signaling the end of the interview.

"Thanks for taking the time to see me," Sean managed.

Jalen paid for his order and followed a slumping Sean out to the car.

"Man, this was the fifth interview since I got out and I keep hearing the same shit as soon as they see I did time." Sean spat onto the black gravel. "I don't see why they getting all high and mighty. Don't nobody want these jobs anyway, 'cause the pay is shit. But I ain't got no choice, cause that's all that's out there for me, and I can't even get that because of the time I spent in prison."

"Yeah, I know it ain't easy, man, but something will work out."

Jalen and Sean rushed back to the apartment. Jalen joined Sean upstairs so he could use Eric's bathroom. When they slung the door open two half-naked women were lounging around the apartment. Jalen could see Eric, halfway under the sheet, sleeping. The shorter woman, wearing one of Eric's T-Shirts, lit a blunt, and camped out on the black leather sofa in the living room. The other one stood in the kitchen, wearing a purple bra and matching thong as she stirred a bowl of eggs.

Jalen felt like an exposed electric wire hit him when he saw how her body shook as she stirred those eggs. He completely forgot he had to go to the bathroom. Her backside shook and jiggled to the motion of her right arm whipping the eggs.

"What's up, ladies?" Sean asked before he took a seat next to the light-skinned one on the sofa. She took a few pulls on the blunt until the fire at the end of it went bright red. She passed it to Sean, who immediately whipped the thick, brown wrapped weed to his lips.

Jalen swiped at the blunt. "Don't you have to get tested by your probation officer?"

Sean shrugged, avoiding Jalen's protesting hand, and took a deep hit.

Jalen sighed and left it alone while the young woman's backside shook and her arm continued to beat the eggs. *She's doing it on purpose.* The sound of the eggs hitting the hot browning butter was making him hungry again. The smell of the cooked bacon flooded the air.

The woman walked over with two plates of food and took her seat next to the other woman who was already faded out with weed. Between puffs with Sean, she managed to polish off her food. Jalen declined her offer to eat from her plate. The girl in Eric's T-shirt rose from the couch, strutted over and sat across Jalen's lap. She took a long pull, and leaned in to blow the smoke in his mouth. Jalen placed his hand over her lips before she could exhale. He rose abruptly. "I don't smoke."

Jalen walked over to Sean and the two exchanged a handshake. "Ay, if you need anything just give me a call. I'm going to the office for a few hours today."

Sean studied him for a full moment. "Thanks for the ride. I'll holla at you lata."

Jalen was glad to be out of there and on to the moment that would change their family's lives.

Chapter 45

Friday night in Philly was an experience all its own. Every one of the cousins was ready to laugh and let go of the past. They wanted the sight of pretty women littering the streets, clubs, lounges, and late night hangouts. Kevin arranged it as a welcome home party for Sean and Damon. He reserved the VIP section at the Hyatt Regency Hotel, where a party was always thrown on the first Friday of the month by a band of local African-American entrepreneurs.

"First Fridays" in Philly was legendary for its ever changing high class, grown and sexy venue and the crowd that staged it. Tonight each cousin was on the prowl for the prettiest woman who would believe that, at least for this night, she was loved.

VIP was sectioned off by velvet ropes and a couple of soldiers serving as security to keep unattractive women and men who weren't family at bay. Eric, Jalen, Kevin, Sean, Damon, and Chub drank and danced with scantily dressed females.

The music of Lauren Hill rained all over the dance floor, warning women to watch out for the men just wanting *that thing*. Her five wins at the Grammy's that year secured her place in Hip-Hop and music history forever. Eric wrapped his arm around the waist of a tall, dark-skinned woman with short curly hair while her girlfriend, wearing a scar across one of her high cheeks and a neon green cat suit and four inch clear platform sandals that showed her skinny legs, swayed to the music *outside* the velvet rope. She peered over Eric's shoulder, eyeing Damon. "How the hell y'all gonna let my girlfriend in and not me? Come on, Yolanda, I'm ready to leave."

Damon blurted out, "Ya girl will be out when she ready. Stop cock-blocking."

"What! Who you think you talking to? You old-ass nigga!"

Damon tossed the hater a mean look and the last of his cognac. The ice cubes ricocheted off of her face and the brown beverage dripped onto her outfit. She swung at Damon across the rope. The family's personal security jumped between them, having to hold her back as she continued to buck and lurch toward him. Her pride matched her stained outfit.

"Did you just throw a drink at me like a bitch?" she sneered. "You learnt that in prison, huh, bitch?"

One of the soldiers reached over the rope and punched her in the mouth while the other ran over and started harassing her. More security ran over, pulling the soldier off the woman.

The woman scrambled to her feet. Her face was swelling and growing red. Suddenly, the lights flashed on. Hotel security rushed in and a stampede started. Partygoers scattered through crowded exits. A young lady in heels too high to run hit the ground. The bloody woman reached into her purse, pulled out a small handgun and aimed straight at Damon.

"She got a gun!" someone yelled.

Kevin's eyes found the man that yelled out the warning and he watched as the stranger ran toward the woman, tackling her as she fired a single gun shot, shattering a bottle of champagne on the bar and grazing Damon's upper shoulder. The stranger wrestled the gun from the woman's hand and it slid away. A security guard grabbed for the gun. He slid; the woman slid. They reached the gun at exactly the same second. She grabbed it. He slammed her hand to the floor in three rapid movements, and the gun dropped. He kicked it toward the open dance floor. Security jumped in and dragged her outside.

The stranger rose to his feet. "I know that guy," Sean said. "Marcus . . . Marcus Gibson!" Sean yelled across the room.

The man cocked his head before slowly walking toward Sean.

"Marcus Gibson?"

The two men half embraced. The party promoters rushed to evacuate Kevin and his entourage through the back door before the police arrived. Sean motioned for Marcus to come with them as they were being hurried out.

"Damn, man you hemmed that girl up like you was a Black Steven Segal," Sean said with a heinous laugh. The SUV whirred up and they all slid inside.

"Sean, how you and that dude know each other?" Damon asked.

"Man, me and Marcus was in the pen together. I got into a beef with some fool up in there and Marcus here got the drop on that nigga."

"Marcus is that *dude,* cousin," Sean said.

"Yeah, I can see that," Kevin chimed in as Chub sped up.

"The police are all over the place. Take us back over the bridge," Kevin ordered.

Chapter 46

The next morning, Kevin curled deeper under the warm blanket, hoping to block out the sound of the 8 o'clock alarm that he knew would ring any minute. Instead of the alarm, his cell phone rang. He grabbed it without poking his head from under the blanket. Tamika groaned, "Damn, do they ever leave you alone?"

I guess not.

"Kevin. This Eric. We need to talk, man."

"This shit can't wait til I at least get outta bed?"

"Naw, man, it can't. Leroy shot one of our people last night outside Jocamo's in Pollock Town."

"Jocamo's? What the hell is a Jocamo's?" Kevin asked.

"It's a strip club." Tamika blurted out from underneath the cover. "And I better not eva catch you up in there!"

"Mind ya business, Mika," Kevin said as he sprang from under the blanket. He grimaced from a sharp pain in his lower back and stumbled out of bed and into the next room.

"What happened?"

"I got a voicemail from this stripper I'm messin wit. She said Leroy was in da club last night, got into a fight with our man, and shot him. The kid's dead, Kevin."

"Get everyone over here in an hour!" Kevin said, hanging up.

Tamika appeared in the hallway. "Now what?"

"Go back to sleep. I'll be there in a little while."

She didn't move. "I used to worry about you being in the streets. Then I had to worry when all that police shit went down. Now we're back to this." She stood there, as if expecting Kevin to answer her. But then, she whirled around and stormed down the hallway to her bedroom and slammed the door.

Kevin didn't know what happened to his mind between the time he heard the door slam and the time the crew came in the front door—Chub, Eric, Damon, Sean, and Jalen single-filed down the stairs into the basement.

At the square table, each man was in his seat. Chub always sat closest to Kevin to his right. Eric was next to Chub, while Damon sat across from Kevin on the other end of the table. Jalen was random. He pulled up a chair from the wall. Kevin spotted each of them, one-by-one. He sensed that Eric had briefed his men before they arrived.

"What happened last night with Leroy doesn't affect the business, or what Jalen and I have planned, but there are rules to this game," Kevin said, pointing his finger at each of them. "And those rules say we can't let anyone, even if they're family, take somebody out in our crew."

Kevin felt Chub's foot tap the linoleum-tiled floor, but soon it could be heard. He watched him sweat out the fate of his only brother—Leroy.

"This is fucked up man, if we don't do nothing, it's gonna look like we not taking care of our people," Damon added. "I mean we family, his brother is sittin at the table with us. Chub, I'm not saying we have to hit Leroy, but we have to do something."

The room went dead silent.

Jalen remained calm and a glaze came over his eyes. It seemed that he was remembering something. Something no one knew but him. He dug his elbows into the leather chair and sat up straight.

"There's a better way to handle this," he said.

All eyes turned to him at once and he took a deep breath. "We've been working the hell out of the burbs without any problems so far. We're almost where we need to be. So close to walking away from all this shit clean. But we can easily wreck the whole plan over some random street fight that has nothing to do with business. If we follow the same tired-ass rules you guys have been following, you're gonna spend the next few months trading shots instead of getting away from this shit."

Chub nodded. This was the first time Jalen had outwardly expressed anger at his family.

"So what's your solution, bruh?" Kevin asked.

Kevin welcomed the offer to take this load off their shoulders. None of them wanted to be responsible for hurting their own blood, even if they didn't see eye to eye.

"Let me talk to Leroy, he'll see me as neutral. If anyone from this side shows up, he'll be on guard. But with me being *Mr. Professor*, he won't be. I'll talk him into paying for the kid's funeral."

Damon interrupted, "That's it? He pays for the damn funeral?"

"No, that's not it, damnit!" Jalen shot back. "We'll hit his pockets too, but not so much that he won't be able to live a life. Let him keep his dignity. That way he'll see we respect him and wish him no harm. This way no one gets hurt, the cops don't get involved, and everyone keeps making money."

Everyone remained quiet and turned to Kevin for approval. "He pays for the soldier's funeral expenses, pays us five thousand and we'll squash the whole thing."

Jalen nodded. "No problem."

Chub threw a look at Jalen and nodded. A gesture of thanks for a peaceful solution and keeping his brother alive.

"Alright that's it. Y'all can leave," Kevin said, slowly standing.

Everyone filed up the stairs. "Chub, hang out for a minute," Kevin whispered. Chub waited quietly until the last person had disappeared up the steps.

"How we making out with those last parties?" Kevin asked.

"We good, man. I got this new addict who used to live in Sicklerville and she's putting us on to her peeps tomorrow. I'ma scope the place out tonight and, if everything's cool, we'll work it tomorrow night." Chub smiled. "We more than halfway through everything. A few more months and we'll be all out. Man, we moving 'round so much nobody can spot us. And them guys buying it up like they stockpiling for the end of the world. This shit's genius. If we could get in good with the police, we'd have enough money to take baths in champagne for the rest of our lives."

Kevin pursed his lips and nodded his head without a word. Then he stared and seemingly couldn't stop. "And all this time, we thought hitting up our city was where the money was at. We slept on the folks that started this getting high shit in the first place. But we not here to turn suburbs out. Let the next hustler figure it out." *We almost home.*

Chapter 47

With the thought of walking away clean still stirring in his brain, Jalen woke up at 8 o'clock the next morning and dialed Leroy at home. Lisa answered.

"Lisa, where's your dad?"

"He's asleep," she said.

Jalen could hear Tasha's voice blaring in the background. "Money nigga, I need more money!"

"Oh, really? Well, wake him up and tell him that I'm coming over," Jalen said. "Tell him it's important."

When Jalen arrived at Leroy's house, he was chasing Tasha in circles around her new Lexus LS 400 in the driveway. Jalen almost laughed at the sight—Leroy in his boxer shorts, t-shirt, and one white tube sock, picking up whatever object he could find to throw at Tasha—a dry bush, a tennis shoe, a beer can. A small trail of blood was on the front of his white t-shirt signifying that Tasha must have gotten a lucky punch that drove him to his frenzied state. Jalen rushed over and yelled.

"Do you have any idea how crazy the two of you look?"

Leroy looked surprised, perhaps thinking about how to save face. He folded his arms across the blood strain, as if to conceal it. His embarrassment gave Tasha just enough time to run into the house, screaming. The children grabbed her around her legs as she slammed the door shut.

Jalen looked at his hung-over cousin, walked over and blocked him from the door. "I'm not the type to get into married people's business, but you're acting like a damn fool. Last time you were beating her in the bathroom; today you're chasing her around the front of the house, throwing plants and beer cans at her in broad daylight. What's going on in your head, man?"

Leroy finally regained his senses. "Man look, she keep nagging me bout my other women and she keep stealing from me."

Jalen looked around the serene community that Leroy had moved his family into and shook his head. *You can take him out of the hood, but you can't take the hood out of him.*

"But you do mess around on her," Jalen reminded him. "You gave her the 'clap' after ramming some nasty chick, remember? You'd better be happy she hasn't left your ass and taken your kids with her and have the state hit you with child support and alimony."

Leroy looked at Jalen like a mad dog. "She ain't going no where long as I'm making money and she don't have to work. She gets to live in this house and drive that car," he punched his big finger through the air at the Lexus with chrome rims.

"All she really had to do is spit me out a boy to carry my name," Leroy said. "The house looks like a damn typhoon hit it and my kids run around terrorizing the white kids they go to school with. You know, she hired some Mexican maid so she wouldn't have to clean? I might as well marry the maid if her ass wasn't so fat and she could speak English. She cook for me more'n Tasha."

Jalen groaned. "Whatever, man! You're going to mess around and kill her one day." He changed the subject. "But I'm not here to be Dr. Phil. I came to talk about what happened last night."

Leroy's eyes glazed over as they walked toward the house.

"Word is already back about how you killed Rick, one of Kevin's people."

"Who the hell is Rick?" Leroy shrugged his shoulders. "I didn't kill nobody!"

"Rick is the dude you shot last night at the strip club. Ring a bell?"

Leroy pulled up the back of his shirt. "That nigga hit me wit a chair. I was protecting myself. I didn't even know he was wit y'all."

"Come on man, even I know that don't mean shit," Jalen said. "All that matters is how it looks. You killed one of his people and people know you and Kevin's not on good terms, right?"

"One of *his*? You mean one of *y'all* don't you?" Leroy smirked. "You workin for both of us right now. I bet you haven't told him 'bout that."

Jalen froze, realizing that this was a sensitive subject. "Yeah, you right. I haven't. That's why I'm here to sort this out so nobody else gets hurt."

"Look. If Kevin wanna war over this petty shit, it's on."

"Wrong answer, idiot," Jalen said.

Leroy turned and stared Jalen up and down.

"If he wanted to hit you or one of your guys, you think I would be here? I'm *Mr. Profe*ssor, remember? I'm over here to make this shit right."

Leroy settled down a little like a whistling teakettle when the flame is turned off.

"Come on, man. The word's out. We all know how you clocking and you on the come up, y'all beefing right now could mess things up for both sides."

Leroy smiled and nudged him with his elbow. "Yeah, *we* doin' alright over here, huh?"

"Look, to kill you and Kevin's beef and for both sides to save face, we need you to pay for funeral arrangements for the kid you killed."

Leroy pondered the offer but Jalen could tell he wasn't ready to immediately jump on board. Jalen continued the coaxing. "Come on, man. Think about it. You don't really want to fuck up what you got going on. Chub is with Kevin. You wanna be responsible for hurting, maybe even killing your own brother? How you gonna look your mother in the face if something like that happens?"

Leroy looked Jalen square in the eyes, as if he was mad that he would even play his brother as his ace. He stomped around for a while, then suddenly stopped. "A'ight man. Fuck it, I bank dudes funeral, but this ain't some shit 'bout me being scared of

Kevin. If Chub wasn't on y'all team I wouldn't give a fuck bout ya'll."

Jalen dropped the final bomb. "And you need to pay ten thousand to Kevin to compensate the man he lost." Jalen went high knowing that when he lowered the amount it would be easier for Leroy to swallow.

"What?" Leroy hissed. "You must be crazy! Kevin always got his hand in somebody's pocket. Fuck that, we just got to start dropping bodies."

Jalen shook his head. Leroy clenched his hands. His muscles twitched involuntarily, and Jalen saw it.

"Come on, cousin," Jalen said "You brought me into your camp to advise you. Look, maybe I can convince Kevin to take five thousand instead of ten. If you stop drinking or find some woman with her own crib and stop paying for motels, you won't even miss it."

Leroy glared. Then he caved. "A'ight. I'ma play ball for five grand."

"So we good? Funeral, five thousand, and everything is cool?" Jalen asked.

"He gonna have to wait 'til the first of the month for the five grand, though," Leroy said.

"No problem. I'll straighten it out." Jalen shook his hand, and walked back toward the car.

Leroy headed back toward the house and turned the knob. It was locked.

Bam! Bam! Bam! Bang! Bang! Bang!

"Tasha, stop playing and open the door!"

From his place in the car, Jalen saw someone peer out the window.

"I ain't gonna hit you. Look, baby, I'm sorry, come on. I want to take you and kids to get some breakfast at IHOP."

Jalen got into his car and started the ignition. *Those two deserve each other.*

Chapter 48

Jalen found himself heading to City Hall for another meeting with Velasquez. His early arrival allowed him to sit in on a redevelopment meeting that Velasquez was hosting. He walked into a room of crackling tension. He took the first seat in the last row, and still the audio was too loud.

The phrase *eminent domain* was thrown around like a football. Jalen realized he was at the right place at the right time. This was the door to the redevelopment plan that he and Velasquez had been discussing.

"Order! We will have order, or this meeting will be adjourned!" Velasquez said, banging the gavel.

"To hell with order! How you going to bring white developers in a African-American and Latino community and move us out with some 'eminent domain' excuse?" One of the community leaders shouted from the boiling crowd. "I've been living here for forty years, my house is paid for, and all of a sudden I don't count?"

"Yeah!" the crowd shouted.

"How do you redevelop an entire community without including the people that live there?" she asked.

The crowd hurled frenzied insults at Velasquez and he pounded the gavel again. Jalen scanned the angry faces, feeling something like a shooting star in the pit of his stomach. He had acquired eight homes: five abandoned shells and three fore-closures for $145,000. Six were for Kevin and the family and two were for himself. In the future the properties are projected to bring in at least fifty thousand each, more than a quarter of a million dollars in profit. He felt bad everyone in the room couldn't benefit like he and his family would.

Eminent domain gave the city of Camden the power to force people from their homes or store-front businesses. The city would gain right-of-way for urban renewal. Guards walked up front and ushered the city officials outside as the angry mob threw balled-up paper at them. Jalen caught sight of Velasquez with his personal assistant and stepson, Rafael, trailing behind. Jalen stood and waved to get his attention. Velasquez acknowledged and pointed toward his office upstairs.

While Jalen stepped into the exit aisle, and was putting on his jacket, he accidentally tripped a young lady in the crowd. While the angry mob herded outside, Jalen reached out to grab her arm, but it was too late.

"Sorry about that," Jalen said.

The young woman bent over and scooped up her manila folders and scattered documents. The slender beauty crouched with her long black straight hair tucked neatly behind her ear partially blocking her identity but for the small beauty mark on her chin—it was *her!*

"Don't worry about it," she said. "Just help me pick up some of this stuff."

Jalen just stood there. When she looked up in disgust, their eyes met.

"Asia Carter?" Jalen said, searching her face.

"Jalen Carthane," she answered.

She was still as beautiful as she had been in high school, except her face had thinned to striking proportions; her hair had been straightened flat and long to the middle of her back.

"What are you doing here?" Jalen asked. "I thought you would be training for the Olympics between having Omar's babies or something."

Asia rolled her eyes. "Oh my God! Please don't mention his name to me."

"Huh? What happened?"

"I see you're seriously out of the loop on current events."

Jalen was afraid he might have offended her until she pulled a small silver flip phone from her purse and asked for his number. "856-495-1234," she repeated, making sure she got it right.

"I'm at work right now and I don't want to get fired after being here just a couple of days, so I'll call you later." She snapped the phone closed.

Her perfume had a soft rosy scent that complimented the mango body spray trapped in his nostrils. It followed him to Velasquez's office, where he took a seat beside Rafael.

"Jalen, in about a month, we're going to sign off on this project and you're going to make yourself a decent amount of money. I'm impressed by what you've done," Velasquez said.

Jalen forced a smile. "Velasquez, I'm not your wife. You don't have to sweet talk me."

Velasquez chuckled and turned to Rafael. "Find my new assistant. I need her to process some documents."

Rafael walked out of the room.

"Jalen, you should see this beauty," Velasquez said, closing his eyes and kissing the tips of his fingers as if he were Italian. "She's smart, too. But I digress. The real reason I asked Rafael to leave is because I have a new opportunity that I thought might interest you."

More dangling, huh, Velasquez?

Jalen sat up in his chair.

"I know this was just supposed to be a formal meeting, but I figured why not ask you?"

Jalen pursed his lips as a gesture to indicate anticipation.

"One of the developers was interested in an apartment building in Camden's downtown area, over by the University."

"You mean the one directly across from the Law School? One of the primary housing units for their students?"

Velasquez grinned. "So you know what I'm talking about?"

Jalen chose not to entertain his rhetorical question. "How many units?"

"Twenty, and the standard rent is six to seven fifty a month for one and two bedrooms respectively."

Twenty units at six hundred each is twelve thousand dollars a month and one hundred forty-four thousand dollars a year. "So

206

why doesn't the developer want the property anymore if it's so great?"

"Off the record," Velasquez said, glancing cautiously at the door, "the potential buyer's been slapped with a sexual harassment suit and his wife is divorcing him. Between lawyer's fees and the possibility of his wife getting half of everything, he's thinking twice about buying anything, especially anything that will have his name attached to it."

"What about the other big boys?"

"They don't know about it yet. I decided to keep it off the table to see if you were interested."

Jalen peered. "Sounds good. Keep it under wraps for a day or two while I think it over. I'll call you." *Is it too good?*

"If I don't hear from you in two days I'll have to pitch it to the other guys. Then it's out of my hands."

"How much, anyway?" Jalen asked.

"Seven hundred and seventy five grand," Velasquez grinned, "Not including my consulting fees."

Jalen nodded. "Speaking of consulting fees." He reached into his pocket, removed an envelope with seventy-five hundred dollars in it, and put it on his desk.

Velasquez quickly flipped through it, smiled, and stuffed it in his inside jacket pocket.

Moments later, Rafael came in, followed by the new personal assistant. Jalen turned to—*Asia Carter!* He turned back to Velasquez. Rafael left immediately and Velasquez waved Asia to his desk. "I need you to go through the rest of these files tonight and process them. I need them ready by tomorrow morning."

"I have class for graduate school tonight in Philadelphia," Asia reminded him. "It will be difficult for me to finish by morning, even if I worked on it from home."

"Velasquez, I didn't know you were such a slave driver," Jalen said, hoping to throw Asia a life preserver.

"Okay, okay," Velasquez said. "I think my friend may have a crush on you, sweetie. Have it done before you go to lunch tomorrow. Now get going to class."

"Thank you, Mr. Velasquez," she said.

Velasquez leaned forward and lightly tapped her backside with one of the files.

Jalen's anger flared. Asia lowered her head, as if that had not been the first time.

"Better be careful or you'll be the next one with a lawsuit," Jalen warned as Asia left the office.

Velasquez laughed. "Naw, not me; I'm a seasoned veteran." His eyes narrowed. "My last assistant tried that little game, but I had Rafael drop her ghetto ass some cash to buy new outfits. When she got back from her weekend shopping spree, I fired her ass. Problem solved."

Jalen stood, deciding it was better to let the conversation die of natural causes. "Well, I've got to go."

"Don't forget, you only have two days," Velasquez warned.

"I'll be in touch." Jalen said, shutting the door behind him.

Jalen walked out and over to Asia's desk. "You okay?"

"I'm fine, it's just a reminder of why I'm studying for my Masters. So I don't have to put up with that kind of crap." She focused her eyes away from Jalen. "Eventually, I'll be out of here and done with his extra testosterone-driven bullshit."

Jalen smiled. "Wasn't expecting that answer."

Asia finally looked up at him. "The plan no one expects are the most effective." Tears rose in her eyes and she blushed. "I can't believe you saw that. I'm so embarrassed."

"Maybe you should quit."

"I can't. This is the only job I could find close to home and I need to help support my father. The money my mother makes and my father's disability just doesn't cut it anymore." She glanced at her watch. "Oh my God, my train to Philly."

Jalen grabbed her bag and threw it over his shoulder. "I'll get you to class on time."

Asia looked at him and smiled. "I see you're still the same gentleman I knew in high school, only now you're all grown up and far more handsome."

Chapter 49

Jalen had just paid the toll on the Benjamin Franklin Bridge. "So fill me in on you and Omar's college—"

Asia flipped her hair and faced him. "Omar is gay. He's probably always been gay, but you can't be a star athlete and a homo."

Jalen was stunned by how blunt she was.

Asia looked at him and started laughing at the expression of shock on his face.

"What? When? How?" Jalen asked in rapid succession.

"Oh God, you don't wanna know," she said staring ahead and shaking her head, her voice no longer slow and deliberate, but just as compelling. "It was the second worst day in my life. The first being the day my father became paralyzed." She paused for a long time, and Jalen allowed her the time she needed. He opened the sunroof and the stars appeared in the sky. Whining trucks crowded them on each side.

"I was in South Carolina, competing in the NCAA Championship in the 200 meter sprint." She reminisced with a smile. "I shot out of those starting blocks and was running neck and neck with an All-American from the University of Texas. You should have saw me Jalen; I was flying. Then I felt this pain shoot through the back of my right leg, and I collapsed onto the track." Asia turned her head away, but Jalen saw tears glistening on her cheek. The smile had disappeared. Jalen heard the pain.

"I knew I would never run the same after that. The trainer said I had torn my hamstring," she whispered. "The coach flew me home because I didn't want to stay for the rest of the meet. A friend drove me to St. Joe's and I went straight to Omar's room.

I used the key he'd given me. The room was dark but I heard something, or someone in the living room. So I crept in and peeked around the corner—" A sarcastic chuckle jumped out of her throat. She took a moment to compose herself.

"And over on the sofa, Omar was half naked, kissing a player on his team. My brain couldn't process what was happening. I just stood there watching him for what seemed like eternity. They didn't even notice me. Tonguing each other like he and I kissed, touching like he touched me. My conscious mind finally recognized it, and I screamed. Omar was with a man and not some girly, flaming homo. He was bigger than me and Omar put together, tattoos everywhere, one of those Timberland and wife beater-wearing homo thugs."

Shit, I wanna scream now.

"But now I don't see how I was surprised. The signs were all there. Needless to say, we went our separate ways and I'm *still* a virgin."

Jalen's jaw dropped and he started laughing.

Asia whipped her head around. "What the hell is so funny?"

Jalen stopped laughing. "Sorry, Asia, but damn. That's a lot to throw on a brotha. Omar's gay. You still a virgin? I thought God stopped making virgins a long time ago." His sarcastic humor didn't fit the moment, but what else could he say that wouldn't be awkward?

The pale moonlight played on Asia's perfectly oval face, tears glistening from her eyes. She was as breath taking as she was the first day he met her. He remembered the day in high school after he lost a game and she and his girlfriend walked on each side of him, holding his arms. He realized how comfortable Asia felt on his arm. The feeling wasn't like the fiery lust he had for other girls, or even his own girlfriend just a breath away. Instead, the attraction was grounded out of respect and admiration, much like he had for his mother, Michelle.

Chapter 50

The closer Jalen's plan came to the end, the more he wanted it to happen. He wanted to take care of his family so they could do whatever they wanted in life without worrying about their past catching up with them. He was in a hurry to leave his newly found low life. The temptation to do and think things out of his character had to go. What good would it be to have the good life and leave his family behind? After all, they were his motivation.

He and Kevin arranged regular conversations to keep each other abreast of their progress from crime to respectability. That day, Jalen walked into Kevin's basement to discuss the development of the deal. He offered up all eight properties to the family, but held back Velasquez's latest offer. The apartment complex deal would be his alone, since he would need to finance it through a bank.

"Eight lots? That's good," Kevin said.

"What about you? You not getting in on this?" Kevin asked.

"Naw, I have my career, and other things will come up," Jalen said. With Kevin's OK, Jalen walked out into the freedom of a morning already warm with sunshine. He headed to City Hall. When he walked into Velasquez's office, he was feeling the power of a deal already done. A new life already started.

"What's the word on the apartment building?" Velasquez asked.

Jalen nodded and placed another envelope with seventy-five hundred on the desk. Velasquez looked at the bills. "Okay, looks good, but we may have had a slight miscommunication."

"About what?"

Velasquez held up the envelope. "My fee *was* fifteen thousand for fast tracking those eight properties for you. The apartment complex's price tag alone is almost eight hundred thousand. Not to mention the unlimited earnings from rent, property values going up, tax write-offs."

Jalen stared at him.

"My fee for this deal is thirty thousand. I'll just hold onto this until you bring me the remaining twenty-two thousand five-hundred."

"I wondered when you'd get greedy," Jalen said.

"Hey, look who's calling a poorly paid civil servant greedy."

Jalen had already given all eight properties to Kevin. He had to make this deal, if he was to reap the benefits of his hard work.

"I'll have the rest when we close." Jalen stood and they shook hands. *You ain't shit.*

On the way out, Jalen stopped by Asia's desk. "What's up, lady?"

"Hello, Mr. Carthane," she said in her professional voice. "I have a message for you. She passed him a Post-It note.

He looked at it and smiled. "I'll call you tonight."

The following day, Jalen was on his way to Pollock Town to pick up the money Leroy agreed to pay Kevin. He pulled up to the corner and saw Leroy with Brooklyn, Tasha's cousin from New York, now Leroy's captain. Runners were busy all around them. Jalen stepped out of the car. "What's up, Leroy? I dropped by to settle up."

Brooklyn looked at Leroy and then at Jalen. "Ay, there's been a change of plans. Since I already paid the funeral expenses, I ain't paying Kevin another dime. You tell him to stay on his side of town and I'll stay on mine and there won't be no problem."

"What?" Jalen asked.

"Nigga, you heard me. If any of them come round here, starting some shit, they gonna get met wit bullets. Plain and simple. Just like you said, Jalen, we got our own nice groove going on over here and I'm not letting none a y'all take a piece of that," Leroy said.

"Just like that? After all we talked about?" Jalen asked.

"I like drinkin and fuckin in motels too much to give that up."

"Come on man, you know we supply you. Who else are you going to buy from? Either way, Kevin's going to get the money. If you don't give it up like this, he's gonna kick up the price on what you buy," Jalen said.

"Naw, that ain't happening either. Me and Brooklyn took a trip to New York and we got a new connect, so we don't need y'all's shit no more."

Jalen played his final card. "And your brother? If Chub comes over here, you gonna blast him, too?"

Leroy looked Jalen in the eyes. "You tell dem fools to keep to their part of town and I'll keep to mine—and just in case Kevin starts to think he's bigger than he really is . . . "

Brooklyn whistled and Jalen lost count of how many people ran up to the corner to surround him. Brooklyn pulled out a big, black Tech 9 semi-automatic.

Leroy put his hand out and lowered the gun. "Chill, Brooklyn, *Mr. Professor* ain't no thug." Jalen and Brooklyn were in the middle of a staring match.

"But don't get it twisted, Jalen. The same goes for you, too. After you leave today, your ghetto pass is revoked. Understand?"

Jalen lifted his arms in pseudo-surrender and walked to his car. His heart felt the heaviness of losing blood. His blood cousin, Leroy.

Chapter 51

Jalen made a bee line back downtown, knowing Leroy and company could ruin the plan he had put together, and this time he wasn't sure if he could stop it. He punched numbers on his cell phone. He was so close to living in a decent neighborhood, even though he had no complaints about the male-modern condo he bought in a gated community near the Waterfront. He was so close to buying his mother a new home. He was so close to having a foundation stable enough to seriously consider taking a wife and starting a family of his own. He was too close to let Leroy stand in his way.

"You get the money?" Kevin asked.

Jalen sighed. "No, he reneged."

"I figured he'd do that," Kevin said. "I'll see you when you get here." Kevin hung up before Jalen could answer.

When Jalen got to the house, Tamika let him in and he went straight downstairs. He was at the mercy of his family and whatever they decided now. He took the first seat at the edge of the table, and everyone became absolutely quiet.

Kevin was the first to speak. "I have a lot to say, so I don't want any interruptions until I'm done. We all are gonna be faced with choices that will determine our future."

The silence was stifling.

"As I was telling all of you, Leroy didn't keep his word. Now, Leroy is and always will be family, but we all know how this is supposed to play out," Kevin said as he rocked back and forth in his chair.

"You guys also know Jalen and I have only weeks to pay up on this redevelopment plan that we told you about. When we do, all of us will have the option of getting away from this lifestyle. I'll be leaving to make some honest money and I hope all of you will come with me. Those of you who choose to stay will have their run of everything I leave behind. This will be my last official business before I leave things to Damon, Chub, and Eric, who have already expressed having no intention of going legit. So this business with Leroy will be left with y'all to deal with." Kevin glanced over to his two cousins and brother, who looked content with their decision to stay in the lifestyle.

"We're going to expand our territory one more time before I leave. This expansion will be into Philly. After talking to Marcus, Sean's new addition to our family, we'll be going over the Ben Franklin to check out a new spot. If it's as good as Marcus makes it out to be, then we'll run them off like we did in East Camden. That means bullets will fly."

The crew looked at each other and then back at Kevin.

"And one more thing. Me and Mika's gettin' married. I finally proposed to her," Kevin said. Smiles swept around the table.

"So that's why you *really* leaving?" Chub asked. "You finally gonna make an honest woman outta Mika, huh? Shiiit, man I can't blame you, I woulda done the same thing." Chub stood and hugged him. The rest of the family stood to congratulate him.

"Yeah man, I am. After all the shit she put up with. It's the *least* I can do to honor her."

Chapter 52

Jalen woke up at 7 a.m. to the music coming from his CD player. It was a testament of love by hip-hop artist Jay-Z. It told a story of how he lost the love who was there for him before all of his fame. Now, he rhymed his regrets for driving her away knowing that his *good girl was gone forever*. Jalen adjusted the volume and rolled out of bed, shaking Asia, who lay beside him. "Good morning, Diossa."

"Good morning who?" she demanded. "My name is Asia mutha—"

"Diossa means 'Goddess' in Spanish," he doused her anger with a hasty explanation.

"Oh, sorry, Jalen. I guess I'm a little on edge after last night. I never did anything like that before," she whined.

Now, it was Jalen's turn to be a bit on edge. He and his friends had joked on numerous occasions about that line before. Usually when a woman said that, it usually meant they *had* done something like that before. But he felt like she had never done it before. Like never, ever done it before. *She felt so tight, so inexperienced, and unsure about everything we did.* She sat there with the covers draped over her all the way up to her neck, clinging to them, making sure not a single piece of her flesh showed. He believed her, she *was* a virgin last night.

"I gotta get outta here. Stay as long as you want, but I'd like to see you again tonight." Jalen grabbed a key from the nightstand and placed it in her palm. He pecked her on the lips.

Asia smiled.

"Take your time getting up and make yourself comfortable, I'll be home late," Jalen said. "My cousin Kevin finally proposed to his girlfriend and we're throwing him a bachelor party."

Jalen dragged himself out of bed, jumped in the shower, and soon left wearing one of his business suits.

At lunchtime Jalen dialed Asia at her job. "Hey lady, how's it going?"

"Hey, you. It's going. Just looking over some contracts for Mr. Boss man."

"Oh really, you see any of my stuff in there?"

"Unless your name is Phillip Mease or Rhondella English, then the answer's—"

"Rhondella English?" Jalen asked, surprised. "That's my Aunt's name."

"Yeah, okay Jalen," Asia replied.

"I'm not joking, Asia! That's really my aunt's name. Remember the cousin we're throwing the party for tonight? That's *his* mom."

Asia's laughter subsided. "Oh yeah? Well she's buying some property, but it's not the redevelopment stuff you're doing. This is an apartment building near the University."

"That's impossible. She can't afford property that big. Are there any other names on the contract? Look for...um...Kevin English or Tamika Randall."

He could hear Asia shuffling papers.

"Tamika Randall is the secondary name on the contract."

Kevin had to be financing it, but put the property in their names. How could both of us have contracts for the same property?" Then it hit Jalen. *Velasquez is hustling both of us at the same time. Fuck! Why didn't Kevin tell me?*

"Asia, I need you to do me a *huge* favor. Find any recent contracts for that property, copy them, and bring them to my house tonight."

"No! Jalen, I could get fired for that."

"I wouldn't ask if it wasn't really important. I think your boss is trying to scam me and my cousin on the same property."

Chapter 53

"I wanna rock, I wanna rock, I wanna rock . . . "

"Doo Doo Brown, Doo Doo Brown . . . "

Jalen fumbled his key in his door as he sang the song stuck in his head after the bachelor party for Kevin's engagement. After a few failed attempts he unlocked the door. He staggered into the living room and met Asia's gaze from a curled up ball on the sofa where she watched TV. "Heeey Asia. Good! I was hoping you were going to be here."

She looked at him suspiciously. "Jalen? Are you drunk?"

"Who me? Oh, nooo. I'm gooood," he said, collapsing into an open space beside her, the smell of alcohol shooting out of his pores and spoiling his breath.

"Jesus, you are drunk. Wait here. I'm going to fix you something."

"I had something already."

Jalen leaned to one side and reached in his side pocket, removing his wallet and tossing it onto the cherry red oak coffee table. It landed on top of a yellow manila file folder. He fell off the sofa while reaching for the folder. On the floor, he flipped it open and copies of the city contracts faced him. He cleared his head, looked hard at the copies, and promised to never get this drunk again in his life. As the man responsible for his family, he should never be this drunk, because even one moment of lost consciousness could ruin all that he has worked for. He studied the documents through a blurry brain, then he picked up his phone and dialed Kevin.

When Kevin answered, Jalen could hear Tamika chastising Kevin in the background.

"Who's that . . . better not be one of those bitches from the tittie bar."

"Jalen, this not a good time, I'm—"

"Kevin, we need to talk about your apartment building downtown. Why didn't you tell me? Man, the world can scam you when you don't communicate with the family that's watching your back. " Jalen's drunken state caused him to ramble.

"Never mind all of that, meet me here in a half hour."

Jalen jumped up from the floor, and regained his balance. Asia returned to the living room with a glass of cloudy liquid.

"What's that?" Jalen asked.

"Don't worry 'bout that. Just drink. It'll make you feel better." Jalen looked at her like she was crazy; his mind was on more serious things.

"Drink it," she encouraged, as she smiled, tilting her head, knowing the extra motivation would weaken his defenses. He gulped the mystery mix down. "Hmm, not so bad."

"I see you found the copies," Asia said.

Jalen flipped his wrist and checked his watch. "Oh shit, I need to make a run, but I'll be right back."

"You just got here," Asia complained.

"The stuff I told you about your boss trying to play me and my cousin is true. It's all in the files. I'll be right back."

Asia leveled him with her eyes, but said nothing.

Jalen staggered out of the door and jumped in his car. The taste of the mystery mix was stuck to his throat. A small smirk formed around his lips as it reminded him of some of the more memorable nights he had back at his University. His stomach growled.

I need something to eat. He made another call and a familiar voice answered.

"Collingswood Diner, how may I help you?"

"I want one order of mozzarella sticks, a pizza burger, and orange juice for pickup."

"No problem, sir. Is…is that you, Mr. Carthane?"

"Yes, ma'am. How are you, Mrs. Carolyn?"

"I'm fine, baby. Your food will be ready in fifteen minutes."

"Thanks, Mrs. Carolyn, see you soon."

It had started to rain when Jalen arrived at the diner and he darted inside to avoid being completely drenched. He picked up his order, slapped twelve dollars on the counter, headed back to his car, and started to eat his sandwich while moisture gathered on the windows.

Oh my God, this is good.

Surprisingly, Marcus walked up to the diner. He rolled down his window to get his attention, but spilled the orange juice all over himself. When he looked up again, Marcus was already inside sitting with somebody in a booth near the window—an older white male with graying hair, wearing a gray suit. Something about the sight made Jalen feel uneasy. He watched as the men ordered. Marcus was doing most of the talking. Jalen glanced at his watch; he only had ten minutes before he had to be at Kevin's house. Mrs. Carolyn walked over to the two men and poured coffee.

Jalen flipped open his phone and called the Diner again.

"Collingswood Diner, how may I help you?"

"Hi again, Mrs. Carolyn. I meant to tell you that a friend of mine is coming by the diner tonight. It's his birthday and I was wondering if you could surprise him. Just put his meal on my tab without letting him know I paid for it? He's a proud person and I don't want to insult him."

"Sure I will, baby. I'll just tell him the diner has a promotion that birthday boys eat free. By the way, how will I know it's him? What does he look like? And what do I say if he asks how I know it's his birthday?"

"He's an old white dude with graying hair and he's always wearing this tired old grey suit."

"Oh, I just took his order, but you don't have to worry about paying for it. We never charge cops and those two have been regulars here for the past couple of months."

Jalen almost choked on his sandwich, but managed to thank Mrs. Carolyn before hanging up.

Cops? Marcus is a cop? He glanced at his watch again. He drove carefully to Kevin's house with a clearing head.

Tamika met him at the door. "Come on in, Jalen."

He rushed to the basement. Kevin was just sitting in his chair rubbing his temples to relieve the stress of his fight with Tamika.

"We got problems, Kevin!" Jalen said, handing him a folder. "Velasquez is playing us against each other for that apartment building. I got these copies from a girl I know at City Hall. Velasquez has been squeezing both of us for the same property and he has no intentions of giving it to either of us. He fed us bogus contracts for a piece of property another developer bid on. Now if you want to play the secrecy game, I'm out."

"Look, man. My fault. I felt I had too much at stake. And just because he asked me not to tell one soul, I didn't tell you. From here on out, we discuss everything, no matter who tell us not to."

"I'm with that," Jalen said. "Now, let me guess. He told you the developer backed out because of some sexual harassment suit, right?"

"Yeah, and I took the bait, promising him thirty thousand for an inside track," Kevin said.

Kevin walked to his punching bag, slipped on the gloves, and began punching away.

"So how do we fix it?" Kevin asked right before Jalen abruptly switched topics. "Marcus is a cop."

Kevin stopped punching the bag and stared at Jalen. "What did you say?"

"Marcus is a cop. I saw him and another cop at the Collings-wood Diner right before I came here."

"A cop? How do you know?"

"Mrs. Carolyn at the diner told me."

"We're getting played by Velasquez, and now we got a rat in the house?" Kevin pummeled the bag. "We supposed to check the spot in Philly in a few days."

"We can't go ahead with that, knowing who he is," Jalen said. "And we can't just cut him loose; he knows too much."

Kevin paced silently around the floor. Finally he spoke. "This is how we gonna play it. We gonna put Philly on the back burner for a minute to sort out this real estate shit. Make sure we don't land in prison. I'll call Marcus and tell him what's up. You gonna fix out our problem with Velasquez. And here's how . . . " Kevin said.

Chapter 54

The next morning Jalen called Velasquez to schedule a meeting in his office that afternoon. When he showed up, Asia escorted him in. "Do you need anything before I leave for the day, Mr. Velasquez?"

"A kiss would be nice," he chuckled under his breath.

Jalen's jaw tightened and his hands clenched.

Velasquez glanced at Jalen, then back to Asia. "I'm just kidding, sweetie. That will be it for today."

Asia strolled out and Jalen pulled out a fat envelope and handed it to Velasquez. "That's the rest of the $30 K," he said.

Velasquez placed the envelope in his inside coat pocket. "Good, everything will be taken care of."

They both stood and shook hands. Jalen showed himself out.

As soon as Jalen reached his car he called Kevin. "I just dropped the money off with Velasquez."

"Cool. I already talked to Marcus. Hit me back tomorrow so we can finalize everything."

An hour later, Jalen walked into his living room. Asia left the kitchen sink and came into the dining room where candles and wine were setup. She threw her arms open to him. She hugged Jalen harder than he had ever been hugged. He would have felt all of it, except the burden of a disintegrating business deal numbed all of his senses. He pecked her lips and flopped on the sofa.

"And I have champagne to celebrate meeting up with you again." She pawed over him and kissed his face. But the scheme he and Kevin had concocted to save their family was the only thing on his mind. He smiled with a distant stare in his eyes.

"I wonder which is worse," Asia said, "to be ignored, or fondled by a disgusting boss?"

The truth from Asia's mouth mentally jerked Jalen back to Velasquez in the second worst scenario in his life, the image of stabbing his father being the first. He could kill Velasquez with his bare hands.

He pulled her onto his chest and stroked her back and the smell of her hair was like fresh rain. He had to do something. Velasquez was messing with his money, his future and the woman he cared about.

"Asia, I need you do one more thing for me. I've got to stop Velasquez."

Asia pulled free and looked at Jalen, a thousand questions flashing in her eyes.

Chapter 55

Sean, Chub, Kevin, and Marcus, and two new soldiers lined the table in Kevin's basement, going over last-minute details for Philly. "We're going to split up into two trucks. Sean and Chub will ride with me while the rest of you will be in the other car."

"OK," Chub said.

"Marcus we'll follow you to the spot in Philly. When we get there, park a block away from the corner and let me scope things out from my truck. I'll call you from there to let you know what our next move's gonna be. A'ight?"

An assortment of mumbles dotted the space, but no one said anything audible.

"Any questions?" Kevin asked.

The crew shut up, making quick glances at each other, shaking their heads nervously. Marcus sat up front in the front passenger seat. One of the new soldiers slid behind the wheel while the other sat in the back directly behind Marcus. They locked the doors and pulled out from Kevin's house. Kevin's truck followed. Chub turned on the radio and the three slowly trailed behind the traitor that was leading them to the Ben Franklin Bridge.

Marcus led the tour through North Philly up Broad Street, past Temple University before turning left onto a side street. There, the city instantly changed. No more pale, preppie college students with burgundy book bags and matching sweatshirts with the large double layered 'T' on the front. All the faces now looked like the occupants of the SUVs, wearing oversized clothing, moving with a city swagger that warned they were not to be trifled with. Marcus's truck pulled in front of a block of row homes and parked. Kevin's SUV pulled up behind him.

Half a block in front of them, a 'corner boy' was taking care of business. The scene looked all too familiar. A different part of town, a different state, but the same hustle. A clean-shaven guy sat on the porch of one house. People came and went as he collected money and allowed them to disappear behind him through the door. Almost immediately, they came back out with hands in their pockets, most likely thumbing the product they just bought. Kevin phoned Marcus.

"They working it out of a house and there's a steady flow of customers. Give it a few more minutes, then pull up and tell homeboy a new crew's takin' over. Tell 'em if they don't wanna get sprayed, don't be 'round tomorrow. Now listen, don't pull any heat unless it's necessary. If they here tomorrow, then we'll light 'em up."

"Alright," Marcus answered and pulled up next to the brother sitting on the porch. He spotted the New Jersey tags. Kevin cracked the window, hoping to catch any part of the conversation. "Ay yo, what you need, Jersey?"

"I need you to clear this block," Marcus said. "Jersey's expanding its borders and y'all in the way. So clear out or get sprayed."

The young man looked at Kevin's SUV and lifted the front of his shirt. "Y'all bitch-ass Jersey boys do what y'all want, we got guns too, ya mean?"

As Marcus pulled away, with Kevin's SUV right behind, Kevin called Marcus. "I take it they wasn't trying to hear you, huh, Marcus?"

"Hell naw. He said they got guns, too."

"No problem, we're not going straight back to Jersey. We gonna stop and grab something to eat, then circle back to see if we stirred up anything," Kevin said.

"A'ight, cool," Marcus said.

A few blocks away, Kevin spotted a cheese steak shop and called Marcus again. "Pull over and send for something to eat for everybody."

Marcus pulled over and Kevin's SUV followed. "Y'all cool?" Kevin asked his two cousins.

"I'll be better once we get Marcus out our camp and off our asses," Chub said.

"Yeah, man. The cops you used to work wit must got it real bad for you Kev. Sending Marcus to jail to play my cell mate got me all fucked up in the head," Sean added.

"Don't worry, he's on borrowed time. I just wanted to check out this spot he scoped. See if it's a trap they hoping we fall into."

"Umm, I don't know. It looked legit to me" Eric said.

"The young boy on the porch didn't look the part and neither did those fake ass fiends going up in the house like they buying shit. The whole place is probably wired and laced with cops," Kevin said.

"So what we gonna do to shake him? We can't just knock off a cop. We won't even make it to trial. The cops'll kill us before we hit the precinct," Chub said.

"Don't worry 'bout it. *We* not killin no cop. Those two new soldiers are no strangers to catching a body. Tomorrow, them and Marcus are gonna be in the same car just like today and as soon as we turn off Broad Street and hit the side streets, one of them's gonna clip him. As far as they know, he's just some slick nigga that was stealing from us getting what he deserves. None of our family will be in that car."

The soldier returned with the sandwiches and hopped into Kevin's truck. Chub beeped the horn signaling the others to come and get their food. Marcus hopped out, approached the SUV and climbed in the back seat behind the driver. The two soldiers stayed in Marcus' car.

Kevin slid over to make room. "Like I said before, we gonna roll back around and see if they still out there, or if they punked out already. If not we'll come back tomorrow and clear the set."

Marcus nodded, grabbed his sandwich and stepped out of the SUV.

One of the new soldiers crawled out of the SUV squinting his eyes, looking past Kevin's truck. "Look out!" he shouted.

Pow! Pow! Pow! Pow!

The soldier ducked and reached in the small of his back for his gun. Everyone in Kevin's truck ducked at the sound of the gunfire. Kevin peered between the two front seats, and through the front window, and saw the soldier return fire past Marcus. He changed his focus to the rear view mirror and saw the soldier firing at what looked like a single man wielding a sawed-off shotgun, not too far behind his truck.

Boom! Click, click. Boom! Leroy's captain, Brooklyn, fired at Marcus, who had pulled his weapon and joined the fight just before getting clipped by shotgun pellets. Marcus ducked between the back of Kevin's SUV and the car parked almost immediately behind it.

The other new soldier crouched close to the floor with Kevin. "Who's got a gun? Mine's in the car."

The soldier outside hit Brooklyn in the shoulder with bullet from his 9mm. the force of the hit spun him around before he took a shot at Kevin's car.

Boom! The shotgun blast crashed the driver's side window, blowing a hole in Chub's shoulder. Brooklyn ducked behind the other end of the car, where Marcus found cover. Sean was finally able to pull his weapon and returned fire through the back window. Brooklyn came out again, brandishing a handgun. He sprayed bullets at anything that moved as he closed in on Kevin's position.

Pow! Pow! Pow! Two of the bullets from Brooklyn's gun dropped the massive body of the soldier outside. Brooklyn took cover once more. Chub tried to start the SUV, but the pain and weakness in his arm wouldn't allow it.

"Chub, get us outta here!" Kevin ordered, unable to see how close Brooklyn was to the truck. Sean stopped firing and gave one powerful yank around Chub's chest, pulling him to the passenger side. He slid over his body and under the wheel. Kevin peeked out of the glassless rear window. Marcus was hit, and from a crouched position behind his SUV, his Glock 9 mm sprayed bullets towards Brooklyn's last position. He pivoted around, meeting Kevin's eyes, just before he met Brooklyn's line of fire.

Boom!

The shotgun blast rocked the SUV and Kevin saw Marcus's body fall.

"Sean! He's behind us! Throw this bitch in reverse!" Kevin ordered.

Brooklyn heard Kevin's command. *Click! Click!* He assumed a firing stance, finger poised on the trigger.

Sean shifted in reverse and the SUV's engine roared, plowing into Brooklyn. It pinned him between the SUV and the car behind it, crushing his legs and body, leaving him sprawled across the hood of the other car. The new soldier jumped and high-tailed it toward the other SUV. Sean put the car in drive and rushed forward, pulling his .38 revolver back out. He aimed at Brooklyn's helpless mashed body through the open space that was once the rear window.

"Kevin, get down!" Kevin followed his order, falling as close to the floor panel as possible.

Pow! Pow! Pow! Click! Click! Sean snatched the remaining life from Brooklyn's body, then flung the wheel to the left and pressed on the gas. He pulled up next to the SUV where the remaining new soldier had scrambled to, rolled down the front passenger window, gave a quick wipe of the gun on his shirt and tossed it toward the SUV. It flew through one of the shot out windows.

Police sirens squealed as Sean gunned the motor and screeched from the scene. The new soldier jumped into Marcus' SUV, turned the key in the ignition and made a U-turn into the oncoming police cars. He tried to whip the car in another direction, but the fast turn caused the vehicle to collide head on with a cop car. The force of the collision sent him into the windshield of the squad car.

As Marcus' brethren from the Philadelphia Police Department scrambled along the asphalt, Sean, Kevin, and Chub looked up at the blurring street signs, hoping to find their way back to Jersey.

"Sean, park the car," Kevin ordered.

Sean pulled off and wheeled into a back alley. It was the middle of the afternoon and the alley had cars sparsely parked next to aluminum trashcans and rummaging cats.

Kevin took off his shirt and used it to pack Chub's wound. Blood was running steadily down his arm and onto the car's leather seats. Chub was breathing hard trying not to wince when the pain tore through his body.

"Sean, grab everything out of the glove compartment, we ditching the truck," Kevin said.

Kevin grabbed a crow bar from the back of the SUV, jumped out, and ran to an empty parked black Nissan Sentra. He smashed the window, cracked the steering wheel column and started the car. "Get in," he ordered.

Sean helped Chub into the back seat and hopped in with Kevin in the front. They rolled slowly out of the alley until they were far enough away to feel safe. Then, Sean floored it, headed back toward the Philly skyline, knowing that it would lead them back to Jersey. Jersey, where their families would welcome them home, oblivious to the fact they had been a part of the slaughter, resulting in one of their own being injured. Jersey, where Kevin would scan the news channels for information on whether or not Leroy's assassin had done the job he hired the two new soldiers to do. Jersey, where Jalen was preparing to do his part to provide his family the option to soon go legit.

Chapter 56

The 6 o'clock morning news would determine the family's future. Kevin had to wait and see. Wait and see if the family could come out of hell alive and free. The phone rang and he answered.

"Yea."

"How did things go?" Jalen asked.

"*All* wrong. Brooklyn showed up blasting everything. He shot a soldier and Chub."

"Is Chub alright?"

"We had to take him to the hospital. Told them we got carjacked. They admitted him and got him patched up, then we darted outta there. No I.D. given, only fake names. Told them the jackers took all of our I.D. The doctor said he'd be all right."

Jalen was silent, then, "What about Sean? He okay?"

"Yeah, he's downstairs sleeping."

"Brooklyn and Marcus?"

Kevin sighed. "Dead. You haven't been watching the news, man?"

"You on the run?"

"Naw. Right now, as far as the police are concerned this is just another random shooting in Philly with an off duty New Jersey cop dead. Now it's all on you to fix this shit with Velasquez and we'll make it out."

Jalen was uneasy now. *It's all on me. What can go wrong on my end? You'll be okay. It's going to work out.* "I'll call you after it's done. What we going to do about Leroy sending Brooklyn?"

"You let me worry about Leroy. You just take care of Velasquez."

Jalen went downstairs where Asia was making breakfast. She was wearing a black fitted skirt, blue silk button-down blouse that was meant to show off her curves. Four-inch black pumps accentuated her shapely legs and Jalen couldn't get enough of looking at her. Yes, she was definitely everything he wanted in a woman.

She looked at Jalen, smiled, and kissed him. They sat down to eat without saying a single word. They had been up most of the night going over the paperwork for the properties.

"Sure you're OK?" Jalen asked.

"I'm sure." She grabbed the back of his head and kissed him on the lips. Though she looked at Jalen with a sense of longing, a wish to stay with him, she quickly walked out of the house. Jalen could take no more chances.

* * *

Thirty minutes later, Velasquez called Asia into his office. "Young lady, you keep dressing like that and I'm gonna give you a raise."

Asia giggled. "Are there any documents that need processing?"

"As a matter of fact, yes. Here, let me show you." Velasquez opened a folder and Asia stood next to him. While opening the folder, Velasquez's hand slid down her buttocks, then to her calf.

"Mr. Velasquez!" she exclaimed.

"Oh don't worry about it. It's just a little office flirting." His hand glided up the back of her leg.

"Mr. Velasquez, that's a dangerous game you're playing."

"I love danger." He was breathing unevenly.

Asia looked around to see if anyone could see what was going on. Her hands shook.

"You're studying for your MBA, correct?" Velasquez's hand continued up her leg.

"MBA. Yes." She stepped back near the glass door.

Vasquez pulled at her hand and motioned for her to come and sit on his lap. Asia could tell by the bulge in his slacks that he was excited. She pulled away. He stood, then walked around to the front of his desk, grabbed her hand, and twirled her around, as if in a dance. He dipped her for a second and raised her up.

"It's a shame you work for me," he said, his eyes locked on her firm, shapely cleavage. "It's against policy for me to even ask you out to lunch or dinner. If not for that, we could have a lot of fun together."

Asia reminded him, "And the fact that you're married."

Velasquez smirked. "My wife is sitting at home getting fat and watching *Oprah*. But if I had a woman like you—" He sucked a lustful breath through his teeth.

Asia nervously took a step back.

Asia turned to one side showing off her well-rounded backside. "Mr. Velasquez, would you even know what to do with me?"

"Young lady, I can show you better than I can tell you." His lips went all mushy and his eyes glazed over.

"So, show me."

Asia took a deep breath, walked to the door and shut it.

Click.

Then she turned and walked back to Velasquez.

Velasquez's masculinity seemed challenged and he opened wet, slimy lips to lay on hers. She pushed away and slapped his face. "No. Don't kiss me." She posed her plump breasts. "I don't want you trying to romance me," she said.

Velasquez grinned and fidgeted with his crotch, coming closer, his nose wet with small beads of sweat. "Oh, okay, you like it a little rough, huh? Well, we can do rough."

He ran his hand up her skirt and she slapped his face with enough force to pay for every insult, every degradation, and every foul remark. He grabbed her wrist and spun her around, pinning her between himself and the wall.

Velasquez grabbed at her breast, trying to lick the back of her neck.

"What I tell you about trying to kiss me?" Asia snapped before she elbowed Velasquez.

She stared hard into his eyes. He lunged at her lips and released a long stroke of his tongue against her face, squeezing another handful of her breast.

"I see I have to just take it from you," he threatened.

Asia grabbed a handful of his hair, pulled his head back violently, then raked her nails down the side of his face and neck.

"Okay, you little bitch," he growled. "Now it's time for papi not to be so nice."

Asia, seductively bit her bottom lips and nodded her head invitingly. He yanked her, abdomen down, over to the front of the desk, forcing her butt in the air.

"Mr. Velasquez, what are you doing?"

Velasquez pulled up her skirt and smacked the exposed flesh around her thong. "Daddy's gonna give it to you. That's what I'm doing." He held Asia on the desk with one hand while he unzipped his pants with the other.

As soon as his pants fell to the floor, Asia placed a foot on them. "Stop it! Somebody help me!" she screamed.

"What are you doing? Shut the hell up!" Velasquez's hand clasped hard over her mouth.

Asia clamped her teeth into the side of his hand.

"Ow! Shit!" Velasquez yelled.

His stepson ran into the office, and saw Asia sprawled over the desk with his stepfather's pants around his ankles and tugging at his boxers.

"Help me, please!" Asia pleaded.

Velasquez seemed glued there. Couldn't move. It seemed like paralysis from shock. When he finally let her up, Asia raced out of his office and the building, not bothering to fasten her clothes.

Chapter 57

Kevin sat in his wife's car in Leroy's part of town, parked a block away from his operation. He sat there for almost an hour but didn't see him.

Where the hell is he? He must be home.

Kevin throttled the car and jumped on Route 42 South. Twenty minutes later, he parked within shouting distance of Leroy's townhouse in a wooded area of Sicklerville, New Jersey. Leroy's Grand Cherokee was parked out front. Kevin reached under his seat, pulled out a .40 caliber dual-action Smith & Wesson, and tucked it in his belt. He got out of his car, dashed into the woods, and circled around to the back of the house.

The living room and upstairs bedroom lights were on. Kevin scanned the back of the house and saw two kitchen windows half open. He looked around the window to be sure he was alone. From there, he could see all the way into the living room, but no one was in sight. He pulled a pocketknife out of his back pocket and cut the window screens.

"Daddy, stop it! Mommy's sorry!"

It was Lisa's little pleading voice.

"Shut da hell up and go to ya room!" Leroy continued to beat Tasha.

"Where's the money I left on the dresser, Tasha? I'm gonna beat ya ass 'til you tell me. I told you 'bout stealing from me."

Kevin raised the window far enough to slide in. He moved carefully around the kitchen, opened the pantry door, and slipped inside.

Don't want Tasha and the kids to see. Got to keep this quiet. Need a silencer. Kevin's eyes adjusted to the darkness, and he continued to search for something to silence the pending gunshot. Finding nothing, he peeked through one of the louvers in the door. *There it is!* Kevin spotted a set of dishtowels and grabbed them.

"Don't come out of that room until you find my money!" Leroy shouted as he walked down the steps.

Kevin dashed back into the pantry.

Leroy sat on the couch, breathing hard as he took a swig of beer.

Kevin pulled out his gun and wrapped the towels around the nozzle. *This'll have to do. Make the shot count and leave.*

"Will you shut up? I can't hear the damn television," Leroy bellowed, as he flipped through the channels.

Leroy increased the TV volume. "Yesterday, Philadelphia police found two armed men dead on Fulton Street from an apparent shootout . . . "

Leroy was quiet. Kevin crept out of the panty, gun wrapped tightly in the dishtowels. He peeked around the corner and saw Leroy looking stunned at the television, beer in his right hand. He aimed the weapon.

"Oh, God, no!" Tasha screamed.

As her voice from upstairs broke Leroy's trance, he reached under the couch cushion, pulled out a Glock 9mm, and ran upstairs.

Kevin crept slowly through the living room and slithered up the stairs. Halfway up, he heard Leroy's voice again.

"Answer me, girl! What the hell's wrong?" Leroy shouted.

"It's your fault he's dead. I hate you!" Tasha answered.

Kevin looked up and saw Lisa standing in the doorway of her parents' room. Leroy screamed at her. She and her younger siblings scurried into another room farther down the hallway. Now they were opposite Kevin.

"Who you think you're talking to? I'm so tired of your ass. You money-hungry bitch."

The sound of slaps, blows, and blood-curdling screams echoed in the hallway.

Then everything went quiet except for Leroy cursing Tasha.

"Fuck! Stupid bitch. Ya teeth scraped my knuckles."

Have to end this tonight. He deserves it. It's either you or him. Kevin looked down at his gun and pulled back the trigger, then tightened the dishtowels around the muzzle. When he looked back up at the hallway, he caught a glimpse of Lisa dashing into her parents' bedroom. *Shit! Can't let the kids see. They didn't pick their parents. They just got stuck with them.*

Bang! Kevin jumped at the sound of the gunshot.

Leroy appeared in the hallway reaching for the middle of his back and collapsed onto one knee in the hallway. His lips started to tremble. Lisa came out right behind him.

Bang!

Leroy fell motionless onto his stomach; his expressionless eyes looked directly at Kevin.

"I told you to stop hitting mommy," Lisa, said as she dropped the gun.

The other children ran to their mother. "Daddy's dying," one of the girls said.

Kevin started to slowly slide back down the steps.

"I'm sorry, Daddy. I'm soooooorrrryyyy!" Lisa cried out.

Moments later, Tasha let out another scream.

"Mommy, I'm sorry. I thought daddy killed you."

"You killed your father! Why did you do that? Now who's gonna take care of us?" Tasha pounded across the room and reached for the phone.

Kevin made it back to the kitchen, removed the towels from his gun, and threw them onto the kitchen table.

"Hello! My name is Tasha Smalls and my daughter just shot my husband! Please send an ambulance!"

Tasha kept talking as Kevin tucked his gun back into his belt, slipped out of the window, ran to his car, and returned to Camden.

Chapter 58

Asia's phone rang. "Asia, it's Rafael. Meet me at Cooper River Park near Jake's Seafood Restaurant in twenty minutes."

In twenty-two minutes, Asia saw Rafael's car pull up. The dark of evening was not quite night. The trees were only slight shadows. Rafael got out the car and walked across the gravel parking lot toward Asia. She hit the button, unlocking the door. She watched Rafael slide into the passenger back seat, and reach into his inside jacket pocket. He handed her a thick envelope.

"That's fifty-thousand of what Velasquez conned you and Kevin out of." He pulled out a larger manila envelope. "This is the paperwork you need to own the apartment building. I completed it for you. So as far as the city of Camden is concerned, we have officially accepted your bid. I'll contact the other developers tomorrow to let them know someone else was awarded the property."

Jalen reached back from the front passenger seat to receive the envelope. He thought deeply about this. Rafael had delivered him from harms way once again. The papers, money, and two tape recordings of Velasquez during and after Asia's attack were now in his possession. He wondered if the good is always rewarded. If so, Rafael had earned the money he was being paid to participate in this scam.

Rafael leaned forward toward Asia and said, "I forgot to ask. Are you okay? I didn't want to rush in too early and not catch him in the act."

Asia looked at Rafael through the rearview mirror and smiled. "You were perfect. That son-of-a-bitch is finally going to get what he deserves. I just hope they put him away for the rest of his life."

Jalen put the documents into the glove compartment and kept the tape recorder out. He rewound the tape, took a deep breath, and pressed the play button.

Click.

"This isn't what it looks like," Velasquez said.

"Well, it looks like you're whoring around on my mother again. And this time it looks like she wasn't a willing participant,." Rafael voiced.

"I know this looks a little crazy, but I didn't do anything wrong. She came onto me, but you're right, what I was doing wasn't fair to your mother and I apologize. It was a mistake. I love your mother and I don't need this little bitch stirring up any trouble by calling me a rapist."

Jalen dug his nails into his thigh and glanced over at Asia.

"You said the same thing last time. You swore it was a mistake and it wouldn't happen again. But look at you now. Nothing has changed."

"Look, damn it!" Velasquez said. "When your ass was being a juvenile delinquent, I didn't judge you. Instead, I saved you. I got you a job here and I keep your mother happy at home. She doesn't even have to work. You owe me!"

"Owe you? I don't owe you anything!"

"Look, you ingrate, how about I make it worth you while? You take care of this for me, and I'll put some money in your hands." The tape went silent for a few seconds.

Rafael's voice came back on. "Okay, I'm listening now."

"Good. You find Asia right now. Go to her house, call her, I don't give a shit. You talk to her and get her to say nothing happened. Offer her money, threaten he;, whatever it takes. I'm not gonna let her ruin my career."

"And what if she doesn't want money and I can't talk her out of pressing charges, then what?"

They heard the squeaking of leather, Velasquez sitting down.

"Well, then you need to get creative. If reasoning with her doesn't work, you need to change her mind. I don't care what you do, just shut her up."

Asia shook her head, closing her eyes.

"Are you saying what I think you're saying?" Rafael asked.

"Change her mind or shut her up for good. In return, you will be well compensated." Velasquez said.

"How well?"

They heard keys rattling.

"I have a little more than sixty-thousand dollars here. If you make this problem go away, it's all yours."

"How do I know you won't shaft me after I do it?

Something like plastic ruffled in the background.

"If she insists on making a big deal of this, here is half now and you'll get the other half when it's done. If she just wants money to make this go away, then you have thirty thousand to negotiate with. If she takes thirty and walks away I'll give you thirty thousand. Agreed?"

"Si, Papa."

The door slammed.

Click.

"There's another tape in the envelope with the money," Rafael said.

Jalen opened the envelope, picked up the tape, and placed it in the recorder. He pressed the rewind button and pressed play again.

Click.

The first sound was a knock at the door. *"So what happened? Did you find her? What did she say?"*

"I found her sitting outside of the downtown police station."

"Shit!"

"Lucky for you, she hadn't gone in yet. She was just sitting outside on one of the benches in a daze. When I walked up to her, she just started rambling about how she didn't know what she was going to do and why these types of things happen to women. I tried to talk her into finding a new job and hinted that you may be willing to help with her relocation fees.

"What did she say?"

"She wants a hundred thousand to keep quiet and you have twenty-four hours to decide. I'm supposed to call her when you do decide."

The sudden sound of a fist hitting wood made them all jump.

"What? This little bitch thinks she can blackmail me? I'm not giving her a hundred thousand anything. Look, you need to get rid of her like we discussed. You call her and meet her. When you do, you make sure that bitch doesn't ever come back. Throw her ass in the Schuylkill River."

Asia turned her head to hide her tears.

A drawer opened and closed. *"Here's another thirty thousand. Now you got sixty to make this problem go away for me. Go! Make it happen!"*

Click.

Jalen looked at Asia. She was still looking out the window. He placed his hand on her thigh to comfort her.

She looked over and rested her head on his shoulder.

"So Rafael, what you gonna do with that ten grand?" Jalen asked.

"I don't know. Maybe do something nice for my mom, or enroll in college. We'll see where the wind blows me," Rafael said.

"They both sound like good ideas, but the college thing sounds real good to me. Maybe then you won't have to carry guns anymore," Jalen said, as he pointed back to the bulge at the front of Rafael's waist.

"Well, you know how it is, you have to be safe these days." Rafael gestured back at the tape recorder. "You're going to square my part with the police?"

"You have nothing to worry about," Jalen said. "We already got Asia processed at the police station for the sexual assault. But this tape is going to be the icing on the cake."

"I wish I could be there to see his face when the cops pay him a little visit after we give them this tape," Asia said spitefully. She reached to start the car.

Rafael extended his hand to Jalen and they shook.

"Who would have known that you would save my life twice?" Jalen said, touching the scar near his eye.

Rafael smiled and stepped out of the car. "Maybe that's why God crossed our paths. You two take care. You two make a nice couple. Put an 'H' in your first born's name for me."

Asia and Jalen blushed. Asia threw the car in gear and pulled off. While they were cruising at 35 mph, heading toward Jalen's place, he dialed Kevin from his cell phone.

"It's done. We'll drop the tape off tomorrow and, if Velasquez has any sense at all, he'll plead guilty and throw himself at the mercy of the court. How's Chub?"

"He's in a little pain, but he'll survive."

"What about Leroy?"

"Dead," Kevin said.

"What? What happened?" Jalen asked.

"Just watch the news; I'm sure they'll cover the story. Don't worry though, my hands are clean."

"All right, later."

Jalen looked at Asia. "Let's go home."

Chapter 59

Three months later Jalen sat in the visitor's room of Camden County Youth Authority. Across from him sat his young cousin, Lisa, with her hands folded and head down. A busted lip and fresh bruise showed on her face. Unfortunately, Lisa's mother lacked the maternal instinct Jalen's mother displayed when he was Lisa's age. The phone call to 9-1-1 and Tasha's signed statement later that night at the precinct sealed her oldest daughter's fate until her eighteen birthday. Only the fact she was a minor acting in self-defense of her mother and siblings saved her from being tried as an adult and additional time being added to her sentence once she matured into adulthood. The jury reluctantly decided that the second bullet she placed into her father's back was done out of malice.

"Lift your head and look at me when I talk to you." She raised her head and looked into her cousin's eyes. He glanced around the room to ensure no one could overhear them. He leaned across the table and whispered.

"I know what you're going through. I haven't been to a detention center like this but the bruises and the guilt I know too well." Jalen turned his face to the side showing the scar and placing an old Philadelphia Inquirer newspaper clipping in the middle of the table. The headline read: *"Local man slain by girlfriend."* She read the clipping and looked back at him, puzzled. Jalen continued his explanation.

"When I was about your age, my mother, your aunt Michelle, went to court because everyone thought she killed my father. My dad was a lot like your dad. Drank a lot and was mean to my mother and one night just like you, I kill—I stabbed my dad trying to protect my mother. Just like you, I didn't want to kill him; I just wanted him to stop hurting her. I'm telling you all of this because I don't want you to think you're a bad person for what you did, even though it was wrong. But what you did, was done to protect your mother, to protect your sisters; you were protecting your family. We always have to protect one another." Jalen took a silent moment to see if there was any sense of understanding. He couldn't tell.

"The next few years are going to be hard, but I know you'll make it through. I did. I had nightmares almost every night until I realized I had to think of high school, college, my future and not the past. So, try to keep your hands clean and try not to get caught up in any more trouble. When you go to school here, pay attention and learn everything you can. That's your ticket out of here. When you turn eighteen and it's time for you to get out, I'll be right there to pick you up and make sure you're okay. We all will. We're your family."

Lisa began to sob. She wiped her tears and nose with her shirt. "Most of the girls scared a me cause they know why I'm here."

"Good. That means they won't bother as much. I'll come to visit you on a regular basis and make sure you get some counseling to help you understand how to forgive yourself. Now if you need anything else, call me, understand?"

She nodded her head while Jalen passed her a new business card.

"What's this?" she asked.

"That's where you'll be working as soon as you get outta here. Remember, we have to take care of one another." Jalen extended his arms and gave her a tight hug. It was the first time they had ever embraced, but the same blood coursing through their veins acknowledged the familiarity. Jalen walked towards the door and looked back once more before passing through the line that separated them.

"You be strong. We'll be waiting for you."

She smiled and clutched the card close to her chest as one more tear fell down her cheek to match the one running down the right side of Jalen's cheek.

Before he knew it, he was back in Camden cruising down Haddon Avenue to meet Kevin. He pulled up to the side of a newly renovated storefront that sat adjacent to a parking lot. Balloons and a small crowd marked the opening of a new African-American-owned business. Jalen stepped out of his new Lexus LS 430 in a rich, navy blue dress shirt and beige slacks. The shades on his face protected his eyes from the bright sunlight and all the fanfare of the grand opening.

When he approached the large ribbon draped across the front door, Kevin, Chub, Asia, and the Mayor of Camden, Gwendolyn Faison, met him. She spoke with the media and applauded Jalen's entrepreneurial effort on behalf of Camden. Jalen and Asia cut the purple and gold ribbon—"C.M.D." Carthane Management & Development Company.

Local reporters crowded around to ask questions. "Mr. Carthane, why the name C.M.D.?"

"The acronym is pretty self-explanatory—Carthane is my last name, my small group will 'M-anage' every building so well that it will never be allowed to bring blight to the city. And as far as 'D-evelopment,' I want to help rebuild our fine city." He smiled.

"Not to mention, those three letters have been synonymous with the City of Camden since I can remember, and I want to display my bond with the city that helped make me into the man I am today."

Cheers from the younger people in the crowd erupted as they chanted "C-M-D, C-M-D!"

"Mrs. Carthane. Now that Hector Velasquez has been sentenced to twenty years in prison, now that you're married and moved on with your life, have you forgiven him for what has transpired?"

Asia's grip on Jalen's hand tightened. "I'm very satisfied with how the City of Camden handled the situation, and I hope his time in prison will be focused on rehabilitation."

Another reporter chimed in.

"Mr. Carthane, how does it feel being the city's first self-made African-American millionaire?

Jalen smiled carefully. "I'm a millionaire? So this is what it feels like?" he said sarcastically. "Let's just say it's a really good feeling knowing that from now on my family will always have the means to sustain a respectable quality of life. I never went into this to become a millionaire. I did it to provide my family with the means to develop good American values and contribute to society." *Sheesh, I sound like a politician.*

Jalen glanced over at his family in the crowd: his grandmother, mother and aunts. Cousin Charles, and as his now *legitimate* silent partner, Kevin. They got together to discuss the eight properties. Together, they decided not to sell them, but renovate and rent. The company was in Jalen's name. Kevin would manage the business office. Sean and Damon shared a two-bedroom apartment rent free in exchange for a respectable salary as the property superintendents.

Even Chub and Eric jumped on the bandwagon, performing all the administrative needs to keep C.M.D's commitment to "good properties." They collected rent, renewed insurance policies, and kept a low profile. Jalen organized the family's calendar, so that someone visits her every other week, giving each person one visit every three months. If that member has some emergency, he or she would make arrangements to switch dates with another member. Lisa would always remember who family was for the next eight years.

As the reporters redirected their questions toward the mayor, Jalen's thoughts drifted. He thought back to his earlier years in Camden when he condemned his family for the life they had chosen. But now, after all he had experienced, he could easily see how even inherently good men fall victim to bad circumstances, sometimes forcing their hand to do whatever it takes to survive.

Survival and self-preservation is every creature's first, natural instinct. He had memorized the order of the food chain a thousand times in science classes from grade school to college but never grasped how the concept applies to every living creature. Especially to us so-called "civilized" human beings.

Now, he saw everyone from a different perspective and could no longer judge because his soul knew how one becomes tainted.

He realized how easy it had been for him to group people into categories and discard them as the poison that was slowly killing the city that raised him. He could no longer look down on others who found themselves in unfortunate circumstances because only a few small choices separated their social and moral status from his own. Kevin walked up to him with Tamika and their children. "Kinda hard to believe that after all that's happened we're still standing. A little beat up, but still standing."

"Yeah, I think back to when, how, and why all this started, and how fortunate we are to be right here at this spot. Who would have ever thought?" Jalen said.

"But now that the drama is over, we just nine-to-fivers like everyone else. Well, we are. Not you. The reporters gave you a new nickname. We can't call you *Mr. Professor* anymore. So what's your next big plan, *Mr. Millionaire*? We'll be doing all the work. You jus gotta sit home and collect a check," Kevin said. "So what you gonna do?"

Jalen pondered for a moment. "I don't know. Maybe I'll write a book."

Author Bio

    T.H. Moore is a Southwest Philadelphia native who relocated to Camden, New Jersey at the age of ten. Primarily raised by a single mother, he managed to remain on the perimeter of the illegal lifestyle that claimed the lives and souls of many in the area where he grew up.

    Tarik is an active member of Omega Psi Phi Fraternity, Inc., and earned a Bachelor of Science degree from Morgan State University in Baltimore, Maryland. His career as an Information Technology Consultant and Real-Estate investor has provided him the opportunity to travel to countries such as England, Sweden, France, Spain, Mexico, and Brazil as well as several places in the United States.

    Blending experience with imagination helped formulate the basis of, and inspired him to write *The End Justifies the Means*. The novel is uniquely creative fiction, but an equally honest representation of his life and challenges.

    Tarik is the proud father of one son, Jason, and currently resides in Woodlynne, NJ where he is working on his next novel "Cyber Sex".

Printed in the United States
68183LVS00003B/136-165